HIGH ADVENTURE

NUMBER 102

Edited by

John P. Gunnison

Subscription Rate - $45.00 - 6 Issues - Advertising Rates - Full Page - $75.00. The publisher has made every effort to contact the present owners of any copyrighted material. Our apologies to those who hold such rights but whom we failed to contact because ownership was unknown or addresses were incomplete. Appropriate credit will be given in future editions if such copyright holders contact the publisher.

Printed in the United States of America

ISBN: 1-59798-176-1
ISBN-13: 978-1-59798-176-7

First Adventure House Edition September 2008

BLIND MAN'S BLUFF

By G. WAYMAN JONES

A returning wanderer, a substitute corpse, a faithless girl, a vague-minded musician and a murdered man are all parts of the grim jigsaw of crime that Tony Quinn must fit together!

CHAPTER I

Return of the Doomed

TONY QUINN, Special District Attorney, flipped the switch of his inter-office communicating system in answer to its buzz. One of the clerks spoke.

"There is someone to see you, sir. He won't give his name. He's—well, rather startling looking, sir. He can't hear me now, of course, but he looks as if—as if he'd just stepped out of a casket after being hit by ten or twelve speeding autos."

"My, my." Quinn clucked his tongue. "He certainly must be something to behold. However, he won't bother me with his appearance. I can't see. Or have you forgotten, Jerry?"

The clerk gasped. "I—well yes, sir, I did for the moment. I'm terribly sorry, sir."

"Forget it," Quinn chuckled. "I'm used to the idea. What does he want?"

"He refuses to say, sir. Except that it is very important."

"Hold him there for three minutes, then send him in," Quinn directed.

He turned to the bald, slender man beside him.

"Silk, as usual, you'd better go into the next room. Most of the time, as of course you

---

AN EXCITING COMPLETE BLACK BAT NOVEL

know, people who want to see me so badly and who refuse to identify themselves, are coming in to give me the sordid details of some crime they have committed. They talk better when I'm alone."

"Yes, sir," Silk replied. "I do know. And as usual too, the door won't be closed tightly. With all the enemies you have, sometime or other, some of them are apt to try and take advantage of a man they think is blind."

Quinn nodded absently. Until Silk walked out of the room, Tony Quinn's eyes had been alive, vital and sparkling. They were a deep blue and keen. Now, swiftly, they changed. They became dead-looking, staring, and rigid. The eyes of a blind man. They were like that when the door opened and his visitor came in.

Those apparently blind eyes saw the man, and for a second Quinn almost gasped at the startling appearance of the visitor. He carried a thick, heavy cane on which he leaned. He was thin to the point of emaciation. His bald head was bony, and his face beneath it resembled a skull more than a human countenance. The cheeks were sunken and the flesh tight as a drum skin. His eyes seemed enormous until Quinn realized their sockets had receded and only gave them that deceptive appearance. But they were cold, deadly eyes that seemed to look through one.

HIS complexion was the color of wax. In fact, he reminded Tony Quinn of a horror museum's wax dummy without the color the artist uses in trying to make his mannikins resemble flesh and blood. A wax dummy—that fitted the man exactly, except that he moved. After a fashion.

His arms and legs seemed to be stiff, as if they had been baked. He didn't exactly drag himself along, but he barely lifted his feet off the rug. His lips were almost nonexistent. A sharp, straight line framed the mouth and that was all.

When he spoke, his voice sounded like an ancient gramaphone with a bad needle.

"Do I astonish you, Mr. Quinn?" he demanded arrogantly. "Most people stare at me as if I were a side-show freak. Well—go ahead and grimace."

Quinn leaned back, his eyes well to the left of the position which the visitor had taken.

"I'm sorry, my friend," Quinn said, his features impassive. "I don't know what the devil you are talking about."

The man's eyes blazed and those excuses for lips moved in a hideous grin.

"What are you trying to give me?" he demanded. "I don't look human, do I?"

"I can't say," Quinn replied. "I'm totally blind."

The visitor blinked slowly and owlishly several times while the idea seemed to soak through that high, bony forehead of his. Then he moved forward with that sluggish pace and found a chair.

"Thank heaven," he muttered. "Thank heaven you are blind. That's a horrible thing to say to you, a blind man, but I mean it. I can talk to you without being conscious of my own ghastly appearance. You don't even know I'm a freak. Fine—fine. I couldn't be better pleased."

"Now that we've disposed of those amenities," Quinn said, "will you state your business?"

The visitor didn't pay much attention to that.

"You think being blind is bad," he said. "If you could only see me! See what's left of what used to be a man. Not an unhandsome man, either. Once I had a fine head of hair. Now I am bald. Once I had a husky frame and a strong, rugged face with lips, and filled-in cheeks like that of any other man. I wish they'd blinded me while they were at it. They did everything else."

"They?" Quinn asked.

"Japs. Those dirty little beasts who call themselves men. I was a prisoner for more than three years in Bilibid. That's a Jap prison camp in the Philippines, if you need to know."

Quinn nodded. "I see. It must have been a ghastly experience, Mr.—Mr.—"

"Bradley is the name. Matt Bradley. A ghastly experience you say? That's not half of it. But you have no idea how the human body clings to existence. They tortured me with about every device their devilish minds could think of. I'm a physical wreck of a man now. The doctors did what they could. It wasn't much, let me tell you."

"I sympathize with you, Mr. Bradley. Deeply so. Many of our people were hideously treated by the Japs."

"But not like me." Bradley's voice grated like a wooden wheel on dry gravel. "They especially didn't like me, the dirty little animals! And yet, they weren't even certain of my identity. I passed under another name in the camp. You see, I once helped the Chinese in their unequal fight against the Japs. I helped them with all my heart and as much cash as I could spare. The Japs knew it. They suspected who I was, but they weren't positive. That's why they didn't kill me. It would have been better if they had, because someone else has killed me since."

"I beg your pardon?" Quinn frowned deeply. "Your last remark hardly makes sense."

The man laughed harshly. "I suppose it doesn't. This is the story, Mr. Quinn. I

men, you surely must understand that they reached Manila as rapidly as they possibly could."

"All right,—maybe they did and maybe they didn't," Bradley barked. "It's beside the point anyway. As I say, I was rescued, patched up somewhat, and allowed to come home. It so happened that I wanted to surprise my people. My people! A fine lot they turned out to be. It was late at night when I arrived and I checked in at a hotel. I saw a man I knew, but he didn't recognize me, and when I told him who I was he informed me, quite politely, that I was a con-

THE BLACK BAT

flew to the Philippines just before those devils struck. I was taken the moment they entered Manila. Oh, I'd have fled if there had been a chance, but they dropped one of their filthy bombs on the building I was in. It exploded in the room next to mine and knocked me out. Practically burned me to a crisp as well. However, I survived the bomb and all the punishment those fiends could conjure up. I was rescued. Heaven knows it took them long enough to come after me, but they finally did."

"Just a moment," Quinn cut in icily. "If you happen to refer to MacArthur and his

temptible fraud. He said that Matt Bradley had died more than three years ago and was buried at Woodlawn Cemetery."

QUINN'S impassive features twitched slightly, a sign of interest.

"Go on," he urged.

"I waited until the following morning. This very morning to be exact. Then I went to that cemetery, studied the records and found my own tombstone. There is someone buried under it and I resent that. I'm not dead. I am Matt Bradley, and I'm certain someone simulated my death for reasons advantageous to himself or herself."

Quinn made a few notes. "There might have been another Matt Bradley," he suggested.

"No," Bradley snapped. "It's my family plot. My parents are buried there too—and my sister. Well, I made a bit of an investigation. I am dead. My estate—a considerable one—has passed into the hands of three heirs. Nit-wits I knew I should never have trusted. They're living in my house, spending my money."

"And these people are?" Quinn prodded.

"One is my nephew. Don Thayer, the lying, chiseling tramp. I particularly hate him because he not only took my money and my home, but my fiancé as well. He married Wilma, who was promised to me. I ought to kill him, and maybe I will."

"Forget such ideas," Quinn told him sternly. "If those people wrongfully appropriated your estate, there are laws with which to punish them. Who are the others?"

"My lazy brother, Sam Bradley. I think he was waiting for me to die. I carried him for years, even with his drinking and gambling. Then there's my cousin, the saintly and righteous skunk. Never drank, never looked at a girl, never smoked. Just buried his nose in books and music. He almost drove me crazy with his piano playing. Thinking of that was the only consolation I had while the Japs held me. I used to think of his incessant and infernal playing when they tortured me. It made the punishment a little easier to take. Because he wasn't there and his piano didn't drum in my ears."

"And his name?" Quinn's pencil was poised.

"Clint Henderson. And there is another doublecrosser to squawk about too. My business partner, Hal Salisbury. I discovered he simply took over the plant."

"All right," Quinn said. "I have information enough. Now listen to me, Mr. Bradley. If you intend to go home and raise the roof over this, take it easy. If you kill anyone, you'll be punished. If they have wrongfully robbed you, it's my job to take care of them. Quite obviously, they have, if what you have said is the truth."

"Do you think I am a liar?" Bradley screamed.

"I didn't say that," Quinn answered patiently. "So far, I must act solely upon presumption. But, as I was saying, if all this is true, someone rigged a funeral to establish your death legally. If that happened, a crime has been committed. I shall look into it at once. Now, where can I find you?"

"At my home." Bradley arose, unbending like a hinge to do so. And he wasn't much fatter than a hinge. "I'll drive those vermin out!"

"You'll do nothing of the kind," Quinn said with grim authority. "You may go home if you wish, but I want every one of those people there. And do me a favor. Forget, if you can, all that you have been through. Pretend you don't know a thing about your alleged death. Just act as if you were mighty happy to be back home. Remember—no violence."

Bradley's lips parted again. "As you wish." He bowed his head slightly. "I suppose I am a bit on the venomous side myself. And, Mr. Quinn, do you mind if I say once more that I'm glad you can't see. If you could, you'd probably have me put away. Yes—it is that bad."

"I'm sorry," Quinn said again. "Have you no one to assist you?"

"Yes—and the funny part of it is he's blind too. The Japs really gave it to him. We were in the same camp. He has no one— no family, no friends as close as I am. He was kind to me and I intend to make it up to him. He is waiting outside. He can't see me either. I have to have someone who doesn't wince every time he sees my face. When shall I expect you?"

"Presently," Quinn said. "But, Mr. Bradley, you can't blame me for checking up a trifle. Your story is rather weird. Suppose you wait in the outer office for a little while. Be sure to make your blind friend comfortable. In fact, I'd like to meet him afterwards."

"I'm in no hurry," Bradley said, with a smirk. It was hideous to watch him. If this man was on the level, he deserved all the sympathy possible, even if he was so intensely bitter.

When the door closed on Bradley, Silk hurried into the room.

"That was some story," he said, with a note of sarcasm in his voice.

"It does sound fantastic," Quinn admitted, "and yet it has a ring of truth to it also. Anyhow the whole thing can be checked up on easily. Silk, Bradley mentioned the name of Don Thayer, his nephew, and added that he had married a girl named Wilma. Wilma Thayer! She's one of Carol's friends."

Silk whistled. "So she is. Carol has often spoken of her."

"Slip outside," Quinn ordered, "and get hold of Carol. Tell her this man Bradley's story and have her go see Wilma at once. Don't let her waste a moment. I want

Silk was clambering over the roof when Bronco thrust out an arm through the window, bringing up his gun (CHAPTER X)

Carol in the home of the Thayers when Bradley arrives."

CHAPTER II

Frankenstein's Brother

SILK took his hat on the fly and hurriedly left the office. Tony Quinn leaned back, and those amazing eyes of his were clear and alive again. He started going over the affair in his mind. The story Bradley had told him was just eerie enough to be true.

This monstrosity of a man now waiting in the outer office probably had been illegally declared dead and his estate taken over.

Thinking of the man, Quinn's fingers unconsciously touched the small, but deep scars surrounding his own eyes. He knew what it meant to be burned. Those scars had been caused by acid which had been flung into his face when some crooks had been trying to destroy incriminating evidence against them. Quinn had been a hard-hitting regular District Attorney then, and had been trying the case. He had attempted to save the evidence, and the acid had instantly blinded him.

He had resigned as District Attorney, of course, and had spent months trying to find a doctor who might restore his sight. There was none. Not even in pre-war Europe where he had gone as a last, forlorn hope. Returning to America, dejected and filled with despair, Tony Quinn had settled down to the life of a blind man.

He had not been the type of man to give up, however. He had learned to use his other senses and, in time, they had become acute. Yet he had lived in a world of darkness.

Silk Kirby had come into the life of the District Attorney just before Quinn lost his sight. Silk had been a confidence man, as smooth as his name, but having fallen on hard times he had descended to taking on his first second-story job. He had come to rob Quinn, but after a talk with his would-be victim who discovered him, Silk had become a reformed character, without reservations.

From the first moment, Quinn was a great man in Silk's estimation, and he had remained that to this day. For Silk had never returned to his former underworld companions. Instead, he had remained to work for Quinn, and now he occupied not only the position of loyal servant, but of devoted friend.

It was when Tony Quinn had given up hope of ever seeing again had a visitor one night. A pretty and charming girl named Carol Baldwin. She had come with a strange offer. Her father, a police sergeant, she had explained, lay dying from a gangster's bullet, in a faraway Mid-western town. He had followed Quinn's career intently and admiringly, and now it was his dying wish to donate his eyes to Tony Quinn so that the former District Attorney could go on with his battle against the evil of the underworld.

A little known surgeon in the police officer's home town performed the operation, using techniques later on adopted by famous specialists. The operation had been a success. Carol's father had died—that had been inevitable—but Tony Quinn could see again.

All during his career as a District Attorney, he had realized how the red tape of the law retarded the work of anyone who battled against crime. So Quinn decided to keep the recovery of his sight a secret, to live as a totally blind man and devote his life to a fight against crime.

He had become eminently successful under the name of the Black Bat, which he had adopted at the offset of his new life. It had not been long before that name had become well-known, and feared, by those who robbed and killed and cheated.

The Black Bat was an eerie being to underworld denizens, to whom he soon became a Nemesis. A soft-footed creature, clad wholly in somber black, and wearing a close-fiitting hood that covered his features perfectly, he shortly showed law-breakers that the Black Bat knew more about crime than they did. Also, he could shoot straight and fast, and battle them with some of their own methods when necessary.

The Black Bat had another advantage over criminals who were his prey. His months of blindness had sharpened his hearing and sense of touch to a remarkable degree. And, as if Nature wanted to recompense him for his blindness, a strange addition to normal vision had come to him with his returned sight. He could see in inky darkness as well as in broad daylight. Even faint colors were visible to him where normal vision would have been blacked out.

Carol Baldwin, after her father's death, enlisted in the small band of crime fighters under the Black Bat's guidance. She soon proved that his confidence in her was not misplaced. She was shrewd and clever. Unafraid and enterprising. The Black Bat trusted her implicity.

THE fourth member of the little group was a giant of a man named "Butch" O'Leary. He had owned another first name at one time or another, but his enormous bulk had fastened the appellation of Butch upon him, and so he was known. Butch was not brainy, but he was faithful and strong and had his own uses for the Black Bat's purposes. His loyalty to Tony Quinn, after the former District Attorney once had done him a big favor, was unquestioned.

These three persons alone knew that Tony Quinn was the Black Bat. Police Commissioner Warner, of Quinn's home city, suspected it, but realizing the usefulness of the Black Bat, he preferred not to think of it. The Black Bat often adopted methods in his work which could be construed as highly illegal—but effective.

For that reason Captain McGrath, a short, bulky police officer who did not look on the work of the Black Bat so leniently, had sworn to put the self-appointed criminals' Nemesis behind bars some day. McGrath's tenaciousness was sometimes exasperating, but mostly his activities added zest to the dangerous game. McGrath didn't just suspect that Tony Quinn was not blind, and that he was the Black Bat. In his own mind he was certain of it—but was without the proof he needed to make an arrest.

As the Black Bat, Tony Quinn had made many pay for their crimes, killers and thugs who might otherwise have escaped punishment. Yet as he sat behind his desk now, he doubted that any case he had ever undertaken had quite the quality of weirdness which the matter of Matt Bradley seemed to offer. Quinn's position as special District Attorney gave him a reason for being interested, and he was, intensely and deeply. He had already started the ball rolling. Now he asked his clerk to send Matt Bradley in again, for Silk Kirby had by now had time to reach Carol Baldwin. She probably was on her way now to the home of her friend, Wilma Thayer, the home the gargoyle Bradley claimed as his own. . . .

Carol had, in fact, already received Silk's call, and had gone to work immediately. Stopping only long enough to repair her make-up, she hurried out of her apartment and took a taxi for the beautiful Long Island estate just outside of Flushing where Wilma Thayer lived.

Carol was a slim, vivacious, unusually pretty blue-eyed blond girl. Her figure could vie with the most perfect in the front lines of great show choruses. No one would have suspected the dynamite packed in her five-feet-three of height. And she was cool and composed, apparently with nothing on her mind but a call on a friend when she arrived at her destination and asked her taximan to wait.

Wilma Thayer came to the door to greet her. At once Carol knew that Matt Bradley had not reached the house yet, because Wilma was unworried and glad to see Carol.

"It's a surprise, this visit from you," Wilma said eagerly, "but I'm so glad you're here, Carol! Don is home, but he's doing some work in the garage. Clint is buried in some new music. Sam is off to one of his favorite cafés, I suppose . . . Or no—I remember now. Sam didn't feel good this morning, so he took a pill and went back to bed. Anyhow, it's lonely around here."

"Then I'm glad I stopped by," Carol said. "I was on an errand further down the island, and suddenly I thought of you. So here I am."

Carol surveyed the big house with its gables and ells, a cheerful, homey place, for all of its size. The estate that surrounded it stretched for acres behind the house, the entire place neatly enclosed by a white fence. It was as charming an estate as Carol had ever seen, and she wondered how anyone could be lonely here.

They entered the big living room and sat down. Wilma offered Carol a cigarette, lit it and her own, and both girls relaxed. For half an hour they talked of people they both knew, discussed a show they had seen, and made some tentative plans to attend the theatre together some evening.

Once Clint Henderson, the man Matt Bradley had told Tony Quinn was a cousin, plodded into the room, searching for some music. He walked with his head and shoulders bent, like some gnome out of a fairy story book. He didn't notice the two girls at all.

Don Thayer came in soon afterward. His hands and arms, to the elbows, were smeared with grease. His face was covered with it too, but he was a good-looking young man. Muscular, broad-shouldered and slim-waisted.

"Well, Carol!" He extended a hand, then drew it back with an embarrassed laugh. "Guess I'm a little too oily to shake hands. But I'll get cleaned up in no time. How about a fast game of tennis? The court was just rolled."

"Splendid!" Carol agreed, wondering just

how these people would take it when the supposedly dead owner of this property arrived.

SHE knew that the estate left by Matt Bradley had made Clint Henderson, Sam Bradley, Don Thayer and Wilma, independently wealthy. It was going to be hard to take, and Carol found herself hoping that Matt Bradley would turn out to be a fraud.

Yet, like Tony Quinn, she sensed that his story was weird enough to be true. It was something a man couldn't simply make up out of the whole cloth and hope to get away with. It was too easily checked.

Matt Bradley would be here soon. Carol shuddered, thinking of Silk's description of the man.

A car stopped out front. Don, on his way to the staircase, stopped and turned around. Wilma looked up too. Matt Bradley didn't ring the bell. He merely opened the door and walked in. With him was a wild-looking creature who also carried a cane—a shiny white enameled one. The long, heavy gray hair of Bradley's companion covered his face like a poodle's. He was stooped, and obviously none too strong. Just as obviously he was blind.

Don Thayer, annoyance on his face, stepped up to the pair.

"It's customary to ring the bell," he chided. "What do you want?"

Matt Bradley's gravelly laugh filled the house.

"So you don't recognize me! I didn't think you would, Don. In fact, if my features were as they used to be, I still believe you wouldn't wish to recognize me. And Wilma! My darling, faithful Wilma. You'd wait for me forever. That's what you said, but I wonder just how long you did wait after you thought I was dead."

Wilma grasped Carol's arm so hard that Carol winced.

"Who—are—you?" she asked in horror.

"You too?" Matt Bradley derided. "You don't remember me either? Why Wilma, my dear, we were to have been married. Remember? I'm your promised husband. Matt Bradley!"

Wilma said nothing. She merely leaned against Carol and her knees folded. She slid toward the floor, but Carol seized her in time. As she half-carried, half-dragged Wilma back to a couch in the living room, Carol looked over her shoulder, glaring at Matt Bradley.

"At least you could have been gentle about it," she snapped.

Bradley rubbed his hands and smirked. "Gentle, eh? Gentle in the same smooth manner all my property and money were taken away from me? Don, you thieving scoundrel, I'll—"

Don recovered his wits. "Now wait a minute!" he said belligerently and moved toward Bradley.

Instantly the blind man raised his white cane. Bradley nudged him.

"It's all right, George. Don never had any more courage than a scared rabbit." He looked at young Thayer steadily. "So you don't believe I'm your loving uncle, Don. How nice of you. And considerate. You look at me once and decide I can't be your uncle. Spendid, I must say. But I am Matt Bradley. I am your uncle and the party is over."

"I don't believe you," Don said stonily. "This is some kind of a scheme."

"Ah—so!"

Bradley suddenly lifted one leg. Straight out, it didn't seem to articulate at the knee. He pulled up his trouser cuff and an oddly shaped scarlet mark was visible.

"I was born with that," he said. "You once said it was Satan's mark put upon me. Your mother was my sister. She died on April seventeenth, Nineteen-hundred-eight. Her husband, a thorough-going rat like you, his son, died in an auto accident less than a year later. You had a sister who died in infancy. Rather than grow up into something like you, I imagine.

"Then there is Clint Henderson, my loving cousin who hasn't the brains to earn a dime. If he shatters the peace of this house with his accursed piano playing, I'll throw him out."

Don Thayer was backing away slowly, the light of incredulity growing in his eyes. Matt Bradley, his hideous mask of a face cracked in a grin, went on.

"My brother Sam isn't here to greet me. Unless a miracle has happened, he must be sleeping off a hang-over upstairs—in his room which is the second to the last one on the right hand side of the right wing. And you, Don. The only really clever one of the lot. Clever, but you were kicked out of college in your junior year. A little trouble over cheating in an examination, wasn't it? Then you went to work in a brokerage house and lasted four months. Cheating again, I presume. Now, you infernal idiot, do you believe I'm Matt Bradley?"

"You can't be!" Don said, in sheer horror. "You simply can't be. Matt is dead. I—saw him buried. I bought a stone for his grave. It just—can't—be, I tell you."

MATT BRADLEY cursed once.
"Do I have to remind you of the time you stole money out of my safe?" he snapped. "Eleven hundred and twenty-one dollars, to be exact. I should have sent you to prison that time. You're a weak-kneed, lily-livered crook, Don. If I've been gypped out of my money, you're the one to blame, and this time I will see you in prison. I'll—"

He raised his own cane and stepped forward. The cane swished through the air. Carol, coming out the doorway, called a warning. Don dodged the blow which had been rendered impotent anyway, as Matt Bradley jerked around at the sound of Carol's voice. Bradley lowered his heavy cane and faced Carol.

"Just who the devil are you?" he demanded. "Someone Don picked up because Wilma ceased to interest him?"

Carol came forward, straight up to Bradley, and looked at him coolly.

"I happen to be a friend," she said. "A very good friend of Wilma's."

"Ah—so," Bradley purred. "Then you, too, doubt who I am?"

"I don't know who you are and I don't care," Carol snapped. "But I think Frankenstein might recognize you. You look like his brother." She turned away, unaffected by Bradley's rasping curse.. "Don, pull yourself together. Wilma needs you."

Don hurried into the living room. Bradley started to follow, with that stiff-legged gait of his. Carol placed herself firmly in the doorway.

"No you don't," she said tartly. "Wilma has been through enough without being scared to death of that face."

The blind man was on Bradley's arm again. He let go and raised his white cane.

"Shall I?" he whispered hoarsely.

"No, George." Bradley seemed incongruously kind to this strange blind man. "Perhaps later I'll let you wrap the cane around her pretty neck, but not right now."

"I thank you," Carol said sardonically, "for your very kind consideration of my neck. Now go away somewhere before I lose my temper entirely."

She turned and walked into the room. Bradley's laugh chilled her, and she had to repress a shudder. In her career as the Black Bat's aide, she had met some weird and dangerous characters, but Matt Bradley and his blind man seemed to be a composite of all of the worst of them.

The heavy gun was raised and brought down in a long swinging blow on Silk's skull (CHAP. VI)

CHAPTER III

Murder Moves In

WILMA was feeling better, but the shock of Matt Bradley's return made her shiver as with a chill. Don stroked her wrists and hands, but he was just as pale as his wife was. Carol remained sensibly practical about the whole thing.

"Do you believe he really is Matt Bradley?" she asked.

"He can't be," Wilma declared. "Matt is dead."

Don, staring at the floor, spoke slowly.

"I could have been wrong. Matt left here just before Pearl Harbor. He stopped off at San Francisco. Later I received word that he had been killed. I went to Frisco and there was a body in the morgue, dressed in Matt's clothes, and looking like him. I never doubted but that it was Matt. So I made the identification and had the body sent back here."

"Didn't anyone else question the identity of the body?" Carol asked.

There was a lot of ground to cover here and she was in a hurry. Things could happen.

Don looked up with a shrug. "You're talking like a detective, Carol, but that's all right. Nobody saw the body. Matt's will provided that he be buried in a metal casket, sealed, and that no one look upon him in death."

"What about sailing records in Frisco?" Carol queried. "If Matt really did sail, there must have been some notation of it."

Don shook his head. "Not necessarily. Matt knew the Japs were going to strike. He knew they hated him and if he did go back, he probably used a phony name to confuse them. That man out there may be Matt. He certainly knows enough to be him. And yet, I can't make myself believe. . . . Oh, what's the use?"

Carol shook him hard. She knew Don was something of a weakling. Perhaps all those accusations Matt Bradley had made about him were true.

"Come off it," Carol said crisply. "This is no time to go into a blue funk. Perhaps your other uncle—Matt's brother—would be able to help determine his identity. Or Clint, your family musician. You're not going to give up without a fight, are you?"

Don arose. "I'll talk to Sam," he said heavily. "He came home spiffed early this morning, but he should have sobered up by now. He'll know, I'm sure."

Don went out of the room, with Carol following him as far as the door. There was no one in the hall. Matt Bradley and his blind companion had vanished. The front door was ajar. Probably they had gone out to look over the estate, though of course it would have to be described to the blind man. Anyhow it would have been like that mask-faced visitor to see if his estate had suffered any damage.

Carol went back to Wilma. "Brace up," she urged. "If things get too tough, you can come home with me for a while. At least you don't have to endure Matt and his sarcasm—if he really is Matt Bradley . . . Wilma, were you engaged to him?"

"Yes," Wilma said. "Yes, I was. Matt never was a gay type, but I was sure I loved him. Then Don came and I wasn't so sure, but Matt didn't happen to be the kind who would stand by and let Don take me away from him. When—Don wired that Matt was dead, I felt relieved. I know now that life with Matt would have been impossible."

"I should imagine," Carol commented dryly. "Do you think this man is Matt?"

Wilma looked straight at Carol. "I don't know. I'm not sure of anything. He doesn't look like Matt, of course. The Matt I remember had a heavy shock of black hair and he was strong, rather heavy-set. This man doesn't speak like Matt, either, but he does know so much. I could make sure. Little things happened when I was going with him that only Matt would know. Yes, I could be sure."

Carol heard a faint scraping sound and looked around toward a window at the back of the room. It was open about a third of the way and she thought someone could have been listening. She arose quietly and moved toward that window. Peering out she saw only George, the long-haired blind man, picking his way along with the aid of that murderous white cane. She went back to Wilma.

"You won't have to go through any unpleasant interviews with Matt," she said. "There is another way to prove if he is telling the truth. A job for the police, but they'll have to be called in anyhow."

"I—don't know what you mean?" Wilma looked half ill again.

"It's quite simple. The body buried as Matt Bradley can be disinterred. If it isn't Matt, then we can safely assume this—this person who just arrived, must be Matt. I have a friend with some influence in the District Attorney's office. I could see him."

"No!" Wilma cried in horror. "No, Carol, don't! You can't help me in that way. Please don't let the police know about this. Please!"

Carol looked her astonishment. "All right, Wilma. Cool off. I don't intend to do anything you don't want. It was just a suggestion. Out of our hands anyhow, I imagine, because Matt is bound to ask for an identification of the body in the grave."

Wilma arose. "I—I'd have to talk with Don first, Carol. It's his problem too."

"I'll see him," Carol said firmly. "You're too distraught."

CAROL hurried up the stairs, leaving Wilma in the living room. This was something of a mess. She liked Wilma, and wanted to help her, but she had never been especially attracted to Don. Carol disliked young men who were wealthy and refused to work.

But she detested this man who called himself Matt Bradley, and she found to her surprise that she actually feared the blind man who accompanied him. This George—whatever his last name was—had had the appearance of a killer when he had lifted his white cane. And Carol possessed few doubts but that a blind man could maneuver well enough to kill.

She wondered about the scraping sound near the window too. It could have been George, but he must have moved fast to get so far away from the window before she reached it. Maybe—and Carol gave the idea more than passing thought—George was not blind at all, but merely a good actor. One who rivaled Tony Quinn.

Her high heels clicked as she ran up the steps. There was nobody in the corridor on the second floor. She knew where Don's room was, and the door seemed to be open. Someone else came up the steps. It was Wilma, and she joined Carol. They walked to the open door.

Carol glanced into the room—and gulped. Don was lying on the floor. The back of his head was caved in just as if it had been an eggshell and some massive thumb had deliberately crunched a hole through it. Blood had gushed out all over the place.

Wilma looked at Carol for a second, and her knees began to buckle. At that moment a tall, ruggedly built man emerged from one of the other rooms. He had rather bleary eyes and wore a bathrobe over his pajamas. This was the Sam Bradley whose sole dis-

tinguishing feature was that he drank too much.

"Sam!" Carol called. "Take Wilma. Hurry! Don has been murdered!"

Wordlessly Sam obeyed. Carol raced down the steps and into the library. She closed the door, lifted the phone and dialed Tony Quinn's office. This was something she could do in only a direct emergency. Silk answered.

"The boogey-man arrived," Carol whispered. "So did murder! Don Thayer has been killed. I'm calling the police as a routine measure."

She quickly deflected the cradle, let it up again and dialed Police Headquarters. She made a brief report of what happened to a desk officer. Then she hurried out of the room. She came to a sudden stop. Matt Bradley was standing in the hallway. He seemed greatly agitated, but before Carol could even wonder whether or not he had been listening, a man Carol had not seen before entered the house.

He was tall, gray at the temples, and a handsome man. His clothes were carefully tailored and he presented a picture of good grooming.

He stared at Matt Bradley as if he didn't believe his eyes.

"Good gosh!" he ejaculated. "Who the devil are you?"

Matt Bradley's strange lips parted in that customary grimace which passed for a smile.

"Hello, Hal Salisbury," he greeted. "How does my business partner feel, and do you think your books can stand an accounting? Because I'll have them checked. Half of what you've earned these last three or four years is mine."

"Are you—Matt Bradley?" Hal exclaimed.

"I'll prove it to your satisfaction," Matt answered. "But not right now. I heard a scream. What's happened?"

"Don has just been murdered" Carol said, quietly, "and if I were you, I would start thinking of alibis. Good ones."

Matt Bradley said nothing. Hal Salisbury gaped for a moment.

"Great Jehosephat!" he said then, and sat down very, very slowly as if he expected the seat of the chair to come up and meet him.

Just as Carol had known would be the case, and as Tony Quinn had known before her, Matt Bradley lost no time in obtaining a permit to open the grave where a body that was supposed to be his own was interred. It was done that very night, after the corpse of the murdered Don Thayer had been removed from the big house, and while the police were still investigating.

The digging was done by the light of a powerful lamp rigged up from a fire truck, borrowed by the Police Department. The outer burial box was opened, revealing a huge, solid metal coffin within.

On the brink of the grave stood a group of men. Predominating by his ugly appearance alone, was the man who called himself Matt Bradley. His blind companion stood beside him, holding his arm and looking down into the grave as if he could see. Sam Bradley was there too, on the other side of the open grave. He was cold sober, but acted as though a couple of drinks might have been most welcome.

HAL SALISBURY, Matt Bradley's business partner, was beside Sam. His face was ashen and it was quite clear that all of this was deeply distressing. Clint Henderson had stayed home with Wilma. No amount of persuasion could have made him accompany the party.

Tony Quinn, with Silk, was in a car drawn up close by the grave. Captain McGrath drifted over to the special District Attorney. McGrath seemed perturbed.

"This is one swell case you dropped in my lap, Mr. Quinn. I got nowhere this afternoon when I got to the Bradley home. Those people are all peculiar, and the oddest one is that—that monstrosity of a man. What do you think we'll find in the coffin?"

"A corpse," Quinn's lips moved slightly, but he didn't smile.

"Sure," McGrath agreed complacently, not noticing the irony in Quinn's voice. "But whose?"

"I haven't the slightest idea," Quinn answered. "However, the man who says he is Matt Bradley was anxious for this disinterment. He must be sure he is Matt Bradley, and therefore you'd hardly expect him to be in the casket."

McGrath grimaced. "I'm none too sure. He looks as if he came out of one. What did you think of the set-up at the house?"

"Too well set up," Quinn replied. "Too many alibis and none backed up. I intend to return after we've finished here. Better come along, Captain."

"How could I stay away when you assign me to the job?" McGrath said, with a shrug. "Say—could it be there is more to this mess than meets the eye, and that the Black Bat might sort of move in—maybe?"

Quinn laughed. "You'll have to find him and ask him. Captain, how many times must I deny that I'm the Black Bat? He has the faculty of sight. He must have, by the way he gets around. And I'm blind. Totally blind. Incurably blind. Your own doctors have examined me and attested to that. Why keep up this farce?"

"Listen!" McGrath dropped his voice. "As far as I'm concerned, it is no farce, and I'll land you yet. That's no threat, but a promise. I'm sick of it too, being given the run-around all the time . . . Well, looks like they're ready to open it up. Be back soon."

"What's the verdict, sir?" Silk said, the moment McGrath withdrew. "About the murder of Don Thayer, I mean."

"I don't know," Quinn confessed frankly. "Any of them could have killed him. Except Wilma, of course, who was with Carol. Yet even Wilma could have done it if there was some place where she could have disposed of the weapon. But she is a good actress if she did kill him. Her grief seems genuine enough."

"Matt Bradley—or the man who calls himself that—threatened to kill Don when he was in your office," Silk reminded Tony Quinn.

"And Matt could be the killer," said Quinn. "He claimed he was roving around the estate. The blind man was out of the house and wholly on his own. Also, there is a back stairway either of them could have used. That likewise applies to Hal Salisbury, Matt's business partner. He showed up only moments after the body had been discovered. Brother Sam was in his room all the time— so he claims—but he was closest to the scene of the crime and not under observation of any kind. Cousin Clint—well, he doesn't seem to know where he was himself. He walks around in a perpetual fog of notes and clefs."

"Or seems to," Silk amended. "I don't trust fellows who act as he does. I . . . Oh, oh, they must have opened the casket. Matt is nearly falling into the grave trying to see."

The casket had been opened, with the use of an acetelyene torch. The body inside was intact. Everyone turned away except Matt, who kept staring into the coffin. McGrath hurried over to the car.

"I don't know who that is—in the grave," he reported, "but is certainly isn't Matt Bradley. The dead man was a little fellow about sixty years old. How in the world Don Thayer ever identified him as his uncle is beyond me."

Quinn sighed. "Well, what little chance there was of proving this Matt Bradley here a fraud is gone now. He probably is Matt . . . I guess that's all, Silk. You may drive me home."

The starter whined and the motor purred. Silk shifted gears. McGrath, his head still inside the car door, was eyeing Quinn almost hopefully.

"Sure the Black Bat isn't going to take a hand in this?" he insisted.

"Find him and ask him," Quinn snapped. "I'm going home to bed. When you get enough evidence to warrant an arrest, let me know and I'll prepare the warrant. Until then, Captain, it's all yours."

CHAPTER IV

The Black Bat

VEN Silk was dissatisfied as he drove Tony Quinn away from the cemetery. He repeated McGrath's question. Quinn smiled thoughtfully.

"The Black Bat, Silk, doesn't risk working on affairs like this," he said. "There isn't much to it. Someone at the house killed Don. Matt Bradley is home, and the man buried in his place was a fraud. It's a routine police job. Something to give McGrath a headache, and I hope he gets one."

"Just the same," Silk said, "I think it would be an interesting case."

Reaching home, Silk drove into the garage, helped Quinn out, and left him standing in front until he had the doors closed. Then Quinn took Silk's arm and they walked slowly around to the front of the house, a blind man and his servant. Tony Quinn never relaxed that pose for an instant when there was an iota of chance that prying eyes might notice.

In the house, Silk made Quinn comfortable in the library, then bustled around the house. Finally he drew the window shades carefully. Quinn arose then and walked up to one of the bookcases lining the walls. Touching a control that was well-hidden, he caused part of the case to move away, revealing the entrance to a secret room.

It was a laboratory, modernly equipped with everything needed in the pursuit of criminals and the study of clues. Only Quinn and his aides knew of the existence of this lab. It was provided with a special entrance from the outside also. A tunnel ran from the lab to a garden house at the rear of the grounds around Quinn's house. By this means, he could come and go without being seen, and his aides were enabled to reach him without arousing any suspicion.

Quinn frowned. The lab was dark, but it should have been illuminated. Carol had promised to come there directly after leaving the Bradley estate. There were no signs that she had been here at all. Quinn looked at an electric clock on a bench. Three hours had passed since Carol had made that promise.

Silk entered and Quinn gave voice to his worry.

"Carol should be here, Silk. I don't like this. Call Butch and have him get over here right away. Then run over to Carol's apartment and see if she is there. Do that, instead of phoning her. It's safer."

Half an hour later, the trap-door in the lab opened and an enormous pair of shoulders came through, topped by a head that reminded one of a St. Bernard. Not in appearance, but in proportionate size. The man pulled himself all the way through the trap-door—and he was huge. Thick arms swung smoothly at his sides and the fists at the end of them were like half-sized hams. This was Butch.

"Something doin'?" he asked Quinn with a hopeful grin.   (Turn page)

"I don't know yet, Butch," Quinn said. "Carol seems to be missing. There was a murder this afternoon out at a place in Long Island to which I sent her. Apparently it was a rather well embellished murder, but why anyone who was involved would want to kill Carol or take her prisoner is beyond me. She didn't know a thing. I talked to her out there."

Butch's grin faded. Thick fingers curled into mighty fists.

"Anybody that lays a hand on Carol gets his head busted," he growled. "Just tell me who."

"I wish I could," Quinn sighed. "Silk has gone to Carol's apartment for a look around. He ought to be back soon."

Silk returned shortly with a report that Carol apparently hadn't come back to her apartment.

"I'm getting worried, sir," Silk said soberly. "This isn't like Carol."

Quinn's own lips were grim as he arose and went to a steel locker. Opening it, he took out a suit of jet-black clothes, a black shirt and tie, and somber-colored shoes equipped with crepe soles. He changed into these togs, then slipped a black hood over his face. It was necessary to conceal the tell-tale scars around his eyes, and the hood also was the identifying mark of the Black Bat.

He slid a compact set of highly tempered burglar tools into one hip pocket and a heavy automatic into the other. He drew on thin black gloves, and Tony Quinn had vanished. In his place stood the ominously forbidding figure of the Black Bat.

"Up until the time Carol didn't return here, there wasn't much in this affair to interest me," he said stonily. "But now there is. I'm going to the Bradley estate and have a look around. Silk, you are to remain in the house at all times in the event that Carol calls. Butch, you have another assignment. The only outsider connected with this Long Island murder is a man named Hal Salisbury. He lives at the Crescent Hotel. Has a big suite of rooms there. You will keep an eye on him. Phone Silk if there are developments. I think that's all for the moment."

THE Black Bat made his way, via the tunnel, to the garden house. He emerged onto the grounds and looked around. It was black dark, but his eyes penetrated that gloom as if it did not exist. He walked briskly toward a gate, through it, and onto the side street beside his home. A coupé was parked there. He got in.

Before starting the car, he removed the hood and replaced it with a wide-brimmed hat which, when pulled down, effectively masked his features and would attract none of the attention a close-fitting black hood would draw.

He drove at a sedate speed to the vicinity of the Bradley home out on the island and parked the car some distance away. He left it there and seemed to fade into the shadows that hemmed in the road. There was not a sign of him because his jet-black outfit blended with the night.

He opened a gate quietly, passed through it and circled the house. Once he drew close to a pair of lighted windows and risked a quick glance into the room. It was the library, and Matt Bradley was hunched over a desk, apparently at work figuring what was left of his estate.

Suddenly, the Black Bat ducked. Someone was walking slowly along the driveway leading to the garage. Those uncanny eyes pierced the darkness and he recognized the prowler as George Lane, as he now knew the blind man to be. He was using his white cane, but it made no tapping sounds, so was probably rubber-cushioned. Soon he faded beyond the reach of the Black Bat's vision.

The Black Bat straightened up, moved silently toward the rear door and found it unlocked, evidently for the convenience of the blind man. He stepped into the house and listened. The notes of a piano, beautifully played, reached his ears. The music was classical, but lilting. An odd tune to be playing in a house visited by death such a short time ago.

The more the Black Bat listened, the more he gathered the idea that the player was actually putting a lot of joy into the notes. It was as if he were glad the murder had taken place, and that a dead man had arisen to take his place in the household once more.

The Black Bat made his way to the reception hall. Nobody was about, so he moved toward the library. The door was ajar. He pushed it open a bit further and reached in to snap off the light switch. The room was plunged into darkness that didn't matter to the Black Bat, but it brought Matt Bradley to his feet.

"Who is there?" Matt demanded in that rasping voice of his. "Who is it?"

The door closed with a click. "Sit down, Bradley," the Black Bat said. "Sit down, I said. And stop opening that desk drawer. If there is a gun inside, it won't do you the least bit of good to take it. I have a gun too, and mine is in my fist."

"What do you want?" Bradley said tightly. "Who are you? How did you know I was opening the drawer? It's pitch-dark in here."

"You've been away for some time, Bradley," came the voice of the darkness. "Perhaps you've forgotten about the Black Bat. But I'm still in action, let me assure you."

Bradley sat down then, with a thump. His lips were drawn back in a weird grimace, but he didn't go for the gun almost at his fingertips.

"The—Black Bat," he said. "Yes, I remember you. What do you want here?"

"I like puzzles," the Black Bat said conversationally. "Especially murder puzzles. I learned an interesting murder took place here today. An interesting return from the dead too. Are you really Matt Bradley?"

"Of course I am," the man's voice cracked. "I can prove it beyond any doubts whatsoever. You are going to try to prove who killed my nephew?"

"Just that," the Black Bat told him. "I'm afraid the police won't get far, and murder cannot go unavenged. What happened this afternoon?"

"Don was struck on the head and killed. At the time I was on the estate. I'd just returned and I wanted to see if the idiots had made any changes. I didn't know he was dead until I returned to the house."

"You say that Don was struck with something. A heavy cane perhaps?"

"Perhaps," Bradley admitted. "In fact, the police seemed to think so. They took my cane—and my friend George Lane's—to their labs, but returned them a little while ago. Neither one had any traces of blood on it."

IN THE dark, the Black Bat made his single word a question. "George?"

"He's a friend who was interned with me in a Jap prison camp. He saved my life on a couple of occasions. He knew who I really was, that I had helped the Chinese against the Japs, but he never told the Japs even when they tortured him. Therefore, I intend to take care of him. He needs care. He's totally blind. The Japs did that to him."

"A friend like that is rare indeed and deserves to be cared for," the Black Bat said calmly. "Who else was present when the murder was committed?"

"A boozy uncle, my music loving cousin, Wilma, who is Don's widow now, and a friend of hers," Bradley said. "I don't know the girl's name. Then my business partner showed up. Come to think of it, I never did find out why he put in an appearance. He didn't mention a word of it."

"The strange girl—the friend of Wilma. What happened to her?"

"She went home, I suppose. She left right after dark . . . What is this—a new form of inquisition? Let me say right here that if I didn't want to talk, you couldn't make me. I had a lot of practise in keeping my mouth shut while the Japs had me."

"But you have nothing to conceal," the Black Bat reminded him, then added significantly, "Or have you?"

"You may ask all the questions you wish and I'll answer them truthfully," Bradley snapped. "I've nothing to conceal and, while I dislike my nephew and I'm sure he cheated me, nevertheless I'd like his murderer captured."

"Why?" the Black Bat queried.

"Because the same killer may try to get me next," Bradley said irritably. "How do I know the attack wasn't meant for me? There are a lot of people I'd benefit by obliging them and dying. I—"

Suddenly an arm landed against Bradley's chest and lifted him out of the chair. The Black Bat crashed beside him on the floor just as a gun cracked and the bullet slapped into the woodwork of the desk. The Black Bat whispered a warning to Bradley, crawled speedily toward the partly opened window and looked out. His automatic was ready, but there was no target. He crept back to where Bradley lay.

"It seems that you were quite right about that," he whispered. "I'm not sure if the bullet was intended for me or for you, but I'll give you the honor of having been its proposed target."

"Help me up," Bradley groaned. "I can't make it alone. My legs won't work well enough. Help me up."

There was no answer, and Bradley started screaming. The door flew open. Clint Hendereson barged in, fumbled for the lights and snapped them on. Sam Bradley appeared a moment later and then Wilma, pale and red-eyed from weeping. Bradley was assisted to his feet. He peered around the room.

"He's gone," he said slowly. "He vanished like the darkness itself."

"Who are you talking about?" Sam Bradley was slightly thick-tongued.

"The Black Bat, you fool!" Matt screamed. "He was here questioning me. Then someone shot at me. I was almost killed. Wilma, help me! I want to go to the living room."

Wilma stepped closer, put an arm around him and he leaned heavily on her as he passed through the door flanked by Clint and Sam. He glared at both of them.

CHAPTER V

Strange People

N THE hallway, while Clint Henderson and Sam Bradley looked on, Matt Bradley stopped and faced Wilma. The gaunt face of the man seemed even tighter as he stretched the skin in a leer. He put an arm around Wilma.

"I think," he rasped in that odd voice of his, "that you realize now what a mistake you made in marrying Don. You do admit that, don't you?"

"Yes, Matt," Wilma answered softly.

"And you are still in love with me?" he persisted. "Even when I look like what you see now? I can't help my appearance, but my brain is intact, and so is my heart. You are in love with me, Wilma?"

"Yes," she answered, like a dutiful child.

Matt glanced at Sam and Clint. Sam was staring in amazement. Clint hardly paid any attention, as if a pretty girl, widowed for a matter of hours and admitting her love for a man hideous enough to be almost revolting, was a common, everyday affair.

George Lane, the blind man, came into the house, his cane tapping slightly on its rubber pad. He stood near the door, his head slightly cocked while he listened. A slow smile crossed his face. Then he walked into the spacious living room and sat down. The others joined him, Matt still leaning heavily on Wilma.

"I hope I am fully accepted as the real Matt Bradley from now on," Matt said. "I don't intend making any changes, which means all of you are welcome to live here just as before. But a word of warning. Someone is trying to kill me. I believe it is same person who murdered Don. I don't pretend to know why, except that my return has turned things upside down here."

Sam Bradley found his tongue finally. "I'm convinced you are my brother," he said. "You talked me into that, Matt. Going solely by appearance, I would never have recognized you. The only thing that hasn't changed is your height. I suggest we all cooperate with you fully."

"Fine," Matt nodded. "I'm glad you feel

that way. Clint, what's your stand?"

He had to shout Clint's name before the musician seemed to come out of his semi-lethargy. Then Clint blinked and said:

"The Black Bat was here. That means he thinks one of us killed Don. What is he going to do?" There was genuine terror in Clint's voice.

Matt sat down in a chair beside the one occupied by the blind man.

"The Black Bat," he said, "is a strange creature. But he's on our side in this affair and there is no reason to be afraid of him. Unless," he added pointedly, "one of you is plotting against me. If that happens to be the case, I won't need the Black Bat's services to find it out and mete out my own form of punishment. Wilma, get me a brandy and soda."

Wilma obeyed meekly. Outside the living room, the cellar door in the hall opened a trifle and the Black Bat emerged. He had listened and overheard the entire conversation and it puzzled him tremendously. But he had no time to think of it now. He had to get out of this house quickly. There was still the matter of Carol Baldwin's disappearance and he was fairly certain no leads to her whereabouts could be obtained in this house.

He moved silently toward the dining room, was half-way through it and well on his way when the blind man in the living room spoke loudly.

"There is someone prowling! I heard footsteps. Matt— on your guard."

The Black Bat moved fast then, and before the others could reach the back exit he had faded into the darkness. In a few moments he had left the estate and was driving back to town.

He removed the hood and replaced it with the wide-brimmed hat. He shuddered once. For the first time in his career he had an opponent whose hearing was as keen as his own. George Lane really was blind. The Black Bat possessed few doubts about that because the man's abnormal hearing was practical proof of it.

He drove slowly and mulled over the weird events. First of all, there was that shot. Had it been meant for him or for Matt? He firmly believed Matt was the intended target because the bullet had struck the desk directly behind the spot where Matt had been sitting.

Who had fired it? Clint, Sam or Wilma? None had offered an alibi. Or could it have been the blind man, shooting purely by the direction of his hearing? Or Hal Salisbury, Matt's business partner, who was made conspicuous by his absence? The Bat could check on Salisbury, for by this time Butch must be covering the man's movements. He was glad about the hunch which had caused him to assign Butch to that man's trail.

AS for the murder of Don Thayer, there were no clues at all. Any one of those people could have killed him. Matt had even, categorically, threatened to do just that and he seemed fully capable of such a deed. Wilma's actions were strange too. Her acceptance of Matt's attentions were almost incredible.

But most of all, the Black Bat worried about Carol's whereabouts. She had van-

that none of them had an iron-clad alibi.

There was Sam Bradley to be considered. A heavy drinker. A lazy individual accustomed to living off his brother Matt, and then off Don Thayer. Now he was back to sponging on Matt again. Men had committed murder before to insure the continuance of a soft berth like this.

Clint Henderson seemed to be so engrossed in his music as to act like a near idiot, but that could be a clever pose. Yet there was no apparent motive except for one similar to Sam's. Clint also lived there by the grace of whoever controlled the estate.

All in all, the Black Bat considered Hal Salisbury as perhaps the man with the

CAROL

ished without a trace. She wasn't in Matt Bradley's house as a prisoner for Clint, Wilma and Sam roved the place unrestrained and they all couldn't be leagued together. She wasn't in the cellar, for the Black Bat had inspected that. He felt himself believing Matt when the man stated that Carol had left the house soon after dark. Obviously she had been picked up somewhere else.

Why? The Black Bat asked himself that a dozen times. What did she know? If there had been a scrap of important information, she would have told Tony Quinn when he questioned her in his capacity as District Attorney. Carol had merely backed up the statements of all the others and indicated

strongest motive. Provided that he had assumed Matt Bradley to be dead and had wrongfully usurped money and interest in their jointly owned business. If he had turned crooked, he might be trying to murder Matt so that the discrepancies would never be uncovered. But why had he killed Don?

The Black Bat was at a complete impassé and knew it. Except for Wilma and perhaps, Hal Salisbury, the people mixed up in this affair were all odd in some way. He'd never had to contend with such people and their peculiar traits helped none at all in locating a killer. They only served to confuse the issues completely.

The Black Bat reached the street where he lived in his rightful identity of Tony Quinn. He started turning the corner, but pulled up short under the dark shadows of a big tree. There was a car parked in front of his home and a man was getting out. Captain McGrath!

The Black Bat waited until he saw Mc-Grath enter. Then he drove quickly to the spot where he usually parked the coupé, leaped out and dashed across the grounds to the garden house. Two minutes later he was in the lab, divesting himself of his somber regalia and replacing it with Tony Quinn's clothing.

He knew that Silk would do all in his power to prevent McGrath from entering the library where the secret lab door was located. Tony Quinn, grasping his cane hard, opened that door a crack. He could hear Silk's protesting voice at the outside door, and McGrath's stern one. What McGrath said was ominous.

"I'm searching this whole house, Silk, and you won't stop me unless you're looking for a busted skull. I know Quinn isn't here, and if he is out alone, he'll have to prove where he's been. I tell you he isn't here, and this time there will be no tricks!"

"But, sir," Silk protested, "I merely indicated that I'd been occupied in the kitchen and don't know where Mr. Quinn is at the moment. Let me look for him."

The lab door closed behind Quinn. He quickly crossed the library to his deep, comfortable chair beside the fireplace. He sat down, put a cold pipe between his lips and let his head sink down until the chin rested against his chest.

Captain McGrath stormed into the room and came to an abrupt halt. Silk, coming up behind him, seemed to wilt when he saw Quinn seated in the chair, apparently asleep. Quinn stirred. His eyes opened and stared blankly. A look of alarm came over his face.

"Who is there?" he asked querulously. "Who is it? Silk—Silk where are you?"

"Coming, sir." Silk brushed past McGrath. "I was looking for you. Captain McGrath is with me. He was insisting upon searching the whole house."

"I must have dozed," Quinn said. "McGrath, come over here and sit down. I want to talk to you. This is going a bit too far. Searching my home. For what?"

"For you," McGrath declared arrogantly. "Okay, I slipped. I got another tip-off that was a false alarm, but this hasn't changed my ideas at all. I still think you're the Black Bat and that you were out prowling tonight."

"You're speaking in riddles," Quinn said. "What tip-off?"

McGRATH stirred uneasily in his chair. It had occurred to him that Tony Quinn was an important factor in the District Attorney's office and generally superseded the police. Especially a detective captain. Quinn could make a lot of trouble if he so desired.

McGrath emitted a long sigh. "I received a phone call," he said. "I don't know who was calling. Just a man's voice. I was told the Black Bat was at Matt Bradley's estate and that if I hurried, I might find that Tony Quinn wasn't home and locate proof you are the Black Bat."

Quinn laughed. "All right, Mac, you are forgiven. I know just how much you're hipped on the idea I must be the Black Bat. That name dulls your wits. You'll never find him if you don't start to think calmly. Sometimes I think I ought to help you run him down."

McGrath grimaced. "Don't rub it in, please. Anyhow, I had another reason for coming to see you. I checked up on Matt Bradley and that blind man, George Lane. It's a fact that they were both rescued from a Jap prison camp in the Philippines. It's also true that Matt Bradley was the subject of an intensive search by the Japs because they wanted to kill him. Bradley returned to the Philippines under an assumed name, knowing darned well what was going to happen soon. He kept that assumed name and fooled the Japs with it."

"And George Lane?" Quinn asked. "What did you learn about him?"

"Not too much," McGrath admitted. "The Red Cross had compiled a dossier on each prisoner, but Lane's was brief. I had the gist of it radioed to Headquarters. Lane appeared in Manila about six months before the war broke out. He claims he came direct from China where he had been a salesman. He got into no trouble. Bradley and Lane were locked up in the same prison and became good friends."

"Which isn't much help," Quinn said. "If Bradley was a fraud and Lane his crooked assistant, we'd have an easy time of it. Nothing further in connection with the murder?"

McGrath shook his head. "Nothing. The weapon hasn't been found. I had the canes those two men used gone over in the labs. Blank again, though they could have been thoroughly cleaned."

"Keep at it," Quinn urged. "As for what

happened here tonight, I've already forgotten the incident. Just don't be quite so impetuous after this."

"Thanks." McGrath arose. "You could have made a lot of trouble for me. Mind you, I haven't switched in thinking you're the Black Bat. I never will without absolute proof."

CHAPTER VI

Murder Bent

COLDLY Silk showed McGrath out and returned to the library. Quinn was deep in thought.

"I really got scared that time," Silk said.

"I'm still frightened," Quinn admitted ruefully. "Silk, whoever tipped off McGrath is one of the greatest menaces we've ever had to contend with. How did that mysterious person ever grasp the idea that I could be the Black Bat? McGrath has reasons. He nearly trapped me several times, but this unknown individual —how in the world could he even guess?"

"I wish I knew," Silk grumbled. "I can't figure it out."

"Neither can I, at the moment." Quinn frowned deeply. "Yet I've done nothing so that anyone might become suspicious."

Silk shivered. "It must be the killer, of course, and he's mighty dangerous." Silk gasped suddenly. "Do you think he made Carol talk?"

"No," Quinn answered swiftly. "Carol wouldn't have talked, no matter what happened. I'm convinced of that. She never told anyone I'm the Black Bat. She would have died first."

"It was just an idea," Silk sighed disconsolately. "I know darn well she didn't."

"No word from her?"

Quinn's query was hardly necessary. He spoke while his brain tried to puzzle out some solution.

"None." Silk's voice carried a note of despair. "She's in a jam, sir. Otherwise she'd have got in touch with us somehow before now."

Quinn's hand, gripping the cane, grew white around the knuckles.

"And we're properly stymied," he said wearily. "Nothing we can do. No clues, nowhere to turn. Not even the smallest part of the mystery solved. Silk, I've never been

so worried. The game is getting dangerous, but I don't mind that. It's Carol I'm thinking about. If anything happened to her I'd never forgive myself for letting her work with us. If she is—dead, I'll . . . Darn it, Silk, I've never even thought this way before."

Tony Quinn spent the best part of the next hour trying to figure the angles which had developed. Trying to determine why Carol would have been taken and if she had been murdered. The latter idea shook his nerve badly. He was so on edge that when the doorbell rang he gave a convulsive jump. Silk went to the door.

"It's a man named Tip Farrel," Silk came back to the library door to say. "Says he'll consider it a favor if you'll let him see you. Personally, I don't like his looks."

"Tip Farrel?" Quinn's forehead wrinkled. "I know him. In fact, I sent him to prison eight years ago. I remember it very well because he bragged his fool head off that nobody could convict him. But I did, and Tip was pretty sore about it at the time. I wonder what in the world he wants with me."

"I'll send him away." Silk started toward the door. "You've got enough on your mind without bothering with a man like that."

"No—wait." Quinn called Silk to a halt. "I'll see him in the study. Turn on only the desk light and tilt the shade just a trifle so Tip's face will be illuminated, while I stay in the shadows. Then stand by in the hall, just in case. Tip doesn't happen to be a man anyone can trust."

Quinn arose, used his can to maneuver out of the room and down the hall. He saw "Tip" Farrel near the front door, but gave absolutely no indication of it. Moving slowly and carefully, just as a blind man would walk, Quinn entered the study. It was a medium-sized room, containing, among other pieces of furniture, a large desk. On this stood the solitary illuminated lamp, a tall leather-covered lamp placed on one corner of the desk. Silk had tilted the shade a trifle.

Silk waited a moment or two, then escorted Tip Farrel into the study. Farrel was a lithe, soft-footed man with a lean, cunning face. His eyes were small and hard, his lips were curled in a sardonic grin right now. Silk put him in the chair directly in front of the desk and then withdrew.

But Silk didn't go far. He stood just outside the portieres framing the doorway, and once he tapped his hip pocket to assure himself that the gun was still there and ready.

Silk's attention was riveted upon Tip. He

didn't hear the front door open softly. There was no turn of the knob. Tip had arranged it so a gentle push would force the door open. A burly man stepped inside. He held a heavy gun and reversed it now, to grip the weapon by its barrel. Then he moved slowly and noiselessly toward Silk.

He raised the gun and brought it down. Not in a long, swinging blow which would create a distinct thud as it hit Silk's skull, but in a shorter blow more calculated to stun than anything else.

IT HIT Silk well to the back of his head and pain and blackness exploded inside his skull. He began falling, but the attacker quickly grasped him under the arms, lifted him bodily and carried him further down the corridor.

There he quietly placed Silk on the floor, grinned broadly, and proceeded to wrap a large handkerchief around the butt of his gun. This softened any sound from the second blow which knocked Silk out completely. The attacker then quietly tiptoed back, glanced into the study, and went on to put his back against the front door and hold his gun ready for action. It was all done smoothly and quickly, as if vast experience in this sort of thing enabled the attacker to make every move count.

Inside the study, Tip Farrel was grinning now. He spoke loudly, by prearrangement, to cover any sounds of a struggle in the hallway, if any developed. This move was successful because Quinn heard nothing at all, but he did notice a shadow flit across the wall of the room and he wondered why Silk was moving about.

"It's this way, Mr. Quinn," Tip said. "You made the judge throw the book at me. Okay, that was your job. I don't blame a man for doing what he's supposed to do. I got eight years."

"You were lucky," Quinn grunted. "I thought you'd get fifteen. Come to the point, Tip. What do you want with me?"

"Nothing much," Tip went on, his voice thinning out a little.

Tony Quinn recognized the smug menace in that tone. Tip Farrel was up to something and it portended no good for Tony.

"Then why did you come here?" Quinn asked irritably.

"To kill you." Tip smiled broadly. "To do what I made up my mind to do those years ago when you sent me away. Sure it was your job, and you got paid for it. Nothing personal at all. With me it's different. It is personal, and I wouldn't take a dime for

the job. It'll be a pleasure."

Quinn gave a start of amazement that was not all simulated. Tip Farrel meant that. He was a cold-blooded killer, but coming here was not his idea alone. He was hardly capable of such a deed because Tip played the game carefully. His previous conviction had resulted only after a great deal of hard work. If Tip was murder bent, he was inspired and protected by someone else.

"Do you think you can get away with it?" Quinn asked softly, and at the same time he raised his cane and placed it across his knees. So far Tip had not drawn a weapon of any kind. He was too sure of himself. So sure that Quinn wondered about Silk who remained the only hope. If anything had happened to Silk, Tony Quinn would have a clear-cut choice. He would have to reveal the fact that he could use his eyes, or die.

Tip leaned across the desk. His coat was open and the butt of a heavy revolver was conspicuous.

"Everything is set my way, Quinn," he said. "There isn't an angle missing. Right now I'm at a certain spot and a lot of people are going to swear I never left there. Anyhow, the cops will hardly pick on me alone. The Big House is full of fellows who'd like to be in my shoes tonight."

Tip drew the gun. He was in no hurry. This job was so safe and so utterly simple that he seemed almost bored by it. Shooting a blind man was hardly different from popping at a clay pigeon with a shotgun at ten yards.

"I could have let you have it through the window, or the minute you stepped into the hall and began moving down it," he went on callously. "But I didn't want things that way. I wanted you to know who did the job, and why. I wanted you to sweat a bit. And, believe me, pal, that ain't rain starting to run down your forehead."

That was quite true. Quinn could feel the perspiration forming. He knew now that Silk was either dead, a prisoner, or out cold. Yet he had to make sure. It was necessary to investigate every possible loop-hole before revealing the fact that he could see.

"Silk!" Quinn called loudly.

Tip laughed. "If it's your flunky you're calling, forget it. A pal of mine got him. Everything set, Bronco?"

"All clear," the voice of Silk's attacker came from the hall.

Quinn knew exactly where that man was located. He stood at the front door, peering out and ready to give an alarm if anyone pulled up.

"And so"—Tip leaned back in the chair now and began to bring the gun on a level with Tony Quinn's chest—"we end our little friendship, Quinn. But I wish you had eyes so you could watch this. I'm starting to pull the trigger. It may take a little while before it happens, but you don't care. Another minute or two of life. Curse you, you took eight years of my life away from me! You got this coming!"

TIP'S voice rose to a savage frenzy as he spurred himself on to shoot. Quinn was watching him, although Tip had no realization of it. Quinn's fingers were wrapped around the cane tightly and he had brought it up a trifle.

He slowly started to push his chair back from the desk. Tip grinned and paid little attention. After all, for Tip's money, a blind man couldn't do a single thing to prevent this.

"The hammer is half-way back now," Tip went on. "In about five seconds—"

Quinn's cane suddenly flew out. It swept across the desk, struck the only lamp in the room and it went out the instant it hit the floor. Tip fired one shot, then let out a yell. Quinn's cane that had been aimed for his gun hand missed, and struck him full across the face.

Quinn crouched. He was on better than even terms with Tip now. He could see the killer while Tip was handicapped by the darkness. Quinn mentally thanked Silk for extinguishing the hall light.

But Quinn knew he was far from safe. If he got away from Tip, there was still that other killer at the door. Quinn grasped his cane by the middle and threw it in the direction of the door. It clattered to the floor. Tip's gun blazed and the killer started running forward, certain that the racket had been caused when Quinn accidentally dropped his cane. Tip reached the spot and his foot landed on the cane. It rolled slightly and he pitched headfirst through the doorway.

Tip never knew what hit him. His pal, guarding the door, was on edge and prepared to shoot at anyone who came through the door in a hurry. Tip literally flew through it and the guard fired twice. One slug hit Tip in the right temple.

At that particular instant, Silk reached out and tried to grasp the gunman's ankle. He failed, but the killer was terror-stricken now and wanted nothing but escape. He got the door open and rushed through it.

Silk arose, massaging his head. He saw the dark bulk in an inert heap on the floor and his heart stopped beating. He took a long breath, snapped the light switch, then he leaned weakly against the wall. Tony Quinn was kneeling beside the limp form.

Quinn looked up. "This is a ghastly mess,"

he said, "but thanks to your help, I'm all right. Seems Tip gave his pal orders to shoot anybody leaving the room and he shot Tip. Poetic justice, but not for us. Silk, were you conscious when the last act of this little play was staged?"

"Yes sir. The one who ran away clouted me and I did pass out, but I came to as Tip told you he was pulling the trigger."

"Think carefully now," Quinn implored anxiously. "Did the man at the front door —the one who got away—move into position so he could see me when I knocked the lamp off the desk?"

"No, sir," Silk said. "I'm quite positive he doesn't know what really happened in there. He had his nose pressed against the door window and anyway, from that close to the door, he couldn't possibly see into the room, sir."

Quinn breathed a long sigh of relief. "Then he has no idea I can see. Tip knew it, but he's dead. If he wasn't, and happened to be just a prisoner, I honestly don't know what I'd do with him. . . . Phone Captain McGrath, Silk. We might as well get the whole thing over with."

While Silk phoned, Quinn searched the dead man. In one pocket he found a thin sheaf of bills. Large denomination bills. There was five thousand dollars in his hand. He appropriated it. Some charity would get the money soon. Quinn didn't want Mc-Grath even to guess that Tip had been sent by someone to do this murder.

Quinn himself was sure of that now. Tip had said he wouldn't take pay for the work, but it was evident he had.

A radio car pulled up before Silk had finished telephoning. Startled and sympathetic cops took charge. They found Quinn behind the desk, horror still written across his face. On the floor beside the lamp lay a book-end which he had placed there.

McGrath came in a hurry and with an owl-wise look on his face.

"Tip Farrel." He glanced at the corpse. "Not much lost there, but tell me, Quinn, how a blind man could draw a bead on Tip?"

"I didn't shoot him, you idiot," Quinn snapped. "He had a friend with him. The pal knocked Silk out, but Silk recovered consciousness in time to seize a book-end from the table in the hall and hurl it at the desk lamp. Fortunately no other lights were lit and in the fracas that followed, Tip's pal shot him by mistake."

"Quite a coincidence." McGrath's smile was twisted. "You don't mind if I search you—and Silk too, of course? Then you'll

be glad to allow me to search the premises."

"For what?" Quinn asked tartly.

"The gun," McGrath gibed. "You know, the roscoe that pumped a slug smack through Tip Farrel's head. You're slipping, Quinn. When the Black Bat kills a man, he always puts his trademark on the corpse. That little black sticker which looks like a bat in flight and which has given me many a headache in the past."

Quinn's lips tightened. "You are welcome to search, Captain. Quite welcome. In fact, I insist upon it. Start with me."

<h3 style="text-align:center">CHAPTER VII</h3>

Mystery Gun

McGRATH spent half an hour at his searching job before he gave up in disgust. He faced Quinn again.

"Okay, I'm stumped," he admitted. "But a gun is easy to hide well. I'm not closing the blotter on this kill, Quinn. Oh yes, I realize Tip probably came here to kill you and he got what he deserved, but I can't make my report complete until I know who polished him off. And I think you did."

"Think what you like," Quinn snapped. "But if I were you, I'd look for a pal of Tip's named Bronco. That's meagre information, but Tip was in prison for eight years. He got out only a short while ago and he can't have run across too many men named Bronco. The nickname isn't ordinary. I'd recognize his voice, so if you want to keep that gold badge, you had better start hunting for him. Bring him to me when you find him. And, Captain—if you so much as insinuate I killed Tip, I'll have that badge."

McGrath gulped. "Yes, sir. I'll do as you ask, but I'm betting I won't find this Bronco."

Silk nudged McGrath. "This way out, sir. I must close the front door. Mr. Quinn doesn't like hot air blowing in on him."

McGrath favored Silk with a heavy frown, shrugged, and went out. In a short time, the formalities of removing the corpse were over with. Quinn was in his library staring at the cold fireplace.

"We got out of that by a narrower margin than I enjoyed, Silk," he said, when they were alone. "But it leaves us just where we were. Someone sent Tip, paid him to kill me. We don't know who. The murder at

Matt Bradley's estate is unsolved. Carol is still missing, and McGrath is more suspicious than ever."

"It's Carol I'm most troubled about, sir," Silk said soberly. "Do you suppose Butch has found out anything in following that man, Salisbury, that might lead to her?"

"I don't know, Silk," Tony Quinn replied with a weary sigh. "But I'm sure Butch will call the moment he has anything to tell us. He knows how worried we are."

Quinn fell silent. In the quiet hush, two men stared at the cold fireplace. . . .

Meanwhile, Butch O'Leary was conscientiously obeying orders to keep an eye on the comings and goings of Hal Salisbury. In the exclusive Crescent Hotel where Salisbury lived, Butch was more than occupying one of the chairs in the lobby of the high-class residential hotel. The chair was never meant for anyone of his bulk, but it overlooked the elevators and a side exit, so Butch sat there despite the discomfort.

He knew what Salisbury looked like and that the man was in his rooms. Once on an assignment of this kind, Butch stuck like adhesive. He showed no impatience as two or three hours slipped away, but when Salisbury stepped out of the elevator, Butch was glad of it.

He trailed the manufacturer, and Butch knew how to do this work well. The Black Bat had been an efficient teacher and Silk had added a few details he had picked up. With Butch's training, his size was no handicap at all.

He was close by when Salisbury boarded a bus headed for an outlying section. Butch clambered aboard also. He took a seat far to the rear so he could watch Salisbury better. The manufacturer was nervous and apparently in a hurry, for he glanced at his watch often. Whenever the bus stopped, he grew impatient and tapped the arm of his seat restlessly.

At last Salisbury got off and Butch was somewhat surprised at his destination. It was a bus depot serving a rather sparsely settled community. There were few houses about and the bus depot itself was nothing more than a thin frame shack with a single door and two windows.

Salisbury sat down on one of the benches and fanned himself with his hat. It was a hot night but not that hot, Butch thought, and kept the man under surveillance every moment. Butch was fairly clever about the way he worked too. He let Salisbury get off the bus and enter the depot before he made the startled driver slap on brakes and

let him out after the bus had pulled away several hundred feet.

Butch removed his coat, slung it over one arm, battered in his felt hat to make it look more disreputable, then walked boldly into the depot. Several bus lines were served from this building. There was a ticket seller, half-asleep behind his window, and people arrived and departed in fair numbers.

A FULL hour went by, while Salisbury grew more and more nervous. Butch was stretched out on one of the benches. He had purchased a ticket for a bus that was not due for a long time yet and the ticket was stuck into his hat band. He pretended to be dozing, but every sense was alert.

He opened both eyes when a seedy-looking character walked in and sat down beside Salisbury, but carefully as he could watch, Butch didn't even see a signal pass between the two men. Finally the seedy-looking individual got up to board a bus. Salisbury mopped his face for the tenth time and eagerly eyed the people who entered the depot. He consulted his watch more and more often now, as if an allotted time was expiring and he had things to do.

Finally Salisbury arose and hurried out as another city-bound bus pulled in. Butch slid off the bench and his hat fell off as he did. Bending to pick it up, he noticed a newspaper wrapped package below the bench where Salisbury had been seated.

Butch nonchalantly walked over, seized the package and got aboard the bus. He was alone in the rear seat and had an opportunity to open the bundle. It contained a .32-caliber automatic. Butch grunted and hastily wound the paper around it again. He frowned, trying to think as the Black Bat would think.

Salisbury had not been carrying this package, but it was small enough to have fitted into his pocket. He might have taken a moment when Butch was not watching him to deposit the gun beneath the bench. Or that run-down little fellow who also had been sitting there could have hidden the gun. Butch wondered if there was any connection between the gun and the murder on Long Island.

Salisbury went straight back to his hotel, for which Butch was joyously grateful. He entered a phone booth and called Quinn's home. He told Silk what had happened and received orders to report to the lab at once.

Butch went there as quickly as possible. Tony Quinn was waiting for him. Quinn took the gun, being careful not to touch it with his fingertips. He placed it on a mount, slid it behind a large magnifying glass and dusted the weapon with fingerprint powder. No prints came out.

"Hmm," he mused. "You didn't see which of those two men put the gun there, Butch?"

"No, sir," Butch answered promptly. "I couldn't keep my eyes on them all the time."

"Naturally," Quinn said. "You did very well, Butch. Now if Salisbury put the gun there, it means he wanted to get rid of it. But why in a bus station? The gun was sure

handle the situation according to your own intuition."

"You mean I can bust the other fella one?" Butch asked hopefully. "I ain't askin' for anything more than that. I'm on my way, sir."

Butch disappeared down the tunnel entrance. Silk stood looking down at the weapon.

Quinn picked it up, slipped the magazine out and then sniffed of the barrel.

"It's been fired recently," he observed. "One bullet is missing, because one more

BUTCH

to be found. From what you tell me, Butch, Salisbury went to the bus depot to keep some sort of an appointment. Nobody showed up, so we can assume he was lured there. Why? Obviously, so he would be seen around the place and identified. Then this gun was parked near the spot where he had been seated. Police would certainly check up on anyone who happened to have been near the gun and they'd find Salisbury."

"I never thought of that." Butch frowned heavily. "You mean this little lug was trying to make it look like Salisbury had put the roscoe there?"

"Exactly. Therefore, the gun has a connection. Butch, you had better go back and keep an eye on Salisbury. If he should come out of his suite accompanied by anyone and he doesn't seem willing to go along, you can

slug fills the magazine. Now the single shot so far fired in the case we're interested in— except the one that was fired in this house— was aimed at Matt Bradley or the Black Bat. That bullet may still be lodged in Bradley's desk, so it's time for the Black Bat to pay that house another visit."

Silk blinked. "Do you mean that Salisbury may have fired the shot, sir?"

Quinn shrugged. "Either that, or someone wants the police to think so. In checking the time element with Butch, I notice that Salisbury was not under surveillance at the time when that mysterious somebody fired through Matt Bradley's window."

SILK watched Quinn don the somber regalia of the Black Bat.

"What about Carol, sir?" he asked. "I'll

admit I'm very worried."

"No more than I," Quinn answered tightly. "But we haven't a lead. Not a shred of a clue, so we can do nothing except keep ferreting out every situation which presents itself in the hope that one of these angles will lead us in the right direction."

"I suppose that's true," Silk conceded slowly. "But another thing worries me too. Somebody knows, or thinks, that you're the Black Bat. Tip was sent here to kill you, even paid for the job."

"I know," Quinn admitted ruefully. "They are closer to us this time than anything we've ever experienced. Whoever is behind this, Silk, is clever. He plays his game carefully and leaves no tracks. We may have to smoke him into the open, but so far I don't even know who should be driven out."

"Matt Bradley, perhaps," Silk offered. "We're not even sure he really is Bradley. We do know that the real Bradley isn't buried in the family plot, but that doesn't prove Frankenstein's brother, as Carol called him, is Bradley."

Quinn laced the soft-soled, jet-black shoes.

"I know, but there are others as well. They all have motives for killing Bradley. Yet none has a motive for the murder of Don Thayer and neither do they have any ironclad alibis. Another odd thing is the way Wilma has turned to Bradley. As if he exerts some power over her."

"You mean hypnotism or something like that?" Silk asked incredulously.

"Oh, no." Quinn slid a shell into the firing chamber of his automatic. "People can't be hypnotized to do something that is repulsive to them. I mean that Bradley knows a few things and is making Wilma toe the mark. Perhaps it has to do with her late husband."

Silk wagged his head from side to side. "I haven't been deeply enough into the case to know about that, sir."

"It's simple." Quinn faced Silk. "I think that Don Thayer identified the body buried as Matt Bradley for selfish reasons and that he knew very well it was not Bradley. He may have reasoned that after the Japs attacked Manila, Bradley was a gone goose because the Japs wanted to kill him so badly."

Silk whistled. "But until Bradley's death could be proven, or many years elapse, Don couldn't take over the estate!" he said. "So he identified a stranger, buried him as Matt Bradley and then took over the estate. It's a smooth scheme, but good heavens, it's mighty illegal too."

"That's just it," Quinn said. "Wilma could be in on the deal. Matt guessed it, and is holding Wilma on threats to expose her. Still, that doesn't really prove anything in connection with either the murder, the disappearance of Carol, or all the rest that has happened. Greed is behind it, naturally."

"I wish there was something I could do," Silk said enviously.

"You'll be doing all you can," Quinn said, "by staying here in case Carol gets a chance to contact us—and to keep Captain McGrath off our necks. That fellow isn't only persistent, but he thinks he has his nose to a nice redolent trail right now. The trouble is that he has, and we've got to be careful. Never fool yourself about McGrath. He's smart."

Silk watched the black-clad head and shoulders disappear through the tunnel entrance. The Black Bat was on the move again.

CHAPTER VIII

Murder Attempt

DURING the early morning hours, not long before dawn, the Black Bat approached Matt Bradley's house. He came from the rear of the estate and progressed through the darkness as smoothly as though it had been broad daylight. His uncanny vision detected obstacles which have tripped an average man or, most certainly, slowed him down tremendously.

He walked along an arbored path and suddenly the house was there before him. It was entirely dark. At least the side of it which he could see. On the opposite side, the driveway cut through the estate and the Black Bat kept away from it. If a car should suddenly pull in, he might be spotted.

He came to an abrupt stop. The darkness concealed him and he knew he hadn't been seen, but someone had been looking out of a window on the first floor. The curtains obscured the identity of the person, but the Black Bat was sure he saw someone. He approached that window rather cautiously and gripped his gun. Murder struck swiftly at this house and he didn't intend to be on the receiving end.

But he saw at a glance that the room was empty. It was the music room and Clint Henderson's highly polished grand piano occupied a predominant spot in the room.

The window was opened wide. The Black Bat climbed through it and stood in the center of the room, listening intently. He thought he heard a purring sound, but thought it probably was a car parked somewhere down the street.

He made his way silently to the room where he and Matt Bradley had been shot at. It was dark, but that didn't bother him. He proceeded straight to the desk, knelt, and saw the hole made by the bullet. It had struck the edge of Bradley's chair, had chipped off a bit of wood, and been deflected to enter the desk at a slight angle.

The Black Bat took out his compact kit of burglar tools, selected a long probe and went to work. In several minutes he worried the bullet free, hefted it in his hand and judged it was the same caliber as those in that gun Butch had picked up.

That humming sound came again with annoying persistence, and the Black Bat cocked his head slightly. It was a car motor, but it seemed closer than somewhere out on the street. He went to the library window. This was on the further side of the house. He saw the hood of a heavy car parked in the driveway. The lights were out and it seemed an odd place to leave a car, with the engine running.

The Black Bat stowed the bullet away, moved softly to the rear of the house and let himself out the back door. He rounded the corner—and instantly knew what that parked car with its idling engine meant. There was a piece of garden hose attached to the exhaust and it had been raised up so that it entered one of the second-floor windows.

There was no time to lose. The carbon monoxide generated by the engine may have already filled the room. The Black Bat merely took time to seize the hose and wrench it off the exhaust pipe. Then he glanced inside the car.

Sam Bradley was back of the wheel, slumped low, his head resting against the back of the seat. There was a bottle beside him, almost empty, and the car smelled strongly of whisky. The Black Bat didn't try to awaken Sam.

It was much more necessary to find out who had been the victim of this insidious murder attempt.

He hurried through the house, not caring much if he made undue noise. He located the bedroom and the door was closed, but not locked. He threw it open. There were **twin beds.**

On one lay George, the blind man. On the other was Matt Bradley.

The Black Bat seized George's shoulder and shook him hard. He mumbled, but didn't awaken. His pulse was fairly good. The Black Bat spent another few seconds looking over Bradley. He seemed worse. The pallor of near asphyxiation was settling around his features.

The Black Bat lifted him off the bed and carried him to the window. He opened it wide and held Bradley's head out until the man's color improved and he began to move restlessly in the Black Bat's grasp.

There was a querulous cry behind him. The Black Bat glanced over his shoulder. George was out of bed, shrinking back a little, and fumbling for his cane.

He seemed quite upset, and there was a tone of deep fright in his voice when he spoke.

"Something is wrong!" he cried. "Someone is in the room. Matt! Matt, where are you? Why don't you answer?"

THE Black Bat carried Matt back and placed him on the bed. He was coming out of it rapidly, but another few minutes would have meant his finish. The hose projected through one of the two windows and it had poured those deadly fumes almost squarely upon Matt Bradley's face. George would have died soon after.

The room had been quite well-filled with the fumes.

"George," the Black Bat said curtly, "stay as you are. This is the Black Bat. Somebody tried to kill you and Matt. I got here just in time. Who else was in this room tonight?"

George fumbled for the edge of the bed and sat down.

"I don't know," he whined. "I fell asleep. Is Matt all right?"

"I'm a little giddy," Matt said, and sat up. "Otherwise I feel fair. Black Bat, it takes only a glance to see what happened. You really did save our lives, didn't you?"

The Black Bat closed the bedroom door. So far, no one had been awakened. At least, nothing in the house stirred. He faced Matt and George.

"Yes," he said slowly, "I did save your lives and in repayment I want some information. In a hurry too. Who do you think did this? There is a car just below the window and the garden hose had been hooked up to its exhaust. Who is capable of committing such a crime?"

"Anyone in this house, except George and

me," Bradley said quickly. "By that, I mean Clint, or Sam, or—yes, even Wilma. I don't trust her. Those people hate me because I came back to life. They hate George because he tries to protect me in his own fashion. He's blind, but a blind man hears exceptionally well and senses things."

"They want the estate they possessed for a few years," the Black Bat said. "They got it through fraud, when Don Thayer identified a stranger's body as yours, Bradley."

"How did you know that?" Bradley gasped.

"I merely assumed it," the Black Bat replied with a short laugh. "It wasn't difficult to come to such a conclusion. Was Wilma actively implicated in that deal?"

"I refuse to answer," Bradley snapped, and in so doing, admitted that she was so far as the Black Bat was concerned.

"I won't press it," the Black Bat soothed him. "Do you believe Sam is capable of this attempted murder?"

"Yes—yes!" George broke in. "Very capable of it. He and Matt had a fight tonight and Sam said he wished Matt had been killed by the Japs so he'd be saved the trouble of doing it himself."

"Sam was drunk," Matt interceded, with a rather strange defense of his brother. "He didn't know what he was saying."

"What of Clint?" the Black Bat queried.

"Him!" Bradley snorted. "That man isn't capable of anything, not even making a living for himself. He's music crazy, and has no other interests."

"Wilma?" the Black Bat went on doggedly.

Bradley shrugged, got up and went to a carafe for a drink of water. He had recovered from his bout with the poison gas quite well. George was still coughing and seemed weak. He stayed seated on the edge of the bed.

"Wilma," Bradley said, "once promised to marry me—when I still looked like a human being. I believed her then. I believed in her, and I still do. Wilma would do nothing to hurt me."

"Then that covers everyone quite well, except George here," the Black Bat said.

"Now just a minute," Matt snapped. "I realize we both owe you a great deal. You saved George's life once and mine twice. That bullet was undoubtedly meant for me. But don't insinuate that George had anything to do with this. Good heavens, man, he nearly died too. Perhaps you ought to know about him. He was aware of my real identity when we were prisoners of the Japs. He could have received his own freedom and a lot of money if he had talked, but he didn't.

Not even when they—when they tortured him and blinded him. He stuck by me and I'm staying by him. I want that understood."

"Very well," the Black Bat said noncommittally. "How about Salisbury?"

"I don't know yet—not for sure," Matt answered. "I figured him as all right, but until I check the books, I can't be sure. Somehow I feel that he has changed and, perhaps, cheated me out of a lot of money. Cash he can't replace. Yes, he might like to have me really dead this time. It would save him a great deal of trouble."

"Be very careful," the Black Bat warned. "Whoever attempted this may try again. For the moment, content yourself with removing all evidence of the crime, after I leave. That will be perhaps in ten mintes. Until then, please remain in this room. Both of you."

STEPPING into the hallway, the Black Bat closed the door and moved toward the steps. He saw a door ajar, pushed it wider and his uncanny eyes swept away darkness. This was Wilma's room and she was not there.

He went in to look around. There was nothing of interest until he reached the bathroom. In the medicine cabinet he saw an unlabeled bottle, removed the cork, and sniffed of the contents. It had a familiar odor. He put the bottle into his pocket.

As he stepped out of the room, the house, so far grimly silent, became alive to the notes of a piano played energetically, but well. The Black Bat hurried down to the music room.

Clint, in pajamas and bathrobe, was at the piano, his nimble fingers creating music out of the keys. He seemed to sense the presence of the Black Bat and swung around. For a moment he looked startled at this grim apparition. Then he scowled.

"You are the Black Bat," he said slowly. "You're here to try and find out who killed Don. I didn't, so don't bother me. I'm writing the music for a ballet. There is little time. I must work whenever the mood strikes me, and I do not like to be disturbed."

He turned and began caressing the keys again. The Black Bat's gloved hand slapped him on the shoulder, and Clint gave a nervous jump.

"Murder doesn't care whom it bothers," the Black Bat said stonily. "Neither do I. How long have you been in this room?"

"About fifteen minutes. Why?"

"Let me have your slippers," the Black Bat said. "Take them off!"

His voice became curt and angry. Clint whitened, reached down and removed his slippers. The Black Bat glanced at the underside. There was no evidence Clint had worn them out of the house. No grass stains, no moisture from the dew or bits of dirt from the driveway.

The Black Bat dropped them on the floor, turned and stalked out. Before he reached the door, Clint was playing again. Matt Bradley had been quite right. Nothing mattered to Clint except his music. Unless the music was a stall to cover terror and confusion.

Someone was at the car outside. It was Wilma, trying vainly to drag Sam from behind the wheel.

She gave a little cry at the sudden appearance of the Black Bat.

"Get inside the car," the Black Bat whispered. "Matt and George will be listening from their window."

They both got in. The Black Bat closed the doors, examined Sam briefly and picked up the nearly empty bottle. He removed the stopped and smelled of the whisky it contained. There was something besides whisky in this bottle.

"How did you know Sam was down here?" the Black Bat asked. "And, Wilma, you can trust me. I know all about Don. What he did and why. I don't blame him too much, but I know that you were not involved."

"Thank you." Wilma choked back a sob. "Matt is so sure I helped Don gain possession of the estate. I didn't. I knew nothing at all about it. I—thought Sam was drunk again. He had a furious fight with Matt earlier tonight and he went out with the intention of getting boiling drunk. But I like Sam, and I trust him. I wanted to see if he was all right."

"I see." The Black Bat was frowning under that black hood. "Are you convinced that the man who came back from a Jap prison camp really is Matt Bradley?"

"I'm certain of it," Wilma responded.

"And this blind man, George?"

Wilma shuddered.

"He frightens me. He seems to think we're all Matt's enemies. He seems like a—a madman to me."

"Go in the house," the Black Bat ordered. "I'll carry Sam in. Say that you discovered him in the garage, not in the car. Is that clear?"

"Yes," she answered. "I'll do anything you say."

"Good. Get going then. Matt and George will be down any minute."

CHAPTER IX

The Trail to Danger

AFTER Wilma had disappeared, the Black Bat examined Sam more carefully. The man was more than plain drunk. He was drugged. The Black Bat lifted him over one shoulder and carried him into the house.

He deposited him in a chair, glanced at Wilma's white face, then quickly left the house. In moments more, he was driving back to town, sorely puzzled, and a dozen times more worried about Carol.

This murderer covered his tracks perfectly. He left no loop-holes, and he held all the cards. Thus far, the Black Bat had only the vaguest idea as to who it might be, with little or nothing to back up his suspicions.

It was a house of hate, with Matt Bradley the focal point for all the hatred. And Matt did nothing to try to help himself or the others. If the bullet in the Black Bat's pocket came from the gun Butch had found, that only confused the issue more. Butch was fairly certain Salisbury had not discarded the weapon, so the whole thing might have been framed.

If the Black Bat's analysis of the contents of that unlabeled bottle he discovered in Wilma's medicine cabinet showed that it was a narcotic, and the same drug was mixed with the whisky in Sam Bradley's bottle, then she automatically fell under suspicion. Yet that drug could also have been planted.

The whole affair so obviously lacked clues and leads. The murderer was an expert at covering up his tracks. There wasn't even a motive beyond that of greed on the part of Matt's heirs. But granted this motive existed, why had one of them murdered Don Thayer?

That could more logically have been the work of Matt, out of hatred and a desire for revenge. Undoubtedly Don had gone through a good portion of Matt's money during those years the uncle had been imprisoned by the Japs. Or even blind George could have done it, perhaps thinking he was doing Matt a favor. The blind man's devotion to Matt was plain.

Well over an hour later, the Black Bat had shed his regalia to become Tony Quinn once more, and he was working in the privacy of his lab. Silk knew he was there, but Silk had not come in yet. He was watching for signs of Captain McGrath, or to see if another killer had been detailed to murder Tony Quinn.

Quinn knew two things after he had worked for a time. One of them was that the bullet fired at Matt Bradley had come from the gun which had been left at the bus depot, to be presumed it had been left by Salisbury. The other was that the drug in the unlabeled bottle was a narcotic and that some of it had been placed in the whisky which Sam Bradley had imbibed.

Quinn entered his library and sat down. Silk brought him a cup of steaming coffee. It was already daylight outside.

"Something queer happened while you were out, sir," Silk said. "At four o'clock, almost on the dot, the telephone rang. It was Matt Bradley asking to speak with you."

Quinn whistled softly.

"I told him you were asleep," Silk went on, "and I refused to wake you up unless the matter was urgent. Bradley said he thought it wasn't, and hung up."

"He could have been checking," Quinn said thoughtfully. "I'd left him a few minutes before four, as the Black Bat. Now his suspicions may be aroused even higher."

"And don't forget," Silk reminded him grimly, "that someone suspects you are the Black Bat and sent Tip Farrel here to kill you. If Bradley was checking, he must feel quite sure now that his suspicions were correct. Thank heaven, it wasn't Captain McGrath."

There was no sleep for Tony Quinn. He worked all night, and shortly before nine in the morning he walked into the big building where he maintained his offices. Silk was beside him, as usual. Ten minutes after he arrived, Captain McGrath was announced, and McGrath had a burly character in tow.

"Morning," McGrath grunted. "I followed your tip last night and looked up Tip's friend. This fellow is named Bronco. The only mug in town with a name like that."

"You're a D.A.," Bronco broke in angrily. "Am I pinched or am I not? That's all I want to know so I can get away from this copper. I don't like 'em."

It was the man whose voice Quinn had heard the night before. The man who had slugged Silk and later shot and killed his own companion. Quinn's apparently sightless eyes were directed somewhat to the left of "Bronco."

"Where were you last night, at ten o'clock?" Quinn demanded.

[*Turn page*]

"Have I got to go through all that again?" Bronco complained.

"He told me he'd been at a wrestling match that didn't end until a few minutes before eleven o'clock," McGrath said. "I ran down that alibi. He has people who'll swear he was there."

QUINN looked disappointed.

"I heard the man who was called Bronco speak last night," he told McGrath. "This man hasn't the same voice. And I'm not mistaken. Being blind, I pay particular attention to tonal qualities. You nabbed the wrong man, Captain."

McGrath sighed. "Well, that's that. He's the only man named Bronco, so I'm stuck. Shall I let him go?"

"Just one second," Quinn said. He felt around the surface of his desk, found paper and scribbled a note. He folded this and called to Silk who responded at once. "Check that," Quinn ordered.

Silk went into the next room, returned in a few moments and bent to whisper into Quinn's ear. Quinn nodded.

"All right, Bronco, you may go."

Silk disappeared also—and on a mission. He was to follow Bronco and be careful about it, because Bronco would certainly recognize him. Quinn leaned back in his chair.

"That note, Captain, instructed Silk to take a good look at the man. Silk didn't see much last night, but I hoped it was enough to make an identification. He whispered to me that he doubted this was the man."

"And I lost a night's sleep hunting that bozo," McGrath grumbled. "Okay, it's all in the game. If I was smart, I wouldn't be a cop. That ends it, of course. I couldn't get a line on any other mug who palled with Tip and might have been around when he tried to kill you. Honestly now, Quinn, don't you admit the whole thing has an aroma to it?"

"Such as?" Quinn asked, and grinned.

"If Tip tried to kill you, it was because he was paid. By somebody who not only wanted to get rid of Tony Quinn, but the Black Bat too. Tip was nothing more than a muscle man. You sent him away for a few years, but those mugs never look for revenge once they're out, no matter how much they talk about it when they're sent up. And the story about his pal plugging him. That's hard to take. I think Tip came and told you he knew you were the Black Bat. That he pulled his gun and either you or Silk let him have it."

"Prove that," Quinn chuckled, "and I'll sign the warrant for my own arrest. What

I told you is the truth, Captain. I agree that men of Tip's ilk don't often seek revenge that way, but Tip was an exception. . . . That's all, Captain. I'm rather busy."

"In other words, take the air," McGrath grunted. "All right, but before I do leave, I want this understood. I think you're probably the best D.A. this city ever had. I know you're honest and I'd trust you with anything. But I also think you're the Black Bat, and he tears around without regard for due process of the law. He's made himself liable to arrest and I'll get him, but when I do I'll hate myself from then on. Go on, call me a stubborn old goat. Maybe I am. Sometimes I wonder how I can keep trying to trap the Black Bat, and yet like him so much for what he does."

Quinn fumbled in his desk drawer and found some cigars. He handed McGrath all he could hold in one hand.

"You're a great fellow, Captain," he said. "I like you, too, and I imagine the Black Bat does as well. Now will you get out so I can earn the salary the tax payers donate to me?"

Tony Quinn did go to work. There were people waiting with complaints. Witnesses to be questioned and all the many details usual to the office of a Special District Attorney. They kept Quinn's mind busy until noon. Silk returned then and they went to lunch.

Quinn ate ravenously. He'd had little time for eating until now. Silk told him an interesting story.

"I picked up that crook's trail in front of the building. In five minutes I knew he was apprehensive. He took three different cabs and taxed me to the limit trying to keep up with him. He rode the subway uptown, switched to a downtown express and then used a bus which I had to trail in a cab. Finally, he seemed pretty sure he'd given any possible shadow the slip. It was easier from there on. His name is, believe it or not, Gilbert alias Bronco Dubbs. He's an ex-con and an all-around bad actor. And he is the man who came with Tip. You know that, of course."

"Yes," Quinn said evenly. "I recognized his voice at once. I let him go because in Bronco I place a great deal of hope. Whoever snatched or killed Carol has underworld help. Tip was one of these and Bronco another. I hope you have him well spotted."

"I have. He lives in a small, cheap hotel downtown. Lately, he came into a little money and he is living high and wide. But he shows no inclination to move from that hotel. Have you any plans for him, sir?"

TONY QUINN nodded vigorously.

"Indeed I have," he said. "For ourselves too, and I sincerely hope for Carol. This man is the only lead we have. If it peters out, I don't know which way to turn. If we are compelled to wait until we have the murderer with his back against a wall, he'll hold the trump card. He'll have Carol and you know darned well I'd even let him go to save her."

"Are there any special instructions?" Silk asked quietly.

"You might round up Butch this afternoon and detail him to watch Bronco. Finger the man if you can, so Butch won't make a mistake. I'll be in court all afternoon so you'll have an opportunity to carry out this mission. And tonight, Silk, we're all going out. With guns!"

The afternoon in court was agony. Quinn's mind was too filled with the problem of Carol for him to concentrate on the cases he was prosecuting. The ugly feeling that she might be dead was almost too strong. It threatened to drive him to distraction.

He ate lightly that night and waited impatiently for darkness. Butch phoned in a report saying that Bronco Dubbs had gone to a bar, imbibed rather freely, and was now back in his room. Shortly after, Tony Quinn had disappeared and the black figure of the Black Bat was ready for business.

Accompanied by Silk this time, because the Black Bat felt he might need all the help he could muster, he made his way to where the coupé was parked on the side street. It was dangerous leaving the house unguarded this way, especially since McGrath was up in arms and the mysterious murderer had more than an inkling that Tony Quinn was the Black Bat. Yet they had to take the chance.

The Black Bat, with the large hat concealing his features, stopped the coupé not far from Bronco's hotel. Butch was parked across the street. Silk, acting under precise instructions, entered a drug-store, went to the phone booth and dialed the number of the cheap hotel where the crook lived.

In a few moments Bronco had been called to the phone. Silk spoke in a low, uneven voice.

"Listen and get this straight. You're hot. Too hot to be running around. Quinn let you go, but he knows you were with Tip. You've got to get out of sight. The only place is where the girl is held. Go there as fast as you can and stay under cover. Is that clear?"

"Yeah," Bronco said doubtfully. "Just who is this?"

"I'm the man Tip worked for and I know what's going on. I'll need you later. A job with a lot of money for you. Now will you beat it? And stay where the girl is so I can reach you if necessary."

"Okay." Bronco seemed satisfied. "I'll start in five minutes. Tip said you're an up-and-up sport, so I don't mind working for you. I'll wait your orders."

CHAPTER X

Run to Earth

HANGING up, Silk hurried back to where the Black Bat waited. He made a brief report. For a moment the Black Bat seemed unable to say a word, made silent by the mere possibility that at last they might be on the track of the mysteriously missing Carol Baldwin. Then his lips moved in fervent thanks.

"Bronco was our one and only hope," he said, and sighed deeply. "If he had questioned you on the phone about where Carol is being held, the whole thing would have been stopped in its tracks. I haven't felt free to exert real pressure on these suspects because of Carol's predicament. Now, if we're lucky enough to save her, I'll really push those people around."

Silk nodded, his eyes on the hotel entrance.

"It will probably be easy to clean up if Carol is alive and well," he agreed. "She must be, according to the way that crook reacted. When Carol tells us what she knows, why she was snatched, we'll head in the right direction from then on."

"How could it be otherwise?" the Black Bat declared. "I have my ideas, of course. There is a certain clue which points to one of those people at Bradley's house, but it isn't enough. Not by a long shot. And I may be all wrong. I . . . Here comes Bronco."

The crook emerged from the hotel, carrying a cheap grip. He put it down, lit a cigarette, and looked carefully about. Then he started walking to the corner. Butch came out of the doorway where he had been hidden and took up the chase.

Two blocks away, Bronco hailed a taxi. The Black Bat slowed the coupé and Butch got aboard, cramming himself down in the limited space, but grinning broadly because the way things were progressing he was certain of some action.

Bronco switched cabs once, and finally entered a garage far uptown. Butch instantly covered the rear exit while Silk and the Black Bat watched the front. This might be where Carol was held.

But the crook came out again, this time driving a light sedan. He passed directly by the cheap little coupé and gave it a hard look, but it seemed to be empty. Silk and the Black Bat were slumped low enough to avoid being seen.

They picked up Butch again and followed Bronco at a respectable distance. He seemed to be headed for one of the important highways and soon both cars were rolling at a moderate clip into the suburbs.

The chase occupied a full hour before Bronco suddenly pulled off the road. The Black Bat was ready for just such a thing to occur. Butch, under orders, opened the coupé door, swung out and jumped. The car was not going fast. Butch immediately dived for the brush where he could be hidden and yet watch Bronco.

The coupé in which Silk and the Black Bat were riding picked up some speed and rolled past the crook's car. In a moment it had disappeared over the crest of a hill. The Black Bat stopped abruptly. Silk got out and hurried back. He signaled with a low whistle. The Black Bat turned the coupé around. Silk jumped aboard.

"Butch winked a flashlight," Silk advised. "He's waiting down there and I think Bronco entered that deserted roadhouse. There are no other buildings close by. Butch will know."

The Black Bat left the car at the top of the hill, took to the brush and guided Silk, whose sight could not penetrate the gloom. They joined Butch who reported that the crook had driven his car into the garage behind the roadhouse. All three of them studied the place. It was a flat-roofed, two-story structure with a faded sign indicating that food, drink and dancing could be had here. Another sign stated that the place was closed.

"Butch," the Black Bat said, "you and I are going in. Silk, Bronco would recognize you, so you cover the outside. Probably you can't see it, but there is a fire-escape along the west wall of the building and it goes all the way to the roof. You may have to use it. Apparently lodgings were furnished at this place and hotel laws required the fire-escape. Watch for signals. Either Butch or I will use our flashlights to send any messages. Ready, Butch?"

"I've been ready for a long time," Butch whispered hoarsely. "If those mugs hurt Carol, so help me, there won't be enough of them left to throw in jail!"

"I'll go first," the Black Bat said. "Wait until I indicate it is safe for you to follow. We're going in, through one of the front windows if the door can't be negotiated. I'm convinced that anyone in the place lives at the rear, to keep up the illusion that the building is empty. That gives us a mild break."

THE Black Bat scurried across the highway and blended perfectly with the gloom surrounding the darkened building. Butch began massaging his knuckles in anticipation. Silk drew a gun and calmly made sure it was ready for quick action.

It required no more than five minutes for Black Bat to effect an entrance. Having a hunch the door would be boarded up, he wasted no time on it, but tackled a window instead. It was a large pane of glass, opening in the middle like a pair of small doors. It was necessary only to cut a hole through the glass skillfully to reach in and turn the latch. During this procedure the Black Bat made hardly any sound. Certainly not enough to be heard more than a few feet away.

He called Butch, by means of his flash, and both of them entered the roadhouse. The window opened on the dance floor, fairly big, and dangerously barren now. The emptiness of the place would magnify even slight sounds. Darkness, of course, was no barrier for the Black Bat and he led Butch along the floor as close to the walls as possible. The floor was less apt to squeak there.

When they reached the kitchen, they saw that stairs there led to the second floor. Butch had started moving toward them when a hiss brought him to a stop. Butch pressed himself against the wall. Someone was coming down the steps.

The man was using a small, weak flashlight and was evidently bent on making some sort of inspection tour. He passed close by Butch and didn't notice him. But the Black Bat knew that this man would automatically inspect entrances, and would see the cut-out portion of glass in the front window. The fellow must not be allowed to give an alarm.

Suddenly the Black Bat, a weird and grim spectacle, stepped out directly in front of the advancing man. The fellow froze in his tracks, unable to utter a sound. Butch moved up from behind, clenched one fist and swept off the man's hat. Then his fist smacked down hard against the crook's head.

The man slumped and Butch caught him expertly.

Holding his victim aloft, so that he dangled like a puppet, Butch carried him behind a counter in the main room. There he administered a touch of more permanent anesthesia in the form of a short punch to the jaw. This done, he joined the Black Bat.

"We don't know how many more there are," the Black Bat whispered, his lips against Butch's ear. "In this case we take no chances either. I'm going up those steps. You stay here. If anyone comes down, or enters the place, work whoever it is over as silently as possible."

Butch nodded. The Black Bat started up the narrow stairs, his crepe-soled shoes making slight, slithering noises. The gun in his hand was steady, with a finger hard against the trigger. So far, things were going smoothly. If there were only one or two other men here, besides Bronco, it might be finished off fast.

The Black Bat was at the head of the steps when a door opened directly in front of him. The man who came out wasn't Bronco, but it was clear that he was wondering what had happened to the crook who had gone downstairs, and was intending to find out. He clutched a cheap, nickle-plated revolver.

The Black Bat gave him no opportunity to raise the weapon. He leaped, grabbed the fellow's gun hand and with one violent wrench pulled him across the hall and sent him hurtling down the steps for Butch to dispose of.

But the clatter and the man's yells filled the roadhouse. There was a sudden scampering of feet. Before the Black Bat could swing around, someone had raced a few steps down the hall and bolted into one of the rooms. A key turned in the lock.

The Black Bat called to Butch and they started searching the second floor. All the rooms were empty except the one with the locked door. The Black Bat put his back against the wall beside that door and struck the panel once with the butt of his gun. Instantly, the man inside fired two shots through the door.

"Bronco!" the Black Bat called. "You haven't got a chance. Come out of there with your hands up."

"Come in and get me!" Bronco roared. "Only the next shot I fire will go smack into the head of the girl in here with me."

The Black Bat gave quiet instructions to Butch, left him on guard at the door and entered the room next to that occupied by Bronco and Carol. At least he prayed that Carol was in there.

He raised the single window quietly and leaned out. The window of Bronco's room was only four or five yards away, but there was no way to reach it. The Black Bat looked up. The roof was just above.

HE RETURNED to Butch. The killer in the room was worried at the unexplained silence. The Black Bat whispered instructions to Butch and spoke the last three words in a hoarse whisper which Bronco must have heard.

The words were, "the fire escape."

Butch moved away toward the stairway. In three minutes he was back, nodding that things were arranged. He took up a position near the door.

The Black Bat crept into the next room again and leaned out of the window once more. Silk was on the roof, sent there by the orders relayed through Butch. Silk also had a rope which he had found downstairs somewhere. He lowered the rope and let it swing past the window of the room where Bronco was holding out.

The Black Bat knew crooks of Bronco's type. Sullen men, dangerous when cornered, but always seeking a loop-hole. If Bronco bit at this bait, he would believe the Black Bat or his aide was making an attempt to slide down the rope, and would start proceedings from the window. Bronco was bound to try to resist such a flanking attack. The only way he could do this was by eliminating the man on the roof.

The Black Bat's abnormal hearing detected the sound of Bronco moving toward the window. So far, the presence of Carol was attested to only by Bronco's threatening admission that she was in the room. The window was raised carefully. Bronco must have seen the rope now. Suddenly he poked his head out and looked up toward the roof.

Silk was giving him plenty to occupy his attention, for Silk was in the act of clambering over the roof-top. Bronco thrust out an arm through the window, bringing up his gun.

"Bronco!" the Black Bat called.

The crook emitted a bleat of alarm, twisted his head and swung his gun into position. He fired once. The bullet hissed by the Black Bat. There was just one more shot. It came from the Black Bat's gun and Bronco sagged weakly against the window sill. He made one last attempt to raise the gun again, but his arm couldn't make it. The gun fell from his fingers and Bronco was draped half-in, half-out the window.

There was a terrific crash in the hall. Butch had broken down the door with one lunge at it. His voice made the Black Bat's hair stand on end.

"Carol! She's dead!"

The Black Bat rushed into the room. Carol lay on a cot. An unhealthy pallor beneath her makeup gave her an eerie appearance. But there was a faint rhythmic movement of her chest. The Black Bat felt her pulse. He looked up at Butch.

"Go to the back of this place and get out a car," he ordered quickly. "Stand by with Silk to leave here at once. Carol isn't dead. She's drugged, and we've got to get her to the lab quickly."

Butch vanished. The Black Bat went over to the window and dragged Bronco into the room. The man was dead. From his own pocket, the Black Bat took a small metal box, opened it and removed a sticker, shaped like a bat in flight. He pasted this on Bronco's forehead. The Black Bat always branded the men he was forced to kill so that no one else would get the blame.

Then he picked up Carol and carried her tenderly down the steps. Butch was waiting, and took Carol out to the car. The Black Bat heard one of the two remaining crooks emit a groan. He jerked the man to his feet and shook him back to consciousness.

"I'm going to ask you some questions," he said coldly. "If you don't answer them, I'll kill you. Who paid you to kidnap that girl?"

"Tip Farrel did," the crook said without hesitation. "Somebody else hired him, but I don't know who it was. Honest, all we were supposed to do was guard the girl. We didn't hurt her any. Just put some stuff in her coffee and she'd sleep all the time and give us no bother."

"You're dumb enough so that I believe you," the Black Bat snapped.

He drew back a fist and sent the man on a quick journey to the oblivion of unconsciousness once more. Then he went over to the telephone booth and called the State Police. He said that he was the Black Bat, told what had happened, but did not give Carol's name. Hanging up without answering any questions he ran for the borrowed sedan which Silk was driving. Butch had gone ahead with the coupé.

Silk deposited the Black Bat and Carol near the entrance to Quinn's garden. Then Silk drove away to get rid of the car. Butch was to pick him up.

The Black Bat carried Carol into the lab. There he quickly changed to the clothes of Tony Quinn.

He took steps then to help bring Carol back to consciousness. It wasn't easy. Butch and Silk soon joined him and they waited eagerly for Carol to tell what happened.

"It isn't often," Silk offered hopefully, "that one of us can solve a mystery this way. Carol was kidnaped for a reason. Whatever it is, should be bound to tell us who that Long Island killer is."

CHAPTER XI

Meeting of Suspects

BEFORE Carol's eyelids moved a full hour went by. Finally she was able to gasp out Quinn's name. She recovered rapidly after that. Silk prepared black coffee which she sipped gratefully.

"Feel well enough to talk now?" Quinn asked her.

"Yes, Tony. But, I'm just a little groggy. What day is this?"

"You were snatched two days ago." Quinn smiled at her. "A lot of things have happened since then, but you hold the solution to this entire business. Carol, why were you kidnaped? What do you know that made such a step necessary?"

Carol looked blank, then pressed a hand to her forehead.

"I've tried to think of a reason," she said after a moment. "But there isn't any. I left Wilma the night Don was murdered. I was just out of the gate when two men stepped up and grabbed me. I was gagged, then a little later forced to drink something that put me to sleep. I remember nothing since then."

"You mean," Quinn said incredulously, "that there is no reason for kidnaping you? Carol, there must be! Even if you can't recognize it. Tell me exactly what happened at the house. From the time you arrived there."

"I was talking to Wilma." Carol thought back with some difficulty. "Don came in and seemed gay and happy. Then that—that awful looking man arrived. With his blind friend. And the story they had to tell came out in a rush. It wasn't nice. The man who declared he was Matt Bradley frightened Wilma half to death. I was taking care of her when Don went to his rooms. When he didn't come back, I went looking for him. He was dead. Then everybody seemed to appear. I telephoned you and left soon after you got to the house, talked to them all and then departed. From the moment those men seized me until now, everything is quite blank."

Quinn's eyes narrowed. "Rest, Carol. In a short time I'll need your help. Silk, telephone Captain McGrath and ask him to have everyone connected with this affair assemble in my office as quickly as possible. No one is to be permitted to remain in Matt Bradley's home. Butch, in a few moments you will drive Carol and me to the Long Island house. We want to be close by when they leave. Time is precious."

"What are you going to do?" Carol asked.

"Have you duplicate every move you made in that house," Quinn said. "Silk, give us a few minutes to get started on our way to the house. Then call McGrath. Take the big car and drive out to pick me up. I'm not even going to wear the clothing of the Black Bat this time. We have to take chances. You will pick me up and drive me directly to the office while Butch brings Carol back here to the lab. . . ."

Carol, Butch and Tony Quinn had arrived at the Long Island estate near Flushing, and were well concealed when Captain McGrath led the occupants of Matt Bradley's home out to a police car waiting in front. Clint Henderson carried a roll of music, apparently intending to waste no time. Sam Bradley weaved a little, but seemed to be fairly sober. Wilma walked beside Matt Bradley, helping him in his stiff-legged gait. George Lane, the blind man, was on the other side of Bradley and used his white cane to guide him. They entered the large car and were driven away.

The moment the car disappeared, Tony Quinn was on the porch. There were no close neighboring houses and he could work freely. In his pocket was a black hood to be donned in an emergency, although he looked for nothing to happen.

Getting into the house was simple. He carried keys which fitted the front door lock. Butch was left on guard. With Carol, Quinn entered the house. Immediately she started duplicating every move she had made prior to being kidnaped. Quinn watched it all and shook his head disconsolately when she had finished.

"I can't see a thing," he sighed. "Not one thing which would have made it necessary for you to be snatched. Try again. This time I'll go up to the room where Don Thayer was murdered and see if I'm helped by being in the same location the murderer must have been."

Quinn reached the room, left the door open and, while Carol began her procedure all over again, he glanced around. The rear exit, undoubtedly used by the killer—unless he were Sam Bradley—was half-way down the hall toward the stairway. Quinn slowly backed out of the murder room as Carol started up the steps.

She seemed to be directly behind him and he looked over his shoulder, but she wasn't there. A few seconds elapsed before she reached the head of the stairs. Quinn frowned.

"Carol," he said, "go back and start up the stairs again, just as you did this time."

ONCE again it sounded as if Carol was in the hall while she was really only half-way up the steps. Quinn took her arm and piloted her out of the house where they were joined by Butch. With split-second timing, Silk was slowly guiding Quinn's limousine down the road. Quinn signaled him and Silk stopped.

"You and Butch take the coupé and go back to the lab," Quinn instructed. "I'll join you there as soon as I've talked to the people in my office." (Turn page)

"Jerry Devine Was Hired to Kill a Man—Who Was in Back of It?"

THAT'S the all-important question that puzzles Tony Quinn when he sets out on one of the strangest and most baffling trails of his career in THE MAN BEHIND MURDER—a mystery novel by G. Wayman Jones that will keep you guessing from start to finish!

It's a fast, action-packed yarn of a puzzling series of crimes that seem to make no sense whatever—until Tony Quinn completes the job of putting together the clues and emerges with an answer to the mystery that will astonish you! Learn the identity of THE MAN BEHIND MURDER in our next issue!

"There's one thing," Butch said, and he was frowning heavily. "I've been thinking, out here all alone. Remember the man who sat next to Salisbury in the bus depot and maybe planted that gun under the bench? I'm sure he was one of the two mugs I lambasted at the roadhouse where Carol had been held."

"Good," Quinn said. "That takes care of one little item. See both of you later."

Silk made time on his trip back to the city. In short order he pulled up before the building where Quinn had his office. He parked, helped Quinn out and they found McGrath and the others impatiently waiting at Quinn's office.

"I'm sorry," Quinn said. "Am I terribly late?"

"What's the idea of bringing us all here?" Hal Salisbury asked irritably. "I was taken out of my home by a detective. You'd think I was under arrest."

"Maybe you are," Quinn said softly. "Please step inside. This won't take long."

Silk arranged chairs and they were all seated in a semicircle before Quinn's desk. His blank eyes seemed to be studying the bare wall between Sam Bradley's chair and the one occupied by Matt Bradley.

"It has come to my attention," he said after a moment, "that more than one attempt has been made on the life of Matt Bradley. This information was given to me by the Black Bat."

"Perhaps," Clint Henderson said mildly, "you are the Black Bat. There have been such rumors."

Quinn smiled. "There are people who think so, but I assure you the Black Bat has healthy eyes and I am quite blind. We're not here to argue that point, however. Behind these attempts at killing Matt Bradley lies a clear-cut motive. Greed! Once Matt was legally dead and his fortune shared by his heirs, Don Thayer, his wife Wilma, Sam Bradley and Clint Henderson. Hal Salisbury, as Matt's business partner, simply assumed control of the business they had owned jointly. Perhaps Salisbury has made some settlement. I don't know. But you people, whom I have named, possess a strong reason for seeing to it that Matt is really dead this time."

"Suppose we concede that," Sam Bradley said. "But why then, was Don murdered?"

"I don't know," Quinn replied. "There are a lot of things about Don Thayer I'd like to know about. Mrs. Thayer, you may be able to answer them. What sort of man was your husband?"

Wilma looked startled. She glanced at Matt Bradley's stiff face. He nodded slightly.

"Don was—well, perhaps not the best type of man," she said. "Until I married him, I mean. Before that, he acted like a playboy. He gambled, traveled around the country and visited all the biggest gambling places, race-tracks and sporting events. Some of his associates did not have very good reputations, I imagine. But he reclaimed himself for me. He settled down and did his best to administer Matt's estate ably."

Matt Bradley spoke up. "To give the devil his due, he did do well. My estate wasn't shrunken, as I had thought it might be. I accused Don, before he was murdered, of being a cheat. He had been, but of course I didn't know he had changed. I was bitter and angry. I honestly wish now that I hadn't made such an accusation."

Quinn nodded. "Now we're getting on. Mr. Salisbury, my source of information tells me you took a mysterious trip to a bus depot far out of the city. Why?"

Salisbury paled. "I—well, I received a telephone call asking me to be there at a certain time. I obeyed."

"Why?" Quinn asked sharply. "Would you obey any anonymous phone call?"

"No." Salisbury was growing more nervous by the minute. "No, this was special. The caller—a man—said I could make some fast money by going there. But nobody showed up. I don't pretend to know what it is all about."

"I think you're a liar," Quinn said tartly, "but at the moment I can't prove it . . . Sam Bradley, last night an attempt was made to murder your brother Matt and his blind friend. The attempt, I believe, was aimed solely at Matt. George merely happened to be there and his death would have meant little one way or another."

"I know what you're going to say," Sam broke in. "Wilma told me the Black Bat found me sitting in my car. Drunk as usual. The engine was going and a hose had been rigged from the exhaust to Matt's room. It looks as if I did that, but I swear I didn't."

"You went out drinking that night," Quinn accused. "If you were that intoxicated, how did you drive a car home?"

SAM BRADLEY looked bleak.

"Well, I—I didn't drink a great deal," he protested. "It suddenly came to me that I was making a fool of myself, so I quit. I drove home, but on the way I felt that I needed a drink badly. I always keep a bottle in the glove compartment—"

"And you invariably drink from it every time you are driving home," Quinn accused. "You were afraid to have too much for fear you wouldn't be able to drive, but as you neared your home, you drank more from that private bottle."

"All right, I did," Sam retorted heatedly. "I always did. I'm a fool, but I hurt no one except myself. I did take a drink. I remember driving into the garage, then I must have fallen asleep."

Quinn tapped his fingertips together. "I think," he said, "that is quite all. Except that there should be some way to remove this motive for murdering Matt Bradley. There must be a way."

Matt Bradley arose, with the aid of his cane, and glared at everyone in the room.

"There is a way," he announced coldly. "And I have already taken the necessary steps. If I am killed, the murderer will find out what I mean. Further than that, I refuse to say anything more. And speaking for all of us, I believe forcing us to come here at this house is an imposition. I'm not a well man. I've been through undiluted Hades, along with my friend George. We are trying to recuperate, but not having much success. I'm going home . . . George, take my arm and let's get out of here"

Quinn made no attempt to stop them. McGrath didn't leave. He was thoughtfully rotating a black cigar between his lips and regarding Tony Quinn intently.

"So the Black Bat contacted you, eh?" he said musingly. "Odd, isn't it, how he always pays you a visit at opportune moments? You're not kidding me, Quinn."

"Forget that," Quinn said irritably. "Frankly, I'm disappointed. I expected much more to happen when those people were assembled here. One of them killed Don Thayer and is trying to murder Matt Bradley. The motive is possession of Bradley's estate. But with the exception of George, the blind man, and Hal Salisbury, they all have that motive and it doesn't necessarily point out any definite suspect."

"Look, McGrath said, "If Sam Bradley was found in his car while it was pumping carbon monoxide into Matt's room, then Sam must be the killer."

"Not necessarily," Quinn argued. "The Black Bat told me that Sam drank from a bottle of drugged whisky. He always kept a bottle in his car and the murderer could have spiked it and tried to frame Sam."

"Doped booze sounds like a woman's weapon," McGrath commented wryly. "Wilma Thayer says nothing and does nothing. She keeps out of everything that she possibly can. Maybe that husband of hers didn't reform quite as much as she says, and she busted his skull. Matt Bradley came home. She knew Don would probably be thrown out on his ear and she with him. But if Don died, Matt might take care of her. I've seen people convicted on evidence less strong than that."

Quinn nodded. "It's worth considering . . . Silk, I want to go home Thanks, Captain, for your cooperation."

CHAPTER XII

The Trail

FIVE minutes after Tony Quinn and Silk were home, the phone rang. Quinn answered it.

"Quinn," a tinny voice said, "I know you are the Black Bat. The cops want you and unless you pull out of this thing you're butting into now, and stay out, I'll see they get you. Remember— stay out."

Quinn hung up without uttering a word. He eyed Silk silently for a moment.

"A definite threat to expose me as the Black Bat, Silk," he finally said. "It was the man who murdered Don Thayer, of course. I couldn't recognize his voice. But he is guessing, just as Captain McGrath guesses. Nevertheless, this threat is real and must be handled accordingly. I'll need your help. We've got to destroy the idea that I am the Black Bat. It's bad enough to handle McGrath, let alone a killer who has no scruples at all and who is bound to blast this information all around when we catch him."

"I notice," Silk said, "that you used the word 'when', not 'if'. That means you know who it is?"

"I'm reasonably certain, Silk. There are a few loose ends, but we can't work on it until tomorrow. Meanwhile, go back to practising the voice of the Black Bat. You're good at it, but perhaps a little rusty."

Needing the rest because of recent strenuous physical exertions, and fairly certain that all of his strength would be called on to cope with the problems of the next day, Quinn went to bed early.

He passed at once into dreamless sleep, and awoke at his usual time, refreshed in mind and body. After a leisurely breakfast he drove to his office and began the day's work, like a man interested in no more than his routine labors.

Late in the morning, Matt Bradley arrived at the office. His leathery face and prominent eyes were almost human looking, and the man was both excited and smug.

"I just visited my attorney," Bradley said as soon as he was admitted to the Special District Attorney's private offices, "I wanted you to know what I'm doing in case anything happens. Last night you mentioned something about removing the menace to me, and I've done it. Permanently too. Whoever tried to kill me wants my money. Therefore I had my lawyer draw up a new will. I have disinherited all my relatives. Every last one. My entire estate goes to George Lane."

"But your relatives aren't all killers," Quinn objected. "You're treating some of them unfairly."

"I know that too. George and I have an understanding. When the danger is removed and the murderer found, I'll make another will, a duplicate of the original. With provision for George, of course, but on a minor basis. I can't forget what he did for me."

Quinn nodded. "That sounds like an excellent idea. And I should inform all interested parties of your action. Thanks for telling me. I'll worry much less about you."

Matt Bradley hunched his chair a bit closer, looked around to make sure the door was closed, then dropped his voice to a harsh whisper.

"The Black Bat contacted you with the whole story. Frankly, Mr. Quinn, I'm beginning to wonder if you really are blind and if you aren't the Black Bat as so many say you are. Now wait a minute before you throw me out. If I had the most definite proof in the world, I'd keep it to myself. I fully appreciate what you and the Black Bat are doing for me."

Quinn smiled. "It's becoming a bit irksome, Mr. Bradley, but I assure you that competent physicians have pronounced me incurably blind. I suppose others at your house hold the same suspicions of me?"

Bradley arose with those jerky movements of his.

"If they do, no one has spoken to me of it. I'm going back now and tell them it's no use killing me. They'll get nothing if I die. If anything develops when I give them that news, I shall let you know."

"Please do," Quinn said. "I'll be interested. The office routine settled down. Just before lunch, Quinn was visited by a delegation of a citizen's committee and asked to make a radio address at ten that night. Quinn held his consent in abeyance, saying that pressure of business might not enable him to have time to write an address.

But he felt a great deal better than he had the day before. Carol was out of danger, living at the lab, and she had fully recovered from her unpleasant experience.

AFTER dinner, shared with Carol in the lab, Tony Quinn went over the case with her, particularly that phase which seemed to involve him as the Black Bat so much. Calmly they reasoned out a plot. Carol's suggestions were clever and constructive.

They were deep in these plans when Silk burst in on them.

"Captain McGrath just phoned, sir. Matt Bradley has disappeared!"

Tony Quinn worked swiftly. He donned the clothing of the Black Bat while he gave Silk orders. Then Carol drove him in the coupé to a point close by Matt Bradley's estate. The Black Bat got out, cautioned Carol to stand by, and hurried to the house.

The back door was open and he walked in boldly. Captain McGrath, questioning everyone in the house, made a move toward the gun in his hip pocket as the black-clad figure approached.

"It might be better, Captain," the Black Bat said, "if we worked together on this."

McGrath dropped his bent arm. "All right. Heaven knows I need help. Nobody here has the slightest idea as to what happened to Matt Bradley."

The Black Bat walked up to George Lane, who sat fidgeting with his white cane.

"You were invariably with Matt," he said. "What happened?"

"I don't know for sure," George answered plaintively. "I'm blind. I can't see. We were taking a walk just after dusk. It was in the rear of the house, close, by where the cement driveway ends, I think. I remember my cane hitting the cement and then tapping against grass and dirt. Someone came up behind us. Matt was struck. I heard the blow. Then someone pushed me into the bushes. I yelled for help. After all, there wasn't much I could do."

"We understand that," the Black Bat sympathized. "But you mentioned someone coming at you from the rear. You heard footsteps. Blind men are supposed to have keen hearing. Did you recognize those steps?"

George mopped his forehead. "I—I think so. I've been listening to everyone here walk around. I eliminated everyone, but I remembered how Hal Salisbury walked. Matt and I were talking about him when it happened. Matt said he was sure now that Salisbury's accounts with the business were all off. Matt's accountants had furnished him with a preliminary report."

"I've already sent a couple of men for Salisbury," Captain McGrath explained.

"Good," the Black Bat said. "Stay here with these people, Captain. I'm going to look around a bit."

The Black Bat moved fast. He sensed that speed was most essential, for if Matt Bradley wasn't already dead his predicament must be serious. The Black Bat followed the route described by the blind man. He saw the bush into which George had been thrown and, close by, several blades of grass which were smeared with blood.

He stood there in the darkness and looked around, penetrating the gloom easily. It was safe to assume that Matt hadn't been taken far unless the killer had used a car, and there were no fresh tire marks on the driveway.

The Black Bat hurried to the garage. It was large, capable of accomodating eight cars, and there were servants' living quarters on the second floor of the brick structure.

He entered the garage, bent and studied the floor. He approached the steps to the second floor and examined these carefully. There was a trail—exactly what he was looking for. He went up the steps, gun in hand. The door at the top was locked, but it was flimsy and he crashed it open. Disappointment swept over him as he gazed thoughtfully into a large storage room.

Trunks were piled up against one wall. Again the Black Bat bent low, and he proceeded in this position, straight toward the trunks.

He dragged the trunks down and, using burglar tools, pried each one open. One of those forming the base of the pile was stoutly locked and he spent five minutes forcing it. He raised the lid. Inside was the doubled up form of a man. The head was blood-smeared. His lips were swollen and a cruel gag had been forced into his mouth. Wrists and ankles were securely tied.

The Black Bat lifted him out of the trunk. It was Matt Bradley, and he was still alive. Then the Black Bat saw why. By sheer accident the tail of Bradley's coat had caught in the lid as it had been closed. A faint amount of air had filtered through. If the trunk had been properly closed, Bradley would have suffocated in five minutes.

THE Black Bat untied the man, removed the gag, and Bradley managed to talk after he was given a glass of water.

"Thanks," Bradley said hoarsely. "You didn't waste any time getting here. But I thought I was finished and every blasted evil thing I've ever done came back to me. I've been too harsh, too uncompromising. I'm going to change—especially toward Wilma, and not be influenced by what has happened to me."

"Interesting," the Black Bat said. "But who struck you on the head?"

"I—don't know," Bradley managed. "I was walking with George. Then the blow. I faintly heard George cry out and I'm pretty sure he said Hal Salisbury's name. Looks as if I was on the wrong tangent entirely, going to all that trouble of changing my will to remove a murder motive."

The Black Bat helped him up. "We'll go to the house now. The police have been sent to pick up Salisbury."

"Fine," Bradley said. "But you know, I've been wondering. George is blind. How could he know who attacked me?"

"He told us he thought it was Salisbury's footsteps he heard," the Black Bat explained. "Let's go. I rather think we can wind up this affair shortly now."

Here were gasps of astonishment when the Black Bat led Matt Bradley into the living room. George arose and came forward, frantically waving his free hand in an endeavor to find Matt. The other hand clutched the cane. Salisbury was already there, seated in one of the big chairs, and looking sullen. Clint was intent on more of his music, while Sam Bradley sat nervously on the edge of his chair. Wilma was quietly tearing a lace handkerchief into shreds.

"I don't know why you can do things I'm unable to accomplish," Captain McGrath complained. "I hunted high and low for Bradley. Salisbury was home when the boys got there. He insists he never left his apartment, but that's no alibi."

"He doesn't need one," the Black Bat said. "Salisbury didn't kill Don Thayer, nor did he attempt to kill Matt Bradley. The reason I located Bradley was because the killer left a trail. He couldn't avoid it. Though he took certain precautions, even the rubber end of a blind man's cane leaves imprints in the dust of a long unused garage second floor. Naturally he couldn't see that the floor was dusty."

George Lane was near the door. He turned suddenly and darted toward the cellar door, as unerringly as a man with sight. It slammed behind him. McGrath whipped out a gun. The Black Bat seized McGrath's arm.

"Wait," he cautioned. "George is the man we're after. I've known it for a while. This is his final sally as a crook, and he intends to take some of us with him if he must die. Send men to guard the cellar exit. They are not to try and enter. George may be blind, but he's holed up in a dark cellar and has more advantages than a man with sight."

Every light in the house winked out.

"He's making certain of that advantage," the Black Bat said.

McGrath shook himself free of the Black Bat's grasp. "We have flashlights!" he exploded. "I'm going after him."

"I admire your courage," the Black Bat said, "but this is my job. Mine alone. I think I can handle George. If you went down there with a flash, if you even got down the steps, George would hear you snap on the flash. Perhaps that act can't even be heard by your ears, but George could hear, and he'll shoot at sounds. Shoot as straight as you or I."

The Back Bat drew his own gun, stepped to the cellar door and opened it. He descended three stairs and closed the door behind him. Then, as softly as a mouse, he took a couple of more steps. There was a shot.

The bullet hissed past him. While the cellar still echoed and reechoed to the din, he rushed down the steps and made a dive for the protection of some packing cases. George was somewhere in a far corner. The Black Bat couldn't quite place him even though he could see through the darkness.

At that moment the Black Bat would much rather have faced someone who could see. George Lane was desperate and deadly.

CHAPTER XIII

Blind Man's Bluff

THERE was the sharp tap of a cane somewhere across the cellar. The Black Bat knew what that meant. George was on the move and he rapped the cane so his sensitive ears could pick up the echo that was sent back from the nearest obstacle. The Black Bat knew that a blind man is able to walk within two or three feet of an obstacle and feel it without touching anything. But he also knew that sounds echo back to locate the obstacle even better.

Then the Black Bat saw George, and his gun automatically leveled. At that moment he could have killed the man, but he held his fire. George must be taken alive, if possible.

The Black Bat took a chance and moved a little, to keep covering the blind man. George fired at the sound and only the fact that the Black Bat saw him train his gun saved his life. The Black Bat fell to the cellar floor, and stayed there.

George was behind the furnace now. The Black Bat risked another move. He scurried toward the doubtful protection of a narrow iron pillar. It was in the middle of the cellar floor and left him almost entirely in the open, but he now could watch George.

The blind man came cautiously around the corner of the furnace. Once again, he was a good target, but the Black Bat didn't shoot. He contemplated chancing a rush straight to George, but gave up the idea. George was bound to hear him and open fire.

George went completely around the furnace. It was clear that he was depending upon darkness to protect him, so he must feel certain the Black Bat could not see him at all. There was a work-bench against the far wall. The Black Bat eyed it speculatively. As George got behind the furnace again, the Black Bat ran lightly toward the bench.

George's gun blazed twice. He was shooting with uncanny accuracy. If Captain McGrath had been fighting this battle, he would have been riddled long ago. Only the Black Bat's advantage of seeing in the dark saved him. Reaching the bench he crouched below it, hardly daring to breathe. George was on the prowl again, making little sounds, and never once stumbling over any objects.

The Black Bat risked standing erect. He looked over the top of the bench, picked up a handful of small metal screws and nuts. George was coming closer. Once he tapped the hard crook of his cane to get his bearings.

The Black Bat watched George carefully. Every time the blind man took a step, the Black Bat matched it with one of his, so that George's own movements masked those of the Black Bat. They passed one another and George must have sensed the Black Bat moving past him for he turned and his gun swung straight at the figure in black.

The Black Bat snapped one of the screws in the direction of the bench. George stopped in his tracks and cocked his head. Another tiny metal object landed on the bench. George was not quite sure what it meant, but he accepted the fact that the Black Bat must be close by the source of that noise. He started moving forward again.

The Black Bat tossed another bit of metal. George's gun blazed and the cellar was filled with the concussion and the racket. It was the moment the Black Bat had waited for. The instant when he was close enough to attack while George's ears were filled by the racket of his own gun.

George battled with the fury of the condemned. The Black Bat knocked his gun to the floor and kicked it as far away as possible. Then he proceeded to force George back until he could seize him.

"McGrath!" the Black Bat yelled, and the detective captain opened the cellar door. "Don't come down here. Call in your men. I've got George, but he's dangerous, and you'll need help to keep him subdued. When your men are ready upstairs, I'll bring him up."

George gave a violent wrench and one hand managed to reach the Black Bat's throat. There was nothing else to do. The Black Bat hit him smartly on the point of the jaw and George sagged to the floor. The Black Bat sped toward the cellar hatch, opened it and looked out. McGrath's men were gone.

"Are you okay down there?" McGrath called. "We're all set."

McGrath was waiting when, at least ten minutes later, the Black Bat forced his now conscious and cursing prisoner up the stairs and into the living room. Two uniformed policeman took him over while two others stood by in case George went on another rampage.

THE Black Bat stood near the door. "Yes," he said, "it was George. He had three long years to concoct this plan. Ever since he met you, Matt Bradley, he planned this. He even withstood torture to save your life. Not because he cared much whether you lived or died, except that for him to carry out his scheme you must live. There was nothing particularly brave about what he did in shielding your identity. If he had accepted the terms of his Jap captors, they would have killed him anyway. They have a habit of doing that, and George knew it."

Matt Bradley's scarred and almost hideous face took on fresh lines. Those of horror.

"I've been such a fool," he said softly. "I trusted George so. He was the one who gave me the plan for becoming my heir so the motive for murder would be removed from my relatives whom I wrongfully suspected. But why on earth did he kill Don?"

"Don was a gambler," the Black Bat said. "A gentleman of fortune, like George. I think they met at one time or another and

George, while he knew he had changed in appearance, was afraid that Don would eventually recognize him. And it was a good way to start the ball rolling. To throw fear into you, Matt Bradley. Those attempts on your life were clever fakes. Except for the last one. Once the new will had been made, you were doomed.

"George tried to pin the blame for the last attack on Salisbury. The one in which Sam seemed to be involved was staged, of course. George would have pretended to be awakened by the gas and given an alarm. The night it happened, George heard me approaching the house. He wasn't sure who it was, but he took a chance and rigged the thing."

Wilma moved closer to Matt Bradley.

"But how in the world could George move around so easily?" she asked. "This is a strange house to him. Unless he isn't really blind."

"I can answer that," Matt broke in. "While were were imprisoned for three years, George had a game. I'd tell him every last little detail about these premises and he'd try to describe them to me later. He even knew approximately how many steps he could take to cross a room. He knew everything about this house and the estate."

"All a part of his plans," the Black Bat commented. "Salisbury, when Matt was finally murdered, you'd have taken the blame. You had cheated. You would have breathed easier if Matt were really dead. You were ripe to play the fool for George by falling in with some of his men. You see, George knew his way around and had friends in the underworld of many cities. He got in touch with some of them here."

"I admit it," Salisbury groaned. "I did appropriate money from the business which wasn't mine, and I was afraid of what Matt would do when he found out. Some crooks called me and seemed willing to kill Matt. It's too late to say I'm sorry, but I'll try to show I am by making restitution as fast as possible."

"You may not know it," the Black Bat said, "but the night you kept that appointment at a bus depot, the gun which George used to fire at Matt was planted so it could be traced to you. You were kept on the move so that you'd have no alibis. However, it's up to Matt if he wishes to prosecute you."

The killer began to struggle violently, but his captors held him back. He began to shriek. "All right, you got me! But you can't shut me up. You're Tony Quinn. Take that hood off. I'm no fool. I've been busy too.

Tony Quinn isn't blind at all. Go on—show us. You're Quinn, and you belong in prison, too."

"Don't move, Captain." The Black Bat's gun was raised. "George seems to possess the same ideas you do. But he's wrong too. Clint, go to the cellar and turn on the light switch. Turn on the radio after the electricity is restored. Dial in Station WKJ. Wait a few minutes. I want this business settled once and for all."

McGrath obeyed, a puzzled frown on his face. There was an orchestra on the air. This changed to a forum hour after a short time. It was five minutes past ten by the clock on the radio. This audience was tense, wondering what the Black Bat meant.

"It is my pleasure," the radio speaker said, "to introduce a man who knows crime from every angle. Ladies and gentlemen, Special District Attorney Anthony Quinn."

Then Tony Quinn's voice came on. There was no doubting it. He talked about crime until McGrath snapped the radio off.

"I must be going crazy," McGrath grumbled. "I don't see how—"

He looked back to where the Black Bat had been standing. The doorway was empty. The Black Bat had disappeared. George, the blind killer, began to struggle again.

"You infernal idiot!" he roared at McGrath. "You completely stupid nitwit!"

"Shut up," McGrath growled. "Take him away, boys."

McGRATH did wonder why George was so vehement in his screaming accusation of his dumbness. At that particular moment, McGrath was inclined to agree with him. That had been Quinn on the air. It was easily checked up on. Therefore, Tony Quinn couldn't be the Black Bat. McGrath was more than slightly dazed as he escorted George to a police car. . . .

Later that night, in the privacy of the lab, Tony Quinn chuckled over the whole thing. Carol, Silk, and Butch joined in the laughter.

"You must have done a splendid job doubling for the Black Bat," Quinn told Silk. "McGrath came to the radio station, found me there and apologized. I pretended I didn't know what he was talking about and now George will stop raving that Tony Quinn is the Black Bat. It was close. Carol burned up the roads getting me to the radio station in time after you slipped into the cellar, Silk, and took my place. I had one of the radio station guides take me to the studio and I mentioned that you were outside in the car. Thanks for stalling as long as possible."

"I talked slowly and in detail," Silk said, grinning, "with an eye on the clock. You should have seen McGrath's face."

"I'm sorry I missed it," Quinn said. "Now you three are entitled to a bit of explanation the jury will never hear. I suspected George as soon as I realized the murderer believed Tony Quinn was the Black Bat. You recall that McGrath accused me while I sat in my car near the grave which was being opened. No one at the grave could have heard him except a man gifted with abnormal hearing. George was that man. He heard McGrath and believed Mac was right."

"Tony"—Carol slipped an arm under his as they sat on the davenport in the lab—"I'm still curious to know why I was kidnapped."

Quinn looked down at her. "I didn't know myself until we attempted those experiments at Matt Bradley's house," he told her. "When anyone, especially with clicking high heels, ascends the staircase, the clatter of the footsteps sounds as if they are along the corridor. George heard you coming after he had killed Don. You were still on the stairs, but the strange acoustics made George believe you were in the corridor and had seen him.

"Only a blind man would have been so affected by yours footsteps and from then on, I knew George must be the guilty man. He probably thought you'd blackmail him, so he lost no time in calling in Tip's men and having them take you. I suppose he wanted to question you out of curiosity, so he let you live."

"What a pity that a man bereft of his sight should be a killer," Carol said softly.

"Don't pity him," Quinn said. "George is the type of person who'd never change. He was always a killer and a crook. He used people to gain his own selfish ends. He got Bradley to phone me, thinking I hadn't returned and that would show I was the Black Bat. Going blind even from torture didn't change him. He slipped up the back steps, located Don and crushed his skull with his cane. He had time to wash the cane off afterwards, for George knew the house and the estate and could move about quite freely. If I ever could have summoned any mercy for him it would have been destroyed when he took you prisoner, Carol."

"For me," Carol said softly, "it would have vanished when he paid Tip to murder you."

Silk and Butch suddenly realized this was no place for them, and they departed. The Black Bat had never disappeared more quietly or smoothly. Tony Quinn and Carol never even missed them.

MURDER CAME LATER

By LEE EUMENIDES

When violent death stalks a bleak New England camp, Bob Fisk, salesman, helps the police find the way to a killer!

BOB FISK piloted his somewhat ancient sedan around the bend of the macadam country road. The back seat of the car was filled with sample cases. Samples of goods which would be for sale after reconversion had really set in.

The road bordered the Atlantic Ocean and now and then he had glimpses of the water. It was a winding, rather treacherous road, originally carved out of the mountainside as a cattle trail, then later for the use of wagons, but never for high-speed cars.

As he straightened the wheel he saw the other car coming. It was a coupé. At least, he thought it was. And it approached so fast that Bob Fisk immediately sensed that he would never escape a crash. For two vehicles to pass on this narrow road required caution at low speeds, but with a racing artist like the driver of the onrushing car, a collision was inevitable.

Fisk decided against the outer rim of the road. If he was hit there, car and all might go through the flimsy fence and down into

45

the gorge. He selected the none-too-happy alternative of being crushed to death against the wall of the mountain.

But the driver of the coupé had seen Fisk's car and was trying frantically to avoid a collision. It pulled out, sideswiped the highway fence, then turned in again as the driver probably took a good look down the gorge. The coupé hit the mountainside with a resounding crunch of metal.

Fisk braked to a stop quickly, got out and ran back to the wreck. As he neared it, the door opened and a girl stepped out. She was pale, but Bob Fisk instantly knew those cheeks of hers usually required little artificial color. Her lips were curled as if in mingled fear and anxiety. She was about five feet four, reaching nicely to Fisk's shoulders. Her eyes were a smoky brown.

"I—I'm sorry about—this." She waved a hand vaguely at the two cars. "Could you get me to a fishing camp five miles north of here? It's terribly important, and my car won't run. The front wheels are smashed."

Fisk glanced at the wreck. "And that's not all, Miss. Fishing camp five miles north? Well, I was going in the opposite direction."

"Please!" She looked up at him and he recognized the desperation in her eyes. "It's vital that I reach the camp before—well, I must get there as quickly as possible. I'll pay anything!"

"Come along." Bob Fisk took her elbow. "Never mind paying me. I'll be glad to take you there. After all you did sacrifice your car to avoid hitting me. Although I must say you were not trying exactly to match the speed of a turtle."

SHE wasn't even listening to him, but she did nod, politely, as if she had heard every word. Fisk turned his car around and began driving as fast as he dared. He kept talking about the little New England towns along this sea coast, how he had been selling hardware all around the region for five years, but lately the actual selling didn't amount to much.

"We're feeding the doorknobs, hinges, hammers, chisels and screw-drivers to the Japs these days," he said. "Right now I'm doing what is called, in the trade, missionary work. Build-up for our products after we're allowed to make them again. You see, Miss— Miss—"

"I wish you all the luck there is," she said absent-mindedly. "Can't you go just a little faster?"

Fisk kept quiet for the rest of the trip. Finally he saw the wooden sign indicating that Kirk Ives' fishing camp was to the left, down a badly rutted lane. He tramped on the brakes and took it slowly.

Soon they came into sight of the camp. It lay nestled in a cove with a fairly sandy shore for its front yard. There were two buildings—one a lodge, the other a smaller place apparently used as a guest house.

Some people were approaching the car as Fisk came to a stop. There was a middle-aged man, rather obese, with a face that was fatter than the rest of his body. His eyes seemed to be set in layers of fat. With him was a woman who was built exactly the same. Perhaps she had been attractive once, but that had been several years ago, at least.

They came from the direction of the lodge. Behind them stalked a tall man with gray hair, a man with a professional look, like that of a doctor or a lawyer. From the guest house another man approached. He was about thirty-two or three, and good-looking despite a protruding chin.

"Mike!" the girl beside Fisk shouted at this younger man, and climbed out of the car. "Oh, Mike!"

She ran up to him and he gathered her in his arms, which Bob Fisk noted with something akin to jealousy. He didn't even know who the girl was, but he felt he would like to know her. He got out also, and walked over casually.

All the strain and despair which had filled the girl during the trip was gone now. She glowed with enthusiastic youth. Then she went over and took Bob Fisk's hand, led him to the little group.

"This is Mr. Robert Fisk," she told them. "My car was wrecked and he was kind enough to give me a lift here. Mr. Fisk, this is Mr. and Mrs. Monroe."

Bob shook hands with the obese couple. Then he met the professional-looking man who turned out to be a dentist named Noah Lally. The man who had embraced the girl grinned at Fisk and offered his hand.

"My name is Mike Douglas," he said. "I'm Grace's brother."

"Her brother?" Fisk's grin was wider than Mike's. "I'm very happy to meet all of you."

"Mike, where is Kirk?" Grace Douglas broke in. "I don't see him about." Then, for Fisk's benefit she explained that Kirk Ives and her brother were business partners and that the fishing camp belonged to Ives.

"The last I saw of Kirk," Mike Douglas grunted unhappily, "he was walking near the cliff overlooking the next cove. I hope he fell off and broke his miserable neck."

"Mike!" Grace said sharply.

William Monroe waddled forward and gave Douglas a curious look.

"The fact of the matter is, Mike," he said, "that Fran and myself were wondering if anything had happened to Kirk. The way you looked when we met you running down from the cliff—well, that expression on your face wasn't nice to see."

"And furthermore," Fran Monroe added, in a deep-chested voice, "we saw nothing of Kirk. You have a vicious temper, Mike. I hope you didn't lost control of it."

Grace Douglas was slowly growing pink. "Why do you make such accusations?" she demanded. "It's true Mike has a temper but it's also true that Kirk deliberately—"

"Whoa, Grace," Mike broke in. "We don't have to hang out all the laundry. The trouble between Kirk and me is personal and can be ironed out. I hope."

Bob Fisk stood by mutely while this went on, and realized that the camp was no place for him. There was trouble brewing and in large quantities. He wanted no part of it, although Grace Douglas was a magnetic attraction.

"Well, folks," he said, "I think I'll be on my way. Got to make Manchester by dark if I can." He glanced at his watch. "It's fifteen minutes of noon right now."

Grace came over to him, smiling. "You'll never know how grateful I am, Mr. Fisk. And sorry for the way I frightened you with my car. Thanks again—and I won't forget what you did."

"Think nothing of it," Bob Fisk said, but he didn't get any further.

A BOAT with an outboard motor was churning toward the small dock. A man was standing in it, waving his arms. Wisps of his shouts could be heard, but they didn't make sense. Fisk looked keenly at Mike Douglas. The young man was several degrees paler, as if he knew what was about to happen.

"Why, that's Baroux, the guide!" Dr. Lally exclaimed. "He's alone. Something must have happened to Stevens. They went out to do some fishing together about an hour ago."

Everyone rushed down to the dock. Before the boat reached it, the darkly-tanned, wiry little man in it was telling what had happened.

"Mr. Stevens and me, we were going along the beach. We rounded the point." His arm swept toward the jutting finger of beach that separated the twin coves. "Mr. Stevens he jumped up and said someone lay on the sand. I cannot see, but I turn the boat toward shore. Sure enough, Mr. Stevens has good eyesight. There is a man on the beach. He is dead."

"Who?" Dr. Lally demanded.

"It is Mr. Ives, the boss," Baroux said. "And he is dead all right. There is a bullet through his head."

Suddenly Grace Douglas was leaning weakly against Fisk.

"Too late!" she said, half under her breath. "I was too late!"

Fisk didn't ask any questions. He clambered into the boat.

"Take me to the cove," he told Baroux. "The rest of you stay here until we get back."

Obese William Monroe raised a pudgy arm. "Listen here! Why do you take all this authority upon yourself?"

"This is either suicide or murder," Fisk said curtly, "and we have no evidence to either cause of death. You people knew the deceased. If it is murder, we innocent people don't want the killer enabled to remove and destroy any clues. Certainly you can't suspect me. I only just arrived and the whole thing is a mystery to me. Therefore, who else is better fitted to take charge temporarily?"

"We ought to get the police," Dr. Lally suggested. "And listen—I am a dentist, but I know something about first aid, in case Kirk isn't dead."

"Get in," Fisk invited. "As for the police, that's a rather vain idea. The nearest town is thirty-odd miles away. There is no telephone and all we'd get would be a constable to whom murder is as strange as it is to most of you. Just sit tight."

Baroux shoved off and the motor chugged smoothly. He was explaining as they moved away:

"Mr. Stevens he says he will remain while I go for help. It is a terrible thing—quick death like that. A bullet through the head."

Bob Fisk reached over and pulled up Baroux's trouser cuffs. He glanced at them, but said nothing. He turned to Dr. Lally.

"Mind you, Doctor, I'm no detective. I'm a salesman, and these things are out of my line, but I have an idea some of this trouble is storming around Miss Douglas. We're strangers, but I want to help her. She was anxious to get here fast. I think it was to stop this murder, which means she believes her brother might have done it. What about that?"

Dr. Lally thoughtfully knocked ashes off his cigarette.

"Well, you have no authority, but we're isolated up here and someone has to take charge of things. You're forceful enough to get away with it. So I'll tell you what I know."

"Thanks," Fisk said. "I appreciate it. Shoot."

"Kirk Ives owns this camp," Lally said. "He and Mike Douglas have been partners in a stock firm for some time. I honestly have no proof of this and it's all assumption, but I'm sure there has been trouble between them. Kirk owes—owed, now that he is dead—me quite a lot of money. He was trying to borrow from the Monroes too. That is why he had them up here. They're impossible people, but Kirk knows—knew—the value of entertaining prospects whom he can touch for a loan."

"And where does the bad blood between Kirk and Mike Douglas come in?" Bob asked.

"I don't know," Lally declared. "Whatever it is, it's bad all right. They were at it hammer and tongs all last night and they resumed this morning. They went off together, arguing like a couple of tom-cats. I thought it would wind up as a battle royal, but not like this."

"Why did Kirk need all this money?" Bob queried.

"I don't know that either," Lally replied. "We're coming into sight of the cove now. Yes—there's Jack Stevens waving."

"And who is Jack Stevens?" Bob wanted to know.

Lally shrugged. "A friend of Kirk's. He often comes up here and uses the camp alone. Has full run of the place, so he and Kirk must be good friends. Must have been, I should say. Can't get it out of my mind that Kirk isn't still alive."

JACK STEVENS greeted them. He was about thirty, tall and good-looking. His features were grim right now, though, and he stared at Bob Fisk intently. Fisk got out of the boat, stepped into two feet of water and waded ashore, followed by Dr. Lally who explained to Jack Stevens who Fisk was.

Stevens seemed to accept the young salesman at face value.

"It's horrible," he said and motioned toward the figure sprawled out on the sand. "I found Kirk, just as he is. Beyond lifting his head I didn't touch him or move anything. By the looks of it he was shot and pushed off the cliff. There is a hole squarely through his forehead. Can't see it unless you raise him up."

Fisk knelt and lifted the limp form. Stevens had not exaggerated. Kirk Ives was dead. Fisk looked up.

"See anything of a gun, Mr. Stevens?"

"No," Stevens replied. "I looked too. Unless it's lying directly under his body, there is no gun here."

Bob Fisk turned the corpse over completely. There was no gun hidden beneath it. He arose and looked up at the cliff. It wasn't so high, but high enough to break a man's neck or back if he was pushed off. There were some bad craggy rocks jutting from the wall of the cliff. Fisk glanced back at the dead man and saw that part of his clothes were torn, as if they'd been ripped by some of those crags.

The dead man wore a gabardine suit, even to coat and vest. There was no hat in evidence. The suit was tan, practically the same color as the sand.

Fisk walked toward the cliff.

"I'm going to scale it," he said. "You others can follow if you like. I want to find that gun if I can."

Jack Stevens was shaking his head from side to side.

"I hate to think what this is going to do to Grace," he said. "Mr. Fisk, you're in it up to your neck now. You've taken over the whole thing, which is all right by me. But go easy on Grace."

"So you too think Mike Douglas killed Ives, eh?" Fisk said bluntly. "Dr. Lally seems to. Mr. and Mrs. Monroe all but accused Mike to his face of doing something to Kirk. Hey, Baroux—what's your opinion?"

The guide avoided Fisk's direct look.

"Me, I am just a hired man. I know nothing. Of course, Mr. Kirk and Mr. Douglas did not like one another. That has been plain. They argue all day and night. One time I see Mr. Mike slap Mr. Kirk across the face."

Bob Fisk sighed. It was not going to be pleasant for Grace. The evidence so far was piling up in overwhelming disfavor of her brother Mike. If these people got on a witness stand and gave their testimony, Mike would be convicted on circumstantial evidence alone. Finding the gun might help some to turn suspicion in another direction.

They reached the top of the cliff after some hard climbing, and the three men fanned out to search. Dr. Lally was in the middle. Fisk took the rim of the cliff and Jack Stevens skirted the fringe of brush near the edge of the clearing.

Fisk saw it first. A black automatic lay in plain sight on the grass. He called the others over.

"Don't touch it," he warned. "They don't get many fingerprints off guns, but sometimes there's a latent print or two which helps. Either of you ever seen the gun before?"

"It's Mike Douglas'." Dr. Lally shuddered. "This gets worse for him as we go along."

Fisk nodded. "We'd better go back to the camp. Doctor, could you climb down the cliff again and help Baroux carry the body to camp? Stevens and I will go afoot along the trail."

Lally agreed and disappeared over the edge of the cliff. Stevens and Bob Fisk walked slowly down the well-cut trail toward the camp. Neither spoke much.

Grace saw them coming and ran to meet them. Fisk moved to take her aside, but Stevens beat him to it. Fisk shrugged and hoped Stevens would give her the news gently.

He kept on going until he reached the lodge. Mr. and Mrs. Monroe were on the porch, rocking themselves in the noonday sun and looking lazier than ever.

"Well—it was murder, of course?" Monroe said.

"Yes," Fisk answered. "Murder! Couldn't have been anything else. You mentioned something about seeing Mike Douglas walking away from the cliff."

"Walking," Mrs. Monroe declared with

aggravating complacency, "is a mild way of putting it. Mike ran and he was startled and, I think, frightened when he saw my husband and me. As if he didn't want to be seen anywhere near there. Of course he killed Kirk."

"Why?" Fisk asked quickly.

"I suppose Kirk owed him a lot of money. Like he did Dr. Lally and he would have owed us. Kirk was trying to negotiate a loan. A great deal of money. Of course you know we're wealthy."

"Yes." Fisk eyed them for an instant. "You do look well fed."

He turned and walked away.

GRACE and her brother were in the small guest house when Bob Fisk entered. Jack Stevens had disappeared and Fisk suspected he had gone to the dock to meet and help Dr. Lally and Baroux who were bringing the corpse back.

Bob Fisk sat down. "I'm going to be frank," he said. "It is a case of murder and all the evidence points to you, Mr. Douglas. If I were an officer, I'd arrest you on the face of it right now. You were the last known person to see Kirk Ives. You were near the cliff. You were arguing with him and you have a motive, possibly. The murder weapon has been identified as your gun."

"Yes, I know." Douglas stared at the floor. "Stevens told me about the gun. I looked in my bags. It had been stolen. A weak alibi, of course, but it's the truth. Why doesn't someone go for the police?"

"I'm trying to keep them from doing just that," Fisk said. "Why, I don't exactly know." But his eyes shifted to Grace and he did know why. "Getting the police would mean your prompt arrest. The fact is, things are so dead set against you they seem to be planted. I don't like it at all."

Grace jumped to her feet. "Then you believe in Mike and—and me?"

"Of course," Bob Fisk replied. "That's why we must try to run this down before the police arrive. How about telling me all you know?"

Mike shrugged. "It isn't much. Kirk and I were in business. He had helped himself to the firm's money—thousands of dollars—and couldn't pay it back. We're on the verge of bankruptcy. I called him on it. He promised to make good and didn't, although I think he borrowed some from Dr. Lally. I say I think so because I never saw a dime of it. He was trying to get more out of Mr. and Mrs. Monroe. He owes Jack Stevens too."

"Why are you sure?" Fisk asked.

Douglas looked up. "Well, Kirk has owned this camp a long time. There's deep sea fishing here and inland streams not far away have some excellent trout. Every time he wants to impress anyone, he brings them here. If he is in debt to anyone, the same thing happens. He figures they'll be easier to do business with under a lazy sun and the influence of some fine fishing."

"All right." Fisk nodded. "Now about the last time you saw Ives."

"At breakfast, where we argued. I socked him last night and I felt sorry about it this morning. After breakfast we walked toward the cliff. I told him if he didn't have money enough to make good when we reached town, I'd go to the Prosecuting Attorney."

Fisk whistled softly. "There's more motive for Ives' killing you than for what really did happen. He was all right when you left him?"

"Of course he was. I was still sore and walking pretty fast to get it out of my system. That's when the Monroes saw me. Somehow I think they're glad this happened. I don't trust them."

Fisk thought it over for a moment. "You left Ives alone. Mr. and Mrs. Monroe went on up to the cliff, by their own admission. They could have killed him. Who knew you had that gun?"

"Everyone," Mike groaned. "I'm pretty good with a gun and I showed them some target practise yesterday."

"Bad." The salesman shook his head. "Where was Dr. Lally all this time?"

"Asleep in his room, I suppose," Mike answered. "That's about all he ever did up here. Sleep."

"And Stevens?"

"He and Baroux were going to fish for flats. I don't know when they left. . . . Look here, I'm fagged out. Mind if I take a little walk to air my brains?"

Bob Fisk was more than glad he went. He sat down beside Grace.

"Regular detective, aren't I?" he said, and grinned. "Pretty good too, for an amateur. You, for instance, heard that Mike had gone to Kirk's camp and you suspected Mike might get rough. That's why you were in such a hurry, why you seemed relieved when you found no trouble here, and why you berated yourself for being too late after you learned Kirk Ives was dead."

Grace looked at him steadily. "You're a very good detective," she said. "That is all true, but I was more afraid Mike would beat him up. I never thought it would turn into —murder. It's bad for Mike, isn't it?"

"Very." Fisk sighed. "However, I'm not completely satisfied. There's one little thing that is strange. Don't ask me what. It may be absolutely silly, but I'm going to track it down anyhow. Now let's see—we have Mr. and Mrs. Monroe as suspects. Your brother, of course, and Dr. Lally. Stevens seems to be out of it. And Baroux, the guide. He worked for Kirk and may have had cause to hate him, but he was out in that boat with Stevens. It's all mixed up."

"But you will try to help us?" Grace begged. "Oh, I know you're not a policeman, but you have done so well so far. Please! We need your help."

BOB FISK arose.

"You've got it, for whatever it is worth. I might put Mike in a worse jam than he is now. We have to take that chance. Show me Kirk's quarters. I'd like to look around them."

Grace left him at the door of Ives' quarters. He entered a comfortable bedroom, closed the door and started going through Kirk's things with an uncomfortable idea that he shouldn't. After all, this was a policeman's work. But thoughts of Grace made him keep on. He was still at it when Mike Douglas knocked and entered. Mike sat down on the edge of the bed.

"What do you really think, Fisk?" he asked. "Give it to me straight."

Fisk shrugged. "You did it, according to all the evidence. But in prowling around Ives' things I noticed several odd facts. He has a diamond ring weighing a carat and a half in the drawer—but the stone is a fake. There are code numbers inside his expensive watch, marks pawnbrokers make when they take in an article. In his coat I found a lot of old bills, none of them paid. What on earth did he do with all his money? Or was the business you both operated on the skids?"

"Anything but that," Douglas replied anxiously. "Last year Kirk made a little over fifteen thousand. Yet he was always broke, and he's into the firm right now for twenty thousand."

Bob Fisk whistled. "Add that to the sums he certainly borrowed from Dr. Lally and Stevens and it runs into big money. How long have you known Kirk?"

"Three years," Douglas admitted. "We seemed to hit it off well, and built up a good business. Kirk never talked about his past. What's on your mind?"

"Motive," Fisk answered. "And it runs to blackmail. There's too much money unaccountably spent. That would place a different light on things, but we have to prove it. I think—"

The door opened suddenly and William Monroe waddled in. His wife's bulky frame filled the doorway after he passed through. She spoke first.

"Mr. Fisk, I believe someone should get the police. We all know very well that Mike killed Kirk. If anyone shot Kirk after Mike left, my husband and I would have heard it. Something should be done about it and if you refuse to act, we shall assume you are in collusion with Mike."

"But why?" Douglas protested. "I hardly know Fisk."

"A man like Mr. Fisk doesn't have to know a girl like your sister Grace long before he'll fall all over himself doing things for her. I've seen the way he looks at her. I want

action on this and at once, or we shall take matters into our own hands."

Bob Fisk arose, flung up a window and called to Grace who was slowly walking past the lodge.

"Miss Douglas—take my car. Drive into town and bring back an officer. Watch the curves."

Grace was pale, but she nodded and hurried toward the sedan. Mike Douglas glared at Mrs. Monroe, walked out of the room and looked for Baroux.

Bob Fisk left also, and found the guide cleaning the rowboat.

"He bled," Baroux explained. "I'm washing it off."

"Good," Fisk said. "Baroux, your story is that you and Stevens were going fishing. What time did you leave? Where was Kirk Ives at that time? And Mike Douglas?"

"They had gone to the cliff." Baroux's eyes narrowed a bit. "I wait here for Mr. Stevens. Then we start out. Like I said, we round the point and Mr. Stevens he get very excited. So I steer the boat ashore. That is all there was to it."

"And you actually saw the bullet hole in Ives' head?"

"There is blood." Baroux shrugged. "He is dead, of course. That much I knew. Why do you ask me all these questions?"

"Because I'm a curious man." Fisk grinned. "Thanks. Maybe later on we'll do a little fishing. As soon as everything is cleaned up here."

"You think that Mr. Mike he kill him?" Baroux asked cautiously.

Fisk shrugged. "Nope. I like to take the side of the under-dog. See you later, Baroux."

He started walking rapidly toward the cliff.

He passed along the trail, reached the edge, and looked down. There was still a fairly deep indentation where the body had fallen. He moved directly above that spot. There was nothing to show any signs of a struggle. The gun had been found close by. As Mrs. Monroe had pointed out, she and her husband might not have heard the shot if Mike had fired. But if it had been anyone else, they would certainly have heard the gun.

Bob Fisk paced back and forth slowly, wondering what sort of idiot he was for trying to help a man like Mike Douglas who had so obviously turned killer. But that same doubt lingered. So did thoughts of Grace Douglas. He wondered if she was on her way back yet. It had been a dirty trick, sending her for the police who were bound to arrest her brother. But he hadn't dared send anyone else. He might have selected the killer who could then have got a good head start on the law.

IT WAS the afternoon sun glinting along the rifle barrel that warned Bob Fisk. The barrel protruded from thick branches alongside the trail. He went into a nose dive faster than he had thought any man could do it. He skidded along the ground, heard the sharp crack of the rifle, then he plunged headlong into the brush.

He stayed there for a minute or two while he recovered his breath and steadied his nerves. Then he started maneuvering, but it was no use. The would-be killer had missed his chance and departed.

Fisk returned to camp, staying off the trail. He was boiling mad when he strode across the clearing.

That anger subsided rapidly. His car was back and a state trooper in a natty uniform was talking to Douglas. There were handcuffs in his hands. Mr. and Mrs. Monroe were there. Dr. Lally was absent, but shortly showed up. Stevens leaned against the door. Grace stood beside her brother, plainly frightened. Baroux was not in sight.

Bob Fisk shook hands with the trooper and was impressed. He looked capable and efficient.

"Miss Douglas met me while I was on highway patrol," the trooper said. "I understand you more or less took over up here, Mr. Fisk. That's all right except you went a bit too far. Moving the corpse, for instance."

"And being shot at a few minutes ago," the salesman answered grimly. "Someone armed with a rifle just tried to cut me down. Has everyone been here for the last ten minutes?"

The trooper shrugged. "I arrived about ten minutes ago. No one was about. Why was an attempt made upon your life and who, in this camp, has a rifle?"

"Baroux," Dr. Lally exclaimed. "He has one. And Baroux hasn't shown his face since the trooper arrived."

Fisk turned on his heel and hurried toward the little dock. Baroux was still in the boat, fussing with the outboard motor now. His hands were greasy and at once Fisk thought that this was an excellent ruse to obliterate any traces of gunpowder on his fingers. Baroux insisted stoutly that he had never left the dock.

When Bob Fisk went back, the handcuffs were on Mike Douglas' wrists.

"It's cut and dried," the trooper said. "I've placed this man under arrest on suspicion of murder. I'll take him to town and then return with the medical examiner and an undertaker. Don't you agree, Mr. Fisk, that I'm right?"

"I'm afraid I do," Fisk admitted ruefully.

"Let him talk to his sister for a few moments. And, Officer, if you'll come with me, I'll turn the murder gun over to you."

He and the trooper emerged from the lodge a couple of minutes later. Douglas got into the trooper's car. Bob Fisk slowly placed a comforting arm about Grace as the car pulled away.

"Don't give up yet," he whispered, his lips barely moving. "But don't even show the faintest ray of hope."

The State trooper returned two hours later, accompanied by a doctor and an undertaker. It didn't take long before Kirk Ives' body was being removed to town. The State trooper called everyone together.

"I'm trusting the lot of you to remain here until tomorrow when I'll return and take statements. Mr. Fisk, I shall hold you responsible for them. Expect me tomorrow afternoon."

The young salesman stayed away from Grace the rest of the day. Everyone retired early and Fisk took Ives' room, but he locked the window, bolted the door, and even then slept fitfully. He recalled the attack with a rifle vividly, although he hoped that the murderer was appeased by the quick arrest of Mike Douglas.

Bob Fisk slept late. When he came out, Stevens was walking toward the dock with a fishing rod under his arm. Fisk fell into step with him.

"Mind if I tag along? Baroux promised me some fishing, and it will give me a great appetite for lunch."

"Glad to have you," Stevens said. "Baroux, we'll go to the spot where we were headed yesterday when we spotted Kirk's body."

The outboard motor sputtered, took hold, and the little craft glided away from the dock. They rounded the point. Fisk glanced at his watch. It was approximately the same time that he had arrived at camp the day before. The same time that Kirk Ives' body had been discovered.

Stevens stared moodily at the cove. Baroux kept his eyes averted. Fisk also looked and after several moments, he gasped.

"Maybe I'm seeing things, but it looks to me as if there is another body over there!"

STEVENS leaped up, almost upsetting the boat. He shaded his hands against the sun, then sat down.

"I don't see a thing, Fisk. Are you sure?"

"Sure enough so we ought to make certain," Fisk said. "Baroux, head for the cove."

As they neared it, they did see the form sprawled out on the sand. Baroux sent the craft as close to shore as possible. Stevens and Fisk jumped out. Fisk reached the body first.

"It's Mike Douglas!" he exclaimed. "He must have escaped. Dead—shot through the head! Baroux, take the boat and go to the camp. Tell them—"

"Mr. Mike is shot through the head?" Baroux screeched. "Yes, yes, I see. I will get help. I will go fast!"

He turned away. Stevens suddenly raised the heavy fishing rod he was still carrying.

Before Fisk could interfere, Stevens slugged Baroux across the back of the head. Stevens dropped the fishing rod, whirled, and drew a knife. His lips were drawn back in a snarl.

"This is some kind of trick!" he yelled. "I knew you suspected me! You snooped too much, but it won't do you any good. This time, Fisk, I won't miss. You can miss with a rifle, but not with a knife!"

He rushed at the salesman who stepped nimbly aside, but Fisk underestimated this killer. Stevens was lunging past but, as he did, he went into a dive that carried Fisk down too. Before Fisk could get over the shock of the unexpected tactic, Stevens had the knife raised.

There was a single shot. It seemed to come from far away. Stevens screamed. The knife fell out of his hand and it seemed to have been replaced by a crimson glove. The form that had been lying on the sand was up and running. It was Mike Douglas all right.

But Bob Fisk didn't need help now. He pinned Stevens down and held him there. Looking up, he waved to the State trooper on the edge of the cliff. The trooper started scrambling down.

After Stevens had been handcuffed and his bullet-smashed hand roughly dressed, Fisk lit a cigarette.

"I suspected Stevens from the beginning," he said. "First, because at the time of day when he said he saw the body, it was impossible to look in the direction of the cove without the sun searing your eyes. Also, Ives wore a suit which matched the color of the sand, making the corpse almost invisible. Stevens couldn't possibly have seen anything. He told Baroux that Ives was dead. Baroux, you did not see the wound, did you?"

"No—no." Baroux was rubbing the welt on the back of his head. "But Mr. Kirk he looks so dead and Mr. Stevens he says he has been shot."

"As a matter of fact," Bob went on, "you didn't even get out of the boat. If you had, your trouser cuffs would have been wet, and they weren't. You merely took Stevens' word for it that Ives was dead. You were Stevens' alibi. But Kirk Ives was not dead. Stevens met him on top of the cliff right after you, Douglas, had left in a huff. Stevens slugged Ives, pushed him over, and then hurried back to camp. Mr. and Mrs. Monroe didn't see him because he did not use the trail, but a short cut. Naturally, nobody heard a shot, so it was assumed that Douglas must have killed him before the Monroes were close by.

"It happens that in this case murder came later. Kirk Ives was not dead when Stevens reached the beach. He was unconscious. Stevens waited until Baroux was out of earshot, killed Ives with Douglas' gun which he had stolen on his way to meet Baroux at the dock. Then he conveniently dropped or threw the gun on the cliff-top so I would find it."

The State trooper nodded. "When you told me those things yesterday, I agreed to work with you. Good thing I did. Ives' fingerprints revealed that he was an ex-convict. Stevens blackmailed him, of course, until he was bled dry and growing balky."

Fisk nodded. "That's why Stevens had the run of this camp. Kirk Ives couldn't refuse him. Stevens was worried about me and did his best to put me out of the picture. He was afraid I'd already guessed the truth."

Douglas shuddered.

"Thank heaven you came along. Fisk, if there is ever anything I can do for you, just let me know."

Fisk grinned. "There is. Let me break the news to your sister."

"I'll do better than that." Mike Douglas chuckled. "I'll let you drive her to town. Alone!"

Bob Fisk thrust out his hand. "My pal," he said, and grinned.

TONY QUINN, NEMESIS OF CRIME, IS AT HIS SLEUTHING BEST IN

THE MAN BEHIND MURDER
By G. WAYMAN JONES

Brandon caught up the chair and hurled it at the nearest gunman.

DOTS AND DASHES

By BILL ANSON

One blonde plus two gorillas adds up to—trouble!

WHEN ex-Sergeant Tommy Brandon entered the East Side subway train, he immediately noticed the blue-eyed blonde with the slightly turned-up nose and the kissable red lips.

She was just the sort of girl any ambitious young man would like to take to a party. Her camel's hair coat was in the best of style, and her little tri-cornered hat was as cute as Rip. She wore very attractive suntan hose and sensible half-heel mocassins with square toes.

Tommy Brandon sat down across the aisle.

Not until then did he become aware of the two hard-case civilians in derby hats and tight Chesterfields who were sitting beside her and glowering savagely at him.

"What in the world is she doing with those two touts?" Brandon asked himself as the subway train jerked, shook and started rolling fast.

He looked squarely at the girl, as if expecting a reply.

Her eyes dropped to her square-toed shoes, which promptly began tapping on the floor of the car.

Tommy Brandon glanced quickly away. He was still in uniform, having been mustered out of the Army only the day before, and he still hadn't shaken off the old feeling that he would lose his Signal Corps stripes if he got into trouble with civilians. And the surest way to get into trouble was to make a play for another man's girl.

But the blonde across the subway aisle certainly didn't seem happy with her two roughneck escorts. Tommy Brandon gave them a hard glance, and they shifted uneasily. Once more he looked at the girl, and once more her eyes dropped to her shoes, which again began tapping on the floor.

She was even prettier than Tommy Brandon had first imagined. She was just the kind of girl he'd had in mind to pal up with in his new start in civilian life. That is, after he'd won that job with the Metro Radio Company, and could operate on a pay-as-you-go basis, rather than on his Army bonus.

"It sure would be great," Tommy told himself as the subway train clattered and swayed along the dark tunnel, "if Metro took my invention and put me in charge of the testing room. I'd be a big shot then. Not just another veteran without a suit of clothes and afraid to spend the money for one."

THE subway train ground and jerked to a station halt. The doors opened. Passengers started out, while other passengers tried to get in.

Tommy Brandon glanced at the girl to see if she were going to get off. Immediately her eyes dropped to her square-toed shoes.

Tap, tap, tap went one toe against the subway floor. Tap, tap, tap; tap, tap, tap!

Utter incredulity flooded Tommy Brandon's lean, tanned face. For the first time he caught what she was doing. The blonde was sending out a distress call! Three dots, three dashes and three dots was the SOS!

As the ex-sergeant continued to stare at the girl, she looked up, and a swift, helpless little smile crossed her lips. But it was gone instantly when one of the derby-hatted civilians spoke sharply into her ear. The other man got to his feet, one hand stealing inside a coat pocket, his black gimlet eyes focused on Tommy Brandon.

Brandon might have risen to the challenge, but the blonde's toe was quickly tapping out a Morse message on the floor of the train. The train's doors were closing again, and he could barely hear the girl's rapid taps. She certainly knew how to send code, and Tommy Brandon knew how to receive it, or he wouldn't have been wearing crossed signal flags on the collar of his GI shirt.

"Don't start a fight," the girl tapped out. "Follow me unseen. Get in touch with——"

The train started with a lurch. Standing passengers swayed against the iron-hatted tout. The tout lost interest in Brandon and sat down beside the girl again. There was a short conversation. Then the girl and the two men got up and moved down the subway car toward the door.

Tommy Brandon eased to his feet and slipped to the opposite end of the car, then went on through the end doors to the next car. He kept moving through the crowd to still another subway car, for he didn't want the two men in derbies and Chesterfields to see him when he got off the train at the next station.

"She must be in a fix," the ex-sergeant muttered to himself. "She spotted my insignia and figured I could take code. But who did she want me to get in touch with? Could it be the police?"

The next station was approaching, but Tommy Brandon still had no plan of action. Nevertheless, as the subway train lurched to a halt, nervous as a race horse, he jumped out.

The milling crowd on the platform shielded him as he sped up the iron stairs to the outside street. The sunlight was blinding. He paused for a moment to find a doorway or a parked automobile for a hiding place, and a hand grabbed his arm.

"Well, if it isn't my old buddy, Tommy Brandon!" a voice exclaimed. "What are you doing in New York?"

"Bill Ritter!" Brandon blinked at the chubby, red face of a former side-kick who had been sent home from Iwo Jima a year before.

Ritter was in a snappy blue serge suit, red plaid tie and new gray slouch hat. Out of the Army, it was plainly evident now that he hadn't a care in the world and all the time in the world to waste. He grabbed Brandon's hand in a firm clasp and kept pumping.

A quick alarm seized Tommy Brandon.

"Quick, Bill!" he said. "Come with me. Duck into this cigar store!"

"What's wrong, Tommy?"

"Don't ask questions!" Brandon's eyes were quickly swiveling. "I'm trying to follow a blonde."

"Ho!" Bill Ritter exclaimed. "A blonde, huh?"

He let himself be swiftly piloted into a cigar store. Tommy Brandon whisked him away from the doorway, held him as he peeked out a window. Brandon was just in time to see the two derby-hatted civilians come out of the subway kiosk and steer the girl in the camel's hair coat and tri-cornered hat toward a large dark sedan. The waiting driver of the car nodded as the trio climbed into the back.

"We've got to follow them!" Tommy Brandon said. "Come on, Bill."

"But there's only one girl," Bill Ritter objected. "What's in it for me?"

"She's in trouble," Brandon snapped. "She flashed me the SOS."

Bill Ritter gave Brandon a cynical stare. He guffawed.

"A blonde gives good, staid, old Tommy Brandon the eye, and he falls for it hook, line and sink—— Hey! Tommy! Where you going?"

Tommy Brandon was out the door on the run. He swung into the nearest taxi cab.

"Follow that black sedan," he called at the driver, who turned around to scowl at him. "There's a five-dollar bill in it for you. Get going! It's a matter of life and death!"

"Sure, I know," the taxi driver grunted. "Every trip is a matter of life and death. But I saw the blonde, and it will cost you a tenner if you want to find out where she's going."

"Ten it is!" Brandon replied. "But don't let that sedan get away from you."

Out on the sidewalk, Bill Ritter shouted as the cab drove off, but Tommy Brandon couldn't hear him through the throb of the cab's motor.

IN the next block, a red traffic light halted the hoodlums' sedan. Brandon's taxi stopped behind it, and when the green light flashed on the street signal, dropped back for a safe distance to follow the sedan into a side street and through it to another block. There the sedan drew up before an old loft building.

"Pull up here," Brandon ordered the taxi driver.

"Okay, sergeant," the taxi man said. "This is easy money for a change."

A hundred yards down the pavement, the two derby-hatted men, the blonde between them, entered a doorway. The black sedan drove off.

Tommy Brandon handed a ten-dollar bill to the taxi man.

"Wait for me, will you?" Brandon asked.

"If I don't come out of that doorway within fifteen minutes, call the cops."

"Not me, buddy," the taxi man replied, putting his car in gear. "I ain't looking for trouble."

The cab drove off, and Tommy Brandon felt a sudden, cold chill. Perhaps he was a fool to get mixed up with a strange woman in a city like New York. Bill Ritter had given him the horse laugh, and now it was the city-wise taxi driver who had pulled out. Maybe he ought to drop the whole thing. If a good-looking girl was dumb enough to get into the hands of a pair of touts, was it his business?

"But I'm making it my business," Brandon gritted. "I started this, and I'll finish it!"

He went up the street to the loft building where the girl had vanished. There was an old sign on the door — EASTERN BOX COMPANY — and tacked to the wall was another sign — FOR RENT. The door led into a dark, dirty hallway, with an empty elevator at its far end.

Brandon entered. There was a closed door to his right, and he thought he heard someone moving behind it. As he stepped forward to make certain, his ears caught the thud of a platform on metal.

Brandon whirled toward the elevator. He was just in time to see a derby-hatted man step out from his hiding place in a dark corner of the lift. An automatic pistol was in the tout's hand and a hard grin on his lips.

"Okay, soldier," the sharp-faced little tout snarled. "You asked for it." His voice lifted. "Walt! I got him. I told you he was a sucker for a blonde!"

Tommy Brandon drew back slowly as the office door on his right swung open. The man called Walt looked out, a revolver in his hand.

"Come on in, pal," Walt growled. "Or do you want a slug now?"

As Brandon's hands raised slowly above his head, he could see into the office where the blonde was sitting, her blue eyes wide with terror. Her camel's hair coat was off, and it was now revealed that she wore a red dress. And there was a gag in her mouth. But she wasn't tied, otherwise.

Brandon hesitated, trying to make up his mind whether to go into the abandoned office, or plunge out the door to the street and risk getting a couple bullets in the back.

Tommy had a great respect for bullets. He'd been hit once in the Army. If he went down hard on his face on the outside sidewalk, he certainly wouldn't be able to get the police. And he didn't doubt but that the black sedan and its driver were parked up the street somewhere near, ready to cause him further trouble.

"Sure, I don't mind going into the office," Tommy Brandon said.

He brushed past Walt, and went over to where the blonde was sitting. Relief showed briefly in her blue eyes. Then the touts closed the office door and locked it.

"What's this all about?" Brandon asked her.

"You better shut up, Sergeant," Walt warned. He turned to his companion. "Rocky, watch out for the soldier boy when you tie him up. He might be one of these commandos who plays dirty.

Rocky was slipping across the room to get behind Brandon, who was listening to the girl tap on the floor. Brandon turned as the code message continued. He saw that Rocky was drawing back the gun to strike him on the head. Brandon backed away, listening to the completion of the code.

"Try to stall them until the police come," the blonde had tapped out. "They are after diamonds I have hidden on my person. But they don't know where."

Brandon backed against a wall.

"Take it easy, boys," he said. "What do you want?"

ROCKY glanced at Walt. The two obviously couldn't decide whether to knock him out or shoot him. They certainly didn't want to make too much noise. In the moments that the pair stood making up their minds, Brandon's fingers sought the back wall and tapped out a message on the wood.

"Sit down," Walt snarled at the blonde as she started to get up, and Brandon knew she had received his message.

"She wants to talk," he told the touts. "Take her gag away."

"She don't need to talk," Rocky replied savagely. "We ain't got any more time to waste. We're going to strip her. Turn around, soldier, so you won't be embarrassed."

Suddenly, the blonde darted across the office. Before they could stop her she had jerked a shoe off her foot, and smashed a glass window.

With a howl of rage, both Rocky and Walt were on her. And that was the one mistake Tommy Brandon had hoped they would make when he'd sent his Morse message to the girl.

Quickly, he jumped to the chair she'd just left. He caught it up and, whirling, hurled it at the nearest gunman. The edge of its seat caught Rocky behind the ear and the man pitched forward into the broken glass of the window, his automatic slipping from his grasp.

In that instant, the girl eluded Walt's groping left hand and threw the shoe she still held straight into his face, striking his eye. A yell tore from his throat, and the revolver in his hand exploded, driving a bullet widely past the girl.

By then, Tommy Brandon was plunging forward, swinging at the half-blinded gunman. The blow spun Walt around, and he floundered back into the broken window, his wrist striking a jagged piece of the window glass, cutting him to the bone. A scream wrenched from him.

Tommy Brandon grabbed up what was left of the broken chair, brought it down on Walt's skull. The man dropped to the floor. The blonde tore away her gag.

"Look out, soldier!" she screamed.

But Tommy Brandon hadn't forgotten Rocky, who was scrambling out of the mess of broken glass. Brandon's boot-toe caught him under the chin as the man tried to throw up his recovered automatic. The weapon never went off. Brandon's toe lifted him off the floor, and then Rocky collapsed like a dummy.

Leaping, Brandon snatched up the automatic pistol. He heard the impact of a shoulder driving into the office door. There was no doubt in his mind that the man trying to get in was the driver of the black sedan.

"Better come shooting!" Tommy Brandon shouted, and triggered a warning bullet into the door jamb.

Immediately, a familiar voice shouted from the outside hallway.

"Tommy! Don't shoot! It's me, Bill Ritter. What's happening in there? Where's the blonde?"

With a grin, Tommy Brandon turned to the girl.

"Better get your shoe," he said. "And you might tell me what this is all about?"

She sank into a chair, a feeble smile on her lips.

"They accosted me in the subway," she said miserably. "They had guns and said they'd murder me if I did anything. I carry diamonds for wholesalers, and they knew it. How they knew it, I don't know, because the stones are sewn into the shoulder pads of my dress. My boss thought it a wonderful trick, but it isn't."

Tommy Brandon turned to the door.

"Bill," he said. "Go get the cops, and watch out for a black sedan. And don't ask questions." Then Brandon turned again to the blonde. "But you took a chance on me, didn't you? How did you know I could get the code?"

"You wear the enamel pins of the Signal Corps on your shirt collar," the blonde replied. "You see, I got out of the WACS only last month. I was in radio."

"Well, I'll be darned!" Brandon looked at her wonderingly, admiringly. "So you know radio! You're just the girl I'd like to meet. My name is Tommy Brandon."

"Mine is Tommy, too—Thomasina Gordon," she replied. "Isn't that funny? Can you imagine, both of us with the same name!"

"I can," Brandon said meaningfully, and it wasn't the same first name he was thinking of. "Gosh, I hope Bill Ritter doesn't hurry coming back."

Thomasina Gordon got up from her chair, a mysterious smile curving her lips.

"Before he does come back, Tommy," she said, "I'm going to do something that I kept telling myself I'd do all the time I was riding along with those two horrible beasts."

"What's that?" Brandon asked.

"I swore I'd do this, Tommy, if I ever saw your sweet face again."

Tommy Brandon had to stoop his head to receive the imprint of lipstick on his cheek. Then, his arms went around her.

"And this," he said, "is what I've been wanting to do ever since I saw you sitting on the subway train."

And his lips came down on a very kissable pair of red lips.

The murder case was deadlocked at eleven for conviction and one for acquittal—and foreman Bruce Manning was determined to find out just why Delma Griffith insisted on having her way in

THE RELUCTANT JUROR
By ANTHONY TOMPKINS

PERFUME OF THE INVISIBLE LADY

By ANTHONY TOMPKINS

*Major Ed Craig of the Marines learns that treachery may
lurk in a quiet American home as well as in the jungles!*

THE Marine major who stood in front
of the staid looking mansion had seen
action all over the Pacific. He'd flown
on all sorts of missions, some of them labeled
suicide. He'd lost two planes and made his
way back to his base afoot, through jungles
that were infested with snakes, leeches, in-
sects, Japs and vermin. He'd brushed
shoulders with death a dozen times, but he
never felt quite as frightened as he did now.

He was a little surprised, too. "Shorty"
Talbot had never talked much about his
home, and Major Ed Craig had believed it
to be a normal residence—not a palace set
in lavish grounds and enclosed by a big
fence.

But that wasn't what worried him. In his
hand he carried a small package containing
a watch, a flyer's scarf, a fountain pen and
some cash—all that was left of Captain
Shorty Talbot, who'd pestered the Japs with
hot lead until he'd finally been killed himself.

As Shorty's best friend it was up to Major
Craig to deliver these little personal posses-
sions to Shorty's sister, whom Shorty had
talked about so much. And Major Craig
dreaded it. He would rather have faced a
firing squad—almost.

Yet the thing had to be done. His only
hope was that Jean Talbot wouldn't be the
weepy kind. Craig was always ill-at-ease
around women who wept. He straightened

his shoulders, adjusted his forest-green uniform cap and marched up the path like a man walking to his doom.

He rang the bell and fervently prayed nobody would answer, that Jean Talbot had, perhaps, gone to some point about ten thousand miles away. Then the door opened, dashing all his subconscious dreams. A man stood there, eyeing him.

MAJOR CRAIG gulped.

"I—I'm here to deliver some things that belonged to—to Shorty—" he began.

The man gasped, stepped onto the porch and hastily drew the door shut behind him.

"Major—you came at the wrong time. Miss Talbot was terribly affected by the news and she hasn't got over it completely. She was ill prior to the War Department's telegram. I—I don't exactly know if you should."

"I guess I better, mister," Major Craig said. "You see—I promised Shorty."

"Yes. Yes, of course." The man was slightly bald, slim and fit looking. "My name is Bernie Dunlap. I am—was—Shorty's cousin. I've sort of taken charge here since —well, since it all happened."

"Shorty spoke about you too," Craig said. "Look, let me see Jean for two minutes, and then I'll get going. I'm no more anxious to face her than she is to see me, but maybe it will help. I saw Shorty go down, but believe me, he had plenty of company. He ripped into those Japs like a buzz saw."

"I'm sure of it." Bernie Dunlap nodded and motioned for more caution in Craig's tone of voice. "Wait here. I'll sort of pave the way. Be back in a couple of minutes."

Craig sat down on the porch railing and frowned. He'd hoped that Jean would be like Shorty had been. The type to face danger and adversity and take a healthy swat at it. But Jean Talbot, it appeared, was a mollycoddle. Not that Craig blamed her much. She'd been through a great deal.

Then Dunlap returned.

"She can face it, I think," he said with a nod. "Just get the story over with as rapidly as possible, Major. You'll see for yourself just how ill she's been."

Craig took a long breath and followed Dunlap into a large reception hall. There were no servants in evidence. He trailed behind the slim man into a living room of huge dimensions. Near the fireplace sat a girl, her face devoid of any makeup, her mouth pinched, her eyes watery. Her legs and lap were covered with a blanket, and a shawl was thrown around her shoulders.

She seemed pitifully small and defenseless sitting there and Craig's heart went out to her. He cleared his throat and tried to fashion a smile—but the attempt resulted in a miserable failure.

"Miss Talbot," he gulped, "I—I'm Major Craig. Ed Craig."

The girl smiled. She wasn't good looking, but not ugly either. Craig wished she had put some makeup on.

"Shorty used to write me about you," she said.

"Well, that makes it easier then." Craig handed her the package. "I—brought back his things. Watch, scarf—the things I thought you might like to have. Shorty died instantly. Never knew what hit him, but he took a lot of Japs with him, if that's any consolation."

She opened the package and slowly fondled each item in it. Her eyes were more watery than ever. She tried to smile again.

"Thank you, Major. You can't imagine how much I appreciate this nice gesture— coming out of your way to deliver these things personally. Bernie—don't you think the Major should stay for dinner, at least?"

Dunlap, standing behind the girl, gave a quick negative shake of his head that only Craig could see.

"Oh, no," Craig said, "I really couldn't. I've some business in town. Perhaps I can come back in a day or two when you're feeling a little stronger."

She extended a slim, pale hand toward him. Craig took it and found the skin very cool. He was disappointed. He'd been so sure he'd like Jean. But this girl, so obviously ill and patently sick even of life, wasn't quite what Shorty had described. Craig frowned. Far back in his mind was something—a little detail Shorty had once told him. It should have clicked, especially when he took her hand, but it didn't. To him, it seemed only that something about the girl was wrong.

He shrugged, bowed awkwardly, and followed Bernie Dunlap out of the room. On the porch again, Dunlap offered his hand.

"Thanks, Major," he said. "You did that splendidly. I hope we shall both see you again. Have you a very long furlough?"

"Five days," Craig answered. "I'll be terribly busy."

Craig was almost certain he detected a look of relief flash across Dunlap's face, but it was gone so quickly it seemed never even to have existed.

Craig went to the car he'd borrowed. It was at the curb directly in front of the house. He waved to Dunlap, and drove away, but it wasn't until he passed by a corner which he should have turned, that he realized he was thinking more of Jean Talbot than of his driving.

There was something wrong! That phrase kept ringing through his brain. There was something radically wrong, and he had to know what it was. In the first place, he hadn't liked Dunlap—but perhaps that was natural, for Shorty hadn't liked him either. But Jean —she should have been like Shorty. Full of fun, gayety and sensible enough to face facts, bad as they might be.

CRAIG drove back to the city, some four miles away, and returned the car to a friend from whom he'd borrowed it. He went to the hotel. Although it was jammed, his uniform had given him a certain precedence, and he had a comfortable room. But to the surprise of the desk clerk, Craig checked out. He brought down his bag and hailed a taxi. Some twenty minutes later, he was again on Jean Talbot's front porch.

Dunlap showed surprise at seeing him again. Craig smiled wryly.

"I was a trifle previous," he apologized. "Seems the town is full up. I can't get a room anywhere and there are no trains out. I wondered if you'd—well, put me up for the night, at least."

Craig watched Dunlap narrowly. If the cousin showed too much concern, then he'd know something was wrong. Dunlap, however, acted utterly delighted.

"Jean gave me the devil for not insisting you stay," he explained. "Really, she was quite ill about it. I'm glad you're back. Come in, Major. Jean is lying down, but she'll have dinner with us tonight. I know she will, even though she rarely does come downstairs for meals."

Dunlap led Craig upstairs and showed him into a snug and comfortable room. Pictures of Shorty were on the walls.

"It was Shorty's room," Dunlap explained. "I think he'd have liked your staying here. Jean suggested it. Perhaps she had an intuition that you'd be back."

"Thanks," Craig said. "I'll clean up a bit, and see you later. Incidentally, what's wrong with Jean?"

Dunlap shrugged.

"Partly the loss of Shorty. He was the only relative she had left, except me, and cousins don't count for very much. More important, of course, Jean was hurt in a serious auto accident. It was fortunate she wasn't killed. Her recovery has been very slow, but we have one of the best specialists attending her. He comes from out of town, and he is sure she will recover in due time."

Craig removed his coat and tie, washed and shaved. Everything in the room reminded him of Shorty. Jean should have reminded him of Shorty, too, but she didn't. Not in the least. What was it that he missed about her? It was something Shorty had talked about, he knew, but it wouldn't come back.

Craig looked in the mirror and called himself an assortment of fools. It was silly suspecting all sorts of crazy things when there was no basis for such suspicions.

Dinner was a solemn affair. Where was that spontaneous gayety and laughter which Shorty had said characterized Jean more than anything else? Certainly this girl showed none of it. She had a bird-like appetite, hardly spoke at all, and as soon as dinner was over, she asked Dunlap to help her upstairs.

No servants had appeared, although someone must have cooked that reasonably good meal in the kitchen. Dunlap did all the serving. Craig knew the servant problem was acute, but he hadn't imagined it was this bad.

For the remainder of the evening he talked to Dunlap about air operations in the Pacific Theatre. Dunlap was a good listener. More and more, Craig believed he'd gone off the beam with his wild hunch that something was wrong. What on earth could be the matter? He had here a bereaved and ill sister, and an attentive cousin. It was silly to have thought anything was amiss, but he had to stay here for the night now anyway.

At eleven, he went to bed, scanning through some books which Shorty must have enjoyed in the days before war had come as a blight upon the world. Craig felt sleepy, turned out the light and settled against the pillow. In two minutes, he was asleep.

But anxious, terrifying days and nights in the jungles had made Craig a light sleeper. He woke up—not suddenly or with a jump—but calmly. He'd trained himself to awaken that way, even if danger stalked.

Through half slitted eyes he saw someone. It seemed to be a woman, and she stood facing the clothes-closet door on which Craig had hung his uniform. A faint bit of light came from the one window. Enough light to show Craig that she was gently passing one hand up and down the tunic of the uniform. She was whispering something that sounded like "Shorty." She repeated it several times. Then she turned and walked through the door.

She was almost wraithlike. One moment she was there, the next the spot where she had been was filled only by moonlight—and a perfume that came sweeping across Craig's nostrils. The perfume wasn't pungent. On the contrary, it smelled subtle, expensive and rare. It reminded him of a garden filled with flowers, bursting in color, glory and fragrance.

Craig swung his legs off the bed and padded to the door. It was still ajar. He stepped into the hallway. Nobody was in sight. He returned to his bed, sat on the edge of it and thought he had the whole idea. Jean Talbot was crazy! She'd stroked his uniform, and in her disordered mind figured that it belonged to Shorty and that he was there again, safe in his own bed. There was no other explanation, and perhaps it was enough. Certainly Jean's insanity was sufficient to have given him the impression that something was wrong in this huge house.

FOR an hour, Craig sat there, smoking innumerable cigarettes. Somehow he didn't care about Dunlap, and he was suspicious of him. The man appeared to be almost overzealous in his solicitude for Jean. Craig found himself wondering if Dunlap would come into control of the family fortune if Jean died. Maybe Dunlap was coddling Jean too much, giving her no rest, seeing to it that her weakness and madness became worse and worse.

Craig made up his mind to investigate that angle in the morning. He finally went to sleep, wishing that girl didn't use a perfume that lingered so long as to be impressed upon his brain instead of merely upon his sense of smell.

He slept well—and very late. Comfortable beds were still a phenomenon to Craig. He dressed and went downstairs. Dunlap had the table set, and immediately brought his breakfast.

"Jean is resting again," he apologized. "And while I'm at it, I'll say how sorry I am that we can't do all the things we'd like to do for you. Our servants have gone. There's only old Max left. He's officially the gardener, but he can cook, after a fashion, and we've pressed him into service. I'm the housekeeper and maid. Now do whatever you like, Major. Jean will see you this afternoon."

Craig tackled the grapefruit.

"I think I'll run into town and see if there is anything in the way of rooms today," he said. "Be back later—and thanks. I appreciate all you've done."

But Craig didn't leave for town at once. He went onto the estate and strolled idly along a winding, heavily arbored pathway which led to a big garage far to the rear. The same fantastic doubt he had earlier lingered. There was something wrong! Jean might be insane, but that alone wouldn't explain it. It was something Shorty had talked about.

Craig raked his brain for a clue, but it wouldn't come.

He entered the garage, merely out of curiosity, and he was attracted by what was left of a once sleek, cream colored roadster. It had been smashed into junk. He managed to slide behind the crumpled wheel. On the dash was an aluminum slot into which the car's registration was fitted. He worried the paper out. It was Jean's car.

Then Craig's nostrils twitched. He was smelling the same perfume the visitor to his room had carried with her. It was fainter, perhaps, but it was present nevertheless. He started prowling, and located a wrinkled, tiny handkerchief wedged behind the driver's seat. It bore the initial "J" and still held the fragrance of that perfume.

Craig shrugged. It wasn't any of his business. There were proper legal restraints if Dunlap tried to take possession of the family fortune, even if he succeeded in having Jean adjudged insane. Perhaps she was insane. Her actions of the night before seemed to indicate it.

Craig had his head bent in thought as he stepped out of the garage. He was hardly prepared to have a gun drilled into his ribs.

The pain of the thrust snapped him back to normal. He froze, and turned his head carefully.

A white-haired, bearded man held the gun, and his eyes were blue and wild. He seemed ready at any moment to pull the trigger, like some hopped-up gangster.

Craig's right hand moved imperceptibly, but it got into position. Suddenly, the hand darted. His fingers closed around the old man's wrist and twisted, so the gun pointed harmlessly down at the ground.

Craig clipped him lightly on the chin then and wrenched the weapon loose.

"Suppose," he said, "you tell me what's the idea?"

The old man backed up a few paces.

"I—I figured you was a burglar," he stammered.

"Since when," Craig asked, "do burglars wear the uniform of the United States Marine Corps?"

"I—don't see so well. I—I made a mistake. I—I'm Max. I work here."

"Oh—the gardener." Craig relaxed. "Dunlap told me about you. Come over to this bench and sit down. I want to talk to you. Look—how come you're still here when all the other servants are gone?"

"They were let go," Max sniffled. "Given the gate. I guess maybe there ain't much money left. Just a big house and no money. I seen things like that before."

"Um—perhaps," Craig admitted doubtfully. "What's the matter with Jean?"

"The accident," the old man replied. "It done her in proper, sir. Funny how it happened too. She was always such a good driver."

"Do you think she's gone crazy?" Craig asked bluntly.

The old man straightened, fury in his face.

"I should have pulled the trigger when I had the chance," he snarled. "You—sayin' things like that about Miss Jean. They don't come no better'n her. She's all that keeps this house goin'. With her singing and her laughter. Oh, maybe since Shorty was killed she hasn't done any singing or laughing, and I don't blame her much. But—"

"Okay," Craig said. "Go on back to work. I'll not mention this episode. I—darn it, I forgot something in the garage."

RETURNING to the garage, Craig closed the door. He went directly to the wrecked car and did some studying of the ruins. He discovered an important pin in the drive shaft had been broken in half. It seemed to have been weakened with a substance that had eroded the metal.

Craig straightened up. The old man was peering through one of the back windows and his face was screwed up in lines of intense hatred.

Craig gave up and phoned for a cab. He

went to town and was in time to see the president of the bank which Shorty had mentioned several times. Craig introduced himself.

"Shorty asked me to look out for things," he explained. "Is everything all right with Jean?"

"Well, yes and no." The banker pursed his lips for a moment before going on. "Jean is smart enough. But lately she's been buying a lot of crazy stock, donating rather large sums to charities, and really depleting the family money too fast. Her cousin handles these things, and says they are done against his advice."

"Jean signs papers though," Craig said. "That's quite necessary. Are you certain those papers and drafts aren't forgeries?"

"What on earth gives you that idea, Major?" The banker smiled. "Don't answer. I wondered about the same thing myself, and I had a rather exhaustive comparison made by experts. I can assure you Jean Talbot really signs those papers, foolish as they may be. What made you suspicious, Major?"

"Dunlap," Craig admitted frankly.

"He affected me that way too!" The banker's eyes narrowed thoughtfully. "I half sensed there was something wrong up there. The servants were discharged, although heaven knows there is still a lot of money to pay them. Jean used to have friends up all the time, my daughter included, but for the last couple of months nobody is admitted. Dunlap says Jean was badly affected by the news of her brother's death."

"Stuff and such," Craig growled. "I could express it a trifle more directly in good Marine lingo, but it isn't polite. I'm going back there and make sure Jean isn't in some kind of trouble. Oh, yes—supposing Jean was declared mad or she—died? Would Dunlap get the money?"

"No. Absolutely not. I know the terms of the will. When the last member of the family dies—and Jean is all that's left—without issue, the estate goes to a college. Dunlap won't get a penny."

"Thank you," Craig said. "I'll look in again if anything develops."

He had himself driven back, confident now that things were not right. Maybe that bleary-eyed old gardener was in on it. Perhaps Dunlap had nothing to with it, but in any case, he intended to find out. He didn't announce his return, but went directly to the second floor and searched out Jean's room.

There were cigarette butts in profusion in the ash trays. A glass smelled of Scotch bereft of soda, and sniffing it gave Craig an idea. He stepped to the dressing table. There were the usual bottles and jars on it, but none of them had the aroma of the perfume he was looking for. He scowled, wondering if he'd been asleep last night when the wraith of the girl had appeared. He recalled that his first impression had been that he could almost see through her, and that she'd vanished as if she were quite invisible.

The floor creaked in the hallway. Craig turned toward the door. He moved swiftly to the hall. No one was there. He returned to his room. Again the smell of perfume came to his nostrils—that same haunting fragrance. It was beginning to get his goat. Jean didn't use it, or he would have smelled the stuff in her room. Then who was this invisible, very fragrant girl?

There was a tapping on Craig's door, and Dunlap came in. He looked worried.

"Major, I've a favor to ask of you. It's rather impertinent, but—would you mind moving out?"

"Moving out?" Craig gasped.

Dunlap smiled.

"Oh, it's not your fault." He shrugged, helplessly. "You see, Jean is affected by your presence. You remind her too much of Shorty. She—suggested that you leave, and after seeing how she has suffered since you came, I'm inclined to agree with her."

"Of course," Craig replied. "I understand. But I would like to see her just once more. There is something I forgot about that I want to give her."

"She wouldn't let you leave without saying good-by," Dunlap interposed. "Come downstairs. She's waiting. You can pack later."

Craig went down the steps beside Dunlap. Jean was in the same chair near the fireplace, looking wan and ill. She tried to smile. Craig stepped before her and unbuttoned his tunic pocket. He drew out a medal.

"I'd never have forgiven myself if I left without giving you this," he said. "It's Shorty's. Of course, you know why he got it. He wrote the whole story while I stood over his shoulder reading it. So I won't go into any more details except to say that Shorty understated everything he wrote. If a man ever earned this medal he did and—I'm sure he'd want you to have it."

JEAN took the medal with both hands. "I—I do know the story, of course. His letters—" She broke off, buried her face in her hands, and sobbed bitterly.

Dunlap poked Craig in the ribs. Craig went upstairs, packed hastily, and was back downstairs in five minutes.

When he walked into the living room, Jean had gone, but Dunlap was there, looking extremely serious. He shook hands with Craig.

"I'm sorry you gave her the medal," he explained. "She's worse than ever now. I've just phoned her doctor, and I am going to suggest that he order her away for awhile. I feel like the very devil making you leave this way."

"I understand perfectly," Craig said. "Good-by, and thanks for all you have done for me."

Craig walked briskly along the path. It was very dark, but he had been trained for night fighting, and could see fairly well—well enough to detect the faint shadow across the path. Someone was waylaying him.

He bent to drop his suitcase without making any noise, straightened and walked boldly into the trap.

A heavy cudgel started swinging toward him. It was a murderous blow, with concentrated evil intent. He ducked fast, but not quite fast enough. The club struck him a glancing blow on the left shoulder. It paralyzed his left arm, and sent pain raging up and down his side.

His right arm worked perfectly though, and when the club started to go up for another blow, he parried it with his forearm, and punched its wielder squarely in the face. By now he knew it was old Max, and that Max's beard apparently was meant to disguise his true age and fitness, for Max was a fighting fool, strong, lithe and quick. It wasn't until some feeling came back into Craig's left arm that he could really start fighting on even terms.

A series of savage, fast punches sent Max reeling backward. Craig brought him down with a lunge, and straddled him. He was breathing heavily as he pinned the bearded man.

"Now," Craig said, "we'll have the truth. Did anyone pay you, or order you to attack me?"

"I wish I'd killed you," Max raged. "I wish I'd busted your head open like a rotten pumpkin. I wish—"

"Stop wishing and tell me why," Craig snapped. "Talk, Max, or so help me, I'll work on you as if you were the Jap who shot Shorty down."

"You know why," Max growled. "You came here and made Jean sicker. All you want is some money—lots of money. As if by saying you were Shorty's best friend entitles you to be rewarded. You're almost killing the girl."

"I'm going to let you up, Max," Craig said. "You're dead wrong about this, but I think I know why. My reason for coming here was to try and help. Instead, I interfered with someone's plans. Max, if you mention this to anyone, I'll have you locked up for assault. Now go to whatever quarters you live in and stay there."

Max got to his feet.

"Yes, sir." He bobbed his head in full recognition of the authority in Craig's voice. But he had to add one more malevolent promise. "Just you get away from here, and stay away. If you come back, so help me, I'll kill you."

He plodded off into the darkness. Craig retrieved his suitcase and placed it behind a large bush. He upended the bag so he could sit on it. He didn't dare smoke, although a cigarette would have tasted as good as—he scowled—that perfume he still thought he smelled.

Almost an hour went by and he wondered if the hunch he was working on now was going to fizzle. Then a car pulled up. A man carrying a medical bag got out. He stalked importantly along the path and into the house.

Craig watched the windows intently. On the third floor, where he had never been, a window was illuminated. The curtain was drawn all the way down, however.

Craig left his suitcase and maneuvered to the sidewalk. Someone in the car was whistling softly. It was apparently the chauffeur. Soon, the man with the medical bag emerged from the house, chuckling heartily. He got into the car. As it started to pull away, Craig leaped for the rear door, yanked it open and piled in.

The driver and passenger both turned and stared. Craig stared back, beligerently.

"Keep driving," he snapped. "You're a doctor," he addressed the passenger. "Well, I want to know how Jean is. I'm Shorty—her brother."

The passenger emitted a harsh gasp.

"But you're supposed to be—dead."

"It's quite obvious I'm not," Craig said. "I sent a pal of mine to look over the ground before I showed up. I was afraid Jean might keel over. He tells me she's very ill. What's the matter with her?"

"Well, it's very serious," said the doctor, "and I would hardly advise that you break the news to her at this moment that you're alive. Her heart—"

"You're a blasted liar," Craig said curtly. "Furthermore, this car doesn't have any doctor's registration plates and only an "A" gasoline sticker. Come through, you two—"

THE driver braked the car hard, and at the same time reached for a gun, under his arm. Craig moved briskly. He brushed off the driver's cap, raised a clubbed fist and brought it down like a sledgehammer on the back of his neck. The driver slumped behind the wheel.

The passenger was trying to climb over the seat to get at Craig. Craig let go a blow and the man stopped trying and sat down in a twisted position, blood spurting from his nose. Craig reached over and grasped the medical bag. He opened it. The bag was empty.

"Pull your pal from behind the wheel," Craig ordered. "Do it carefully. Go for his gun, and I'll break your neck. Then slide behind the wheel and drive to town. Make it snappy."

The fake doctor obeyed. Marine majors usually were obeyed. Craig extracted the gun from the still unconscious driver and held it ready. In town, he had the fake doctor stop at the sight of the first cop. Craig did some explaining, stayed there until a police car drove up, and repeated everything again to a dubious police lieutenant. The fake doctor and the chauffeur were handcuffed and removed. Craig appropriated the car.

He drove back to the big house, parked the car some distance away and approached the place from the rear. He found the kitchen door of the house unlocked, stepped inside and noticed a tray of partially consumed food on the table. The coffee-cup rim and a teaspoon were stained with lipstick. From whose lips? Not the girl he knew as Jean. She wore no makeup.

Craig passed through the kitchen, the dining room and started to cross the hall. In the living room sat Jean, a cigarette dangling from her lips. She saw Craig. The cigarette became limp. She half arose. Craig smiled.

"You seem better, Jean," he said. "Much better. Yes, I came back. I think that cousin of yours is up to something. In fact, I'm certain of it. You see, I looked over the roadster which you were driving when you had that accident. The car was rigged so an accident was inevitable."

"Oh—oh," Jean said. "I can't believe that. I can't."

"You were very fortunate," Craig went on. "You might have been hurt more seriously. Disfigured from scars."

A triphammer thought struck Craig a mental blow. Scars! That was it! He seized the girl's right hand and raised it. She didn't resist, but Craig thought he detected a sudden look of relief cross her face. At almost the same time, the stairs creaked slightly.

"Please sit down, Major," the girl said. "I must talk to you before Dunlap returns. I've been suspicious of him myself."

"Sorry," Craig said, "I can't talk right now. I have things to do. That closet in the hall contains something I want. Come along, and I'll show you."

He opened the closet door, turned on the light and pointed. Jean moved closer. Craig gave her a push, and she went flying into the closet. He closed the door, twisted the key and grinned. Then he went up the stairs as swiftly as possible.

He went all the way to the third floor and the moment he reached the landing, he sniffed that perfume again. Catlike, he tiptoed along the hallway to the room which had been lit when the fake doctor had called. He took the knob firmly in his big paw, turned it so that there was no sound, and opened the door about an inch. He could look in.

Dunlap was putting a coat around the shoulders of a very lovely girl—a girl with tawny hair like Shorty's, with the same wholesome lines to her face. She was smiling ruefully.

"But Bernie," she objected, "I think this is silly. Shorty has come home, and you don't want him to see me. Why not? Shorty will understand, just as I would if something had happened to him. You've been very kind to me, but this time I think you're too worried."

"Shorty will stew and worry," Dunlap said complacently. "He'll be only half the fighting man he was. You can't do that to him, Jean. Before he gets back, we'll slip out the rear. It's better that way, believe me."

"Better for whom?" Craig stood squarely in the doorway.

Dunlap let out a shrill cry, looked from the girl to Craig and then back again. Suddenly he started a crazy charge across the room toward Craig. Craig's fist drove him back, and to the floor. Craig closed the door, walked past Dunlap and stood before the girl's chair. She hadn't arisen.

"I'm Major Craig," he explained. "Shorty's best friend. I—"

Craig gasped in dismay. The girl was smiling, but not with her eyes. They were blank and staring, and suddenly he knew all that composed Dunlap's fantastic scheme.

"I'll be back soon," Craig told her. "Stay right where you are."

CRAIG dragged Dunlap up and pulled him along as he headed for the door. Outside, he held him while he did some telephoning. A short time later, the same police lieutenant he'd turned the fake doctor and the chauffeur over to was there.

"Dunlap had a neat scheme," Craig explained. "Jean—the real Jean—doesn't even know Shorty was killed. As soon as Shorty went into the service, Dunlap moved in here to help Jean. He helped her—to the tune of thousands of dollars. He took them by various methods, and then got scared. So he tried to kill her. That didn't work, but the outcome was even better. Jean was blinded. Craig then took absolute control. He intercepted the telegram saying Shorty was dead. He pretended that Shorty was writing letters from the South Seas, letters in which he advised Jean about investments and charity donations. Jean signed the necessary papers. Dunlap got the money and kept it."

"Nice fella!" The lieutenant slapped handcuffs on Dunlap. "Imagine Shorty dying to protect someone like this!"

"Dunlap," Craig said, "thought he was in the clear. Jean's signatures on all the papers were authentic. Then I showed up and stripped his gears somewhat. He had a girl friend living here, probably posing as a nurse. She took Jean's place."

"But how in the world did you ever tum-

(Concluded on page 77)

As the curtains swung open and the gun came through, Peter Lang gave Conroy a mighty shove, hurling him to the floor out of harm's way

THE MURDER OF "Q"

By WAYLAND RICE

*When sudden death stalks the offices of millionaire art
collector Leon Conroy, it's up to secretary Peter Lang
to reconstruct a perfect picture of the baffling crime!*

CHAPTER I

Nameless Victim

AS THE door opened, Peter Lang looked up quickly. This was his first day on the job and he was extra alert. As secretary to Leon Conroy he had to be. Conroy was an important man, an exacting type who demanded perfection in all things, especially secretaries.

The man who walked in was almost pathetic in appearance. No more than five feet two or three, he was stooped, thin and woebegone. His clothes needed a pressing and his hat looked as if it had endured the sun of several summers, the rain of as many springs and the snow of a dozen winters. He wore shell-rimmed glasses with thick lenses through which he squinted apprehensively.

At once Peter Lang knew very well that Leon Conroy would never want to see someone as disreputable as this.

Yet, when the stranger moved closer to Peter's desk, he appeared to be a rather benevolent old man, kindly and gentle. He had a massive forehead, mostly concealed by the too wide brim of the hat. He looked, in fact, like a caricature of an absent-minded, highly intelligent scientist whose life was concerned with test tubes, florence flasks and microscopes only.

"I wish to see Mr. Leon Conroy," the man said in a mild voice. "It's very important."

"I'm sorry." Peter shook his head. "Mr. Conroy sees no one without a definite appointment and he is so busy these days, it might take a month to get one."

"Oh, he'll see me all right," the little man said eagerly. "I'm very sure he will. You must ask him. He won't like it if I'm sent away. Especially after what happened."

Peter felt sorry for the little man. He did seem to have something very important on his mind. Perhaps, if Peter Lang sent him away, Conroy would hit the ceiling. At least it couldn't do any harm to ask.

"I'll see if he can slip you in somehow." Peter arose. "What is the name, please, and the nature of your business with him?"

"I—can't tell you what I want to see him about, young man. It's confidential, but Mr. Conroy will know. Just inform him that Q is here."

"Q?" Peter gaped a trifle. "You mean that's your name? Mr. Q?"

The little man nodded and smiled. "You can put it that way if you wish. Of course, it's not my real name. But Mr. Conroy will recognize it. Please ask him. You'll see."

Peter looked blank for a moment. Then he pointed to a small bench in a corner of the reception room.

"Just sit there, Mr.—ah—Q. I'll be right out."

NERVOUSLY Peter entered Leon Conroy's massive office. He was still a bit hesitant on how to handle this important man whose business consisted of philanthropies, the heading of numerous civic committees, some real estate work and the handling of his own substantial fortunes. Conroy maintained this office with only one secretary as his staff.

Leon Conroy himself was heavily set, about fifty with an iron grey mustache and a ramrod backbone. His eyes were clear blue and cold as a Northern forest lake.

"Well?" Conroy looked up from the papers he was studying.

"There's a man outside," Peter said, wondering if he had made a mistake in entering the office, if he shouldn't have stood in the doorway to make the announcement. "He says that he must see you, that you know him. His name, so he says, is an odd one. Mr. Q."

Conroy slowly laid down the fountain pen he was holding. He leaned back and looked steadily at Peter.

"This is your second day here, Lang, and I am inclined to overlook a certain incompetence in the manner which you handle this job. You were honorably discharged from the Army. You used to be a second lieuten-

ant. You were wounded and I was glad to let you have the opportunity of working for me. I hope you are grateful enough to appreciate my kindness in doing this."

"Thank you, sir," Peter said, wondering if this iceberg of a man really did have blood in his veins that ran to temperatures above thirty-five.

Conroy's voice rose with each following word until it reached the crescendo of a roar.

"You have the gall to ask me to see some half-wit who gives a letter of the alphabet as his name!" he thundered. "I can't see all the crackpots who come here. I can't even risk it because I'm not the most liked person in this country. Nobody with money is. Someone always wants something and when you turn them down, they get sore. This person outside may be one of those. He may even be plotting against my life. You are an idiot, Lang."

"But he claims he knows you and that mentioning that alphabetical letter will act as a password. I really think he means it, sir."

Conroy closed his eyes in a moment of silent resignation at such stupidity.

"What does he look like, Lang?"

"Small, inoffensive, like an underpaid professor employed by some obscure college," Peter Lang said. "Wears big, thick glasses, is seedy in appearance and extremely earnest, sir."

"I don't know him. From your description I'm sure I don't want to know him. Get rid of the man, Lang, and don't bother me with such inconsequential things again. You are inefficient. Get out!"

"Yes, sir." Peter backed up. He wondered just how long he'd be able to stand this job. He'd dreamed about a peace time job, interesting, clean work that required the use of his brain. He'd been thinking of it that very moment when a German bullet had smashed through his elbow, making one arm rather stiff, but still workable for civilian duties. Now he wondered if he really liked civilian life.

Peter closed the door, turned and looked over at the bench on which Mr. "Q" was seated, hunched over as if he were half asleep. Peter shrugged and walked up to the man.

"I'm sorry," he said. "Mr. Conroy can't possibly see you for weeks. If you will give me an indication of what you wanted to discuss with him, I might arrange an appointment some time from now and notify you by letter."

The man didn't move, didn't seem to hear. Peter approached him.

"Hey, wake up!"

The little man didn't respond.

Peter reached down, grasped his shoulder and shook him. The little man started toppling forward. He kept on going until he hit the floor like a sack of corn. It was then that Peter noticed the haft of the knife which had been driven into his back. The blade had gone in all the way to the hilt.

Peter gave a gasp of surprise. He was not terrified. Death had lived so close beside him for so many months that the shock of seeing another corpse was not severe. He felt for a pulse and found none. He straightened, turned and with a hoarse cry dashed into Conroy's office.

Conroy looked up quickly, startled by Peter's noisy haste.

"Well, what now?" he roared. "Don't tell tell me the little man wouldn't go and you haven't the heart to put him out?"

"He's dead," Peter gulped. "Murdered! Somebody stabbed him in the back."

CONROY kicked his chair back, passed Peter at a fast trot and took a single look at the body. He reddened and turned away.

"Why did that have to happen here?" he demanded of no one in particular. "It will mean publicity and that I detest. Lang, you should have gotten rid of him before anyone had a chance to kill him. This proves stupidity on your part. I can't trust you."

"Yes, but he's dead," Peter cried. "He was sure he knew you. Don't you recognize him?"

"I never saw the man before in my life," Conroy thundered. "I'll swear to that. He looks like a lunatic to me. Probably came to murder me and killed himself instead."

"By reaching over one shoulder and stabbing himself in the back?" Peter retorted. "Don't be silly."

"Silly, am I?" Conroy raged. "Lang, you're fired. Get out of here at once. Get out."

Peter shook his head. "I'm sorry, sir, but you can't make me leave at once. The police must be notified and they'll want to learn my story. After that, I'll be glad to leave. I'll be darned glad. I wouldn't stay for any price. Not at five times my salary."

Peter stalked over to the telephone and dialed the police. Things happened fast after that, all of them calculated to make Conroy grow angrier than ever. A police detective-lieutenant took charge and it didn't matter to him that Conroy was an important man. He asked both Conroy and Peter each about a hundred questions. Finally he laid a metal object on Conroy's desk.

"We found that in his pocket. It's a hand grenade, loaded and ready for business. I think this man came here to kill you, Mr. Conroy. I also believe you know the reason why."

"But I don't." Conroy was suddenly on the defensive and not enjoying it. "I never saw him before. He must have been crazy, giving his identity as Mr. Q. That's proof of it."

"Maybe," the detective-lieutenant conceded. "But I'm not satisfied. Your secretary is new and wouldn't know much about it. Lang, you can go whenever you please. Just stay in town and keep in touch with me."

"But I tell you I was in my office every moment that this—this Mr. Q was outside," Conroy protested. "How could I have killed him?"

In spite of personal antagonism, Peter felt obliged to back up Conroy's story.

"That's right," he told the detective. "Mr. Conroy was in his office, just as he told you."

The detective-lieutenant shrugged.

"I'm not accusing you of killing him, Mr. Conroy," he said. "But I believe you know more than you're admitting. I'm afraid you'd better come downtown with us. Perhaps a more official atmosphere might make you more talkative."

Conroy was beet red now, but he knew better than to argue further. He'd already stuck his neck too far out. He did turn to Peter.

"Take over, Lang," he said. "You can stay on for a couple of more days. But this whole affair is your fault. I hold you responsible."

CHAPTER II

Gun from the Curtains

LATER on, after the medical examiner had arrived and was engaged in his macabre duty of inspecting the corpse, Peter Lang stood around and watched him at work. Lang's eyes were speculative and there was a grim look around his firm wide mouth.

Conroy was sitting in a chair, trying to control his anger and impatience. But he was doing a bad job of both, for his fingers twitched occasionally and the flame still smoldered in his close-set beady eyes.

The detective-lieutenant had taken a post, nearby, with one of his arms resting on a low bookcase. He was watching both Lang and Conroy, never removing his glance from them. A burning cigar was between the fingers of the hand which dangled near the bookcase.

Finally Conroy glared at Peter Lang once more.

"It's your fault," he growled. "You should never have left him alone for a moment, Lang. You should have remained here and watched him. It's a fiasco. That's what it is. A fiasco."

Peter didn't bother to glance at Conroy. "Perhaps. But I wouldn't call death a fiasco. I'm curious to know why he was killed. He was a harmless looking little chap."

"That grenade in his pocket wasn't harmless," Conroy retorted.

Peter raised his eyes then. He looked at Conroy.

"I don't think the grenade was in his pocket when he came here," he said slowly.

Conroy gave a start and bent forward. "What?" he barked. "What nonsense is this? What are you saying? What do you mean?"

The police-lieutenant, too, had swung around and was scrutinizing Peter sharply. He took his arm off the bookcase, and put the cigar in his mouth. His brows had drawn together.

"I'll tell you what I mean," Peter said to Conroy. "The grenade couldn't have been in Q's pocket when he came walking into the room, because I would have noticed it. There would have been a bulge, and I was watching out for suspicious things like that. I carried grenades often enough in the war to know something about them. I think it was put in that fellow's pocket after he was dead. I think the murderer put it there. I'd like to get at the bottom of this."

The detective-lieutenant puffed out a cloud of smoke. "You keep out of it," he told Peter. "It's none of your business. This is a police job." He frowned. "I wish you could have identified him for us. We don't even know who he is. There was nothing in his pockets, no means of identifying him. Maybe we'll never learn who he is."

Peter Lang didn't answer that. Conroy kept silent, too. In a little while some men from the medical examiner's office carried the body out of the room, the police officers left and Conroy, still fuming, went away in the company of the detective-lieutenant. Peter Lang was left alone.

He sat down in the swivel chair behind the desk and rubbed his head thoughtfully.

Something told him that the detective-lieutenant was right. It wasn't any of his business to try and solve this murder. The police probably wouldn't thank him if he did. That much had already been intimated to him. Nevertheless he couldn't keep his brain off the enigma. It fascinated him like a problem in chess.

That evening the newspapers came out. They carried front page stories of the murder and a picture of the dead man, made to look as if he'd been alive when it was taken. Peter thought that such handling ought to draw some results.

He ate dinner, returned to the office and succumbed to the overwhelming desire to get started. He telephoned the detective-lieutenant and asked about Conroy.

"We're keeping him here a little longer," the detective said. "I can't believe his story of not knowing the man. It doesn't make sense. Incidentally, we identified the victim. His niece saw the picture and came here. His name was Roland Rawlings. Some sort of inventor, from her story."

"Rawlings?" Peter asked quickly. "Did he live at Five-fifty-six Blakely Road?"

"No. He lived at the end of Acre Lane, in the suburbs. Why?"

"I knew a man named Rawlings once," Peter replied. "Of course, it's another person. I just associated the names. Maybe I'll drop in and see Conroy later."

"Come ahead," the detective said. "But let us know about it first, so we can remove all articles small enough to be thrown. Conroy certainly has it in for you. He acts like a wild man every time your name is mentioned."

PETER laughed hollowly, hung up and reached for his hat. In ten minutes a taxi was taking him to Acre Road. Reaching Acre Road, he got out of the taxi and stood for a moment looking at the small bungalow which had once been white. Now it was more on the gray side, from dirt. The yard was small, uncared for. A dilapidated fence, falling to pieces from neglect, enclosed the property.

At the rear of the house Peter could see a small building. It reminded him of a child's playhouse. Peter grimaced at these signs of poverty and shiftlessness.

The girl who opened the door to his knock, very definitely wasn't shiftless, though her eyes were red rimmed from weeping. Ordinarily, they must have been delightfully gray. Her nose was turned up a little. Perky, Peter thought. Her face was round and smooth, topped by the silkiest brown hair Peter had ever seen.

"Oh, you're the doctor," she said. I thought they were sending an ambulance."

"Ambulance?" Peter stared at her in surprise. "For what? And I'm not a doctor."

She would have closed the door swiftly had not Peter thrust his foot into the crack. He'd come this far to be balked, and there was no backing down now. Especially since his interest in the case was being matched by his interest in this girl.

"Wait," he told her. "I'm not a newspaper reporter either. My name is Peter Lang. I am, or was, Leon Conroy's secretary. Mr. Q,—Roland Rawlings if you like that better—was killed in my office."

She opened the door wide.

"Come in," she said. "You can help me. Rawlings was my uncle. A dear uncle," she added somewhat belligerently. "He had a boarder living here with him. I found the boarder unconscious a little while ago. Someone attacked him."

Peter hurried into the house. The bungalow had three rooms and the girl led him into a small one in the rear where an elderly man was lying on a bed, his head matted with blood, his face gray with the pallor of near death. One of the man's hands was clutching an evening newspaper. His clothes had almost been ripped into rags and dirt had been ground into his hands and face.

He was slowly coming out of the darkness that engulfed him, but it was apparent that he had been badly injured. Peter gently cleaned the man's face with a towel and some water.

The injured man opened his eyes, after a couple of minutes, and was able to say a few words before he lapsed into unconsciousness again.

Peter Lang straightened up and smiled at the worried girl by his side.

"There, did you hear that?" he asked her. "He says he was struck by a car. Nobody attacked him. I kind of thought an automobile did it from the nature of his hurts. The lacerations and the condition of his clothes show he must have been dragged along the road. He's been badly mauled. How did you find out about it? Who brought him here?"

"He wasn't brought," she answered. "I noticed him lying among the bushes when I opened the door to take in the milk. He must have been there all night in the darkness, unconscious, where he dragged himself. I had an awful time carrying him into this room.

Peter nodded. "He needs a doctor."

"There's one coming," she said. "I ran down the road and phoned a hospital."

The ambulance which she had ordered arrived a few minutes later. After the patient had been removed, the girl showed Lang the green overcoat and the shabby green hat which the man had worn and which she had placed on a chair in the living room at the front of the house. She had found them on the porch where he had dropped them before falling unconscious.

Peter inspected the apparel. Then he straightened up and faced the girl again.

"Why did he come here?" he asked her. "Do you know him?"

"Oh, yes, indeed," she said. "He's Mr. Parkes. He lives with us. He's a friend of Uncle Roland and has been a boarder for three years."

Something in her tones caused Peter to give her a sharp glance.

"From your manner I can tell you didn't like Parkes," Peter said. "Why?"

The girl's pretty face clouded and she hesitated before replying.

"Well, there were several reasons," she said. "He was quarrelsome and he used to steal Uncle Roland's things. They used to bicker with each other lots, but Uncle let him stay anyway because he said he was good company most of the time." She nodded at the hat and overcoat lying on the chair. "Those were my uncle's. Parkes must have borrowed them."

"Nice fellow," was Peter's comment.

Then he told her something of which had happened at Conroy's home. Apparently she knew most of the details.

"The police came to see me last night," she said. "And I read the newspaper accounts this morning. It's terrible. I feel awful about it all." Her lips quivered as she spoke.

"My name is Peter Lang," Peter said. "I suppose your name is Rawlings, too?"

"No," she answered. "I'm Joyce Taylor. Uncle Roland is the only relative I have left." She nodded toward an easy chair. "Won't you sit down, Mr. Lang?"

READILY Peter complied with her request.

"Tell me more about your uncle," he said, after they had both seated themselves. "The police say your uncle is crazy and that he meant to murder Conroy. I don't believe either of those things. I think he was as sane as you or I."

"No, he wasn't crazy," Joyce Taylor said.

"But he was a little odd. I've got to admit that. The police say he had a grenade. I can't understand where he got it."

"I believe it was planted on him after he was dead, by the murderer," Peter answered. "There's a lot more to this than the police suspect. I'm convinced it's part of a plot. That's why Parkes was run down by the automobile. He was wearing your uncle's clothes at the time and somebody tried to kill him, somebody who didn't know your uncle was dead."

The girl stared at Peter in surprise. "I thought you said it was an accident?"

"No, I didn't say it was an accident. I said he was run down by a car. What did your uncle do for a living?"

"Well, he worked in a big factory for many years as a specialist on the chemistry of paints," Joyce said. "He retired two years ago on a pension and a small annuity. Since then, he's been puttering around in his laboratory back of the house."

"Suppose we take a look in the lab," Peter said. "Your uncle didn't experiment with explosives, did he?"

Joyce looked at him with suspicion in her eyes.

"You're referring to that grenade," she said. "You seem to be changing around, Mr. Lang. I thought you believed he didn't own the grenade."

Peter shrugged and waved his hand.

"Forget the question," he said airily. "It doesn't matter. You needn't answer it if you'd rather not."

The girl flushed. "But I will answer it. Again I'll tell you I don't know where the grenade came from. Uncle Roland wasn't interested in explosives. Killing or injuring anyone was against all his beliefs. He was experimenting with various kinds of paints for artists, trying to create new colors to put in the tubes. He wanted to match the paints great artists used, centuries ago, in painting their masterpieces. The old masters used crushed rubies, emeralds and diamonds, sometimes, in an effort to put life into their pictures. A few of them succeeded, too."

"Yeah, I've heard about that," Peter said. "Recently the Russians have done some work along in those lines without much luck." Peter straightened up in the chair as a sudden thought struck him. "Say! Maybe your uncle did find something wonderful. He may have wanted a rich man, such as Conroy, to back him. Perhaps he was mur-

dered by some person who was trying to steal his secret."

"I've thought of that," Joyce admitted. "And while I didn't tell the police, Uncle Roland had been acting peculiarly of late. Buying things he has always wanted, and not paying for the articles."

Peter whistled softly. "Now we're getting some place. Your uncle expected to come into some money. He, was so certain of it he bought things on credit. Now, where did he expect this money to come from? Conroy? Did Conroy really know your uncle and have some reason for denying it?"

Joyce's face took on an expression of distaste. "It wouldn't surprise me one bit," she said. "I met Mr. Conroy last night. The police took me to Headquarters in a squad car. He's not a pleasant man. I didn't care much for him."

Peter Lang laughed. "I'm not exactly crazy about him myself." He rose to his feet. "Now, could I see the laboratory, please?"

She nodded. "I guess it will be all right."

She got up and left the room. In a few minutes she came back with a key and together they went through the door of the kitchen in the rear of the house. They approached the small building Peter had noticed from the front of the house. Joyce used her key, opened the door and they went in. There were long benches equipped with bottles and retorts and various mechanical devices. Peter stopped and stared about him. Then he turned to Joyce.

"Mind if I prowl around a bit?" he asked.

"I wish you would," she said. "You're the only person who seems willing to help me. You can see for yourself how interested Uncle Roland was in studying old paint. In that corner are a number of oil paintings he picked up here and there. He was always haunting art galleries and antique shops looking for something with different colorings which he could buy cheap."

"Thanks."

Peter gazed around the small cluttered room, trying to suppress a thrill of exultation.

"Was the answer to "Q's" murder concealed somewhere in this room? Would he find the key to the mystery here? He wondered. Then, with set lips, he began his search.

CHAPTER III

Scratches on the Lock

TACKED against a bare space of one of the laboratory walls were about a score of old paintings. Nothing but the wooden frames and the time-darkened canvas backs could be seen. Peter walked over and examined them one by one.

Some of the frames empty. From each of the paintings that remained, a tiny bit of canvas had been cut out with a sharp knife. He turned to Joyce.

"What was the idea of this?" he asked, pointing to the holes.

She smiled. "Uncle did that himself," she explained. "He had to, in order to analyze the paint."

Peter Lang's face cleared. He grinned.

"Oh, I forgot about your uncle being a chemist," he said. "Of course, he had to, in order to make tests. For a moment I thought vandals had been at work."

Finishing his investigations, Peter set the paintings back as he had found them, faces to the wall. Then he stood for a moment in thought.

He frowned. What could Roland Rawlings, otherwise known as Mr. Q, have discovered which led him to go to Conroy's office. What had made Rawlings believe Conroy would recognize him, or would welcome him under the strange pseudonym of Q?

Puzzled, Peter wandered over to one of the laboratory benches. There was a black case lying open on one of the shelves, the kind of a case which are made for eyeglasses. It was brand new.

A suden thrill ran through Peter Lang. He snatched up the case. The name of the optician was printed on the inside, in gold letters. Peter's heart began to beat rapidly. This was the clue for which he had been hunting!

He glanced at Joyce Taylor. "I think I'd better go over to Conroy's home right away," he said, trying to keep the exultation out of his voice. "I'd better get there right away before the police release him. There may be some interesting things at that place which the detectives have over-looked. Things connected with the murder. Also, Conroy had an adopted son named Mitchell. Nobody seems to know much about him. I believe Mitchell could help us out in solving the mystery, if he chose."

Joyce caught his excitement. Her face flushed.

"What have you discovered?" she asked.

"Nothing that I'm sure of yet," Peter answered. "Right now, I'll say this much. Your uncle didn't go to Conroy's office to kill him. If anything, it's the other way around. Conroy had plenty of motive for killing your uncle. Conroy knew about Mr. Q, all right. I'm sure of it."

Joyce's eyes were dancing. "Let me go along with you. Please!"

She came closer and Peter turned just in time to look right into the depths of those eyes. They were a deep, clear gray, two of the nicest eyes he'd ever looked into. He hadn't counted on her going along and, for an instant, his purpose almost wavered. Then he remembered and caught himself in time. It wouldn't do at all to take her. There might be danger in Conroy's home.

"No, Joyce," he said, using her first name without knowing it. "You wait here. I'll phone you if anything develops."

He turned and walked across to the door of the laboratory with great resolution. He tried to ignore her. But Joyce followed right after him, very close. She didn't seem to understand the situation at all, that he was fighting himself, trying to keep from putting his arms around her.

He took hold of the knob, opened the door and paused on the threshold of the laboratory, turning to speak to her. And there she was again, right at his elbow, lips temptingly close! Nice red lips. Fresh and sweet.

Peter had a weak spell. Luckily—just then—his attention was diverted in the nick of time. His fingers had come into contact with the key plate and it felt rough. Bending down, he examined the plate and found deep grooves in the metal, grooves which weren't intended to be there. He straightened up.

"Somebody has tried to force this lock," he announced. "Perhaps whoever it was got in, too. That's important."

"Is it?" Joyce asked. She appeared to be disappointed about something.

"Yes. Very important. Better be on your guard, Joyce. Expect me back soon."

Leaving Joyce standing in the door of the bungalow, a few minutes later. Peter hurried to Conroy's home. It was a private three-story stone front house in one of the best residential sections. A butler opened the door and two men came to meet Peter. He knew both of them. The weak-chinned, blond young man was Mitchell Conroy, the adopted son. The other man was taller, more robust and quite dark. He was Peter's predecessor, a former secretary to Conroy.

"You know Jerry Hale," Mitchell Conroy said. "I understand you are no longer in my father's employ."

Peter grinned. "Yeah. He tied a can to me."

JERRY HALE laughed. "Well, you stood him for two days. That's something. I stuck it out for almost two years and he nearly drove me crazy. I'll bet I resigned forty times—and then went back again."

"What finally happened to make you quit?" Peter asked.

"That's the funny part about it," Hale said. "When I resigned, it wasn't because Conroy put on too much heat. I just got battle nerves from the job itself. I was sick and tired of studying every person who entered the office, trying to make up my mind whether they had evil intentions upon Conroy."

By this time the three men had gone into a large, richly furnished living room. The fittings were magnificent. There were easy chairs, lamps, deep piled rugs, and splendid tapestries. Mitchell Conroy motioned for Peter to sit down. He settled himself in an easy chair, an affair with deep cushions, wide arms and a high back. Jerry Hale perched himself upon a bench in front of a grand piano.

Peter Lang put his hands together and frowned.

"Evil intentions," he repeated. He looked at Hale. "Do you think Mr. Conroy is really sincere about that? I ran up against that, too. Does Conroy actually believe the entire world hates him because he's wealthy? Or is it just a bluff, an excuse to cover up a deeper fear? Couldn't it be that he has some particular enemy who has been after him for a long time? Somebody who bears a grudge because of an act committed quite long ago? Somebody who has threatened to kill him?"

It was not Hale, but Mitchell Conroy who answered the question.

"Oh, no," said the weak-chinned young man, leaning forward. "If you're playing around with that theory, Lang, you're all wrong. My father isn't afraid of any particular man. He's just obsessed with the idea the whole world is down on him because he's wealthy. It's a morbid thought he's carried for years. He's sure, some time, a fanatic will get in and bump him off."

Hale nodded his head emphatically. "That's right, Lang. Conroy has told me lots of times he expects to be murdered."

Mitchell Conroy got up, went over to a gleaming cellarette and opened it up, revealing an array of bottles. He got out glasses, ice cubes and started to mix three drinks.

"That's why he wasn't surprised when the police found the hand grenade in the pocket of the little man who was murdered," Hale added.

Mitchell came back and served the drinks. "In other words, Dad has hallucinations about danger. Sounds silly to me."

Peter sipped his highball. Then he opened a different line of inquiry.

"Does your father have any hobbies?" he asked Mitchell. "Any interests besides those he conducts at the office? I'd like to know. If I'm going to work for him, I should know what channels his mind runs in."

"I thought he fired you," Hale said swiftly.

Peter shrugged. "Yeah, he did. But I have an idea I'll be hired right back. The same as you always were. What about that, Mitchell?"

The adopted son removed the highball glass from his lips.

"He's wacky about art. He thinks more of grabbing some rare old portrait than he does of making another million dollars."

Peter Lang shrugged. "That lets me out. I barely know the difference between a Michelangelo and a Currier and Ives print. Guess I'll go to Headquarters and try to help get Mr. Conroy out."

But Peter didn't go to Headquarters. That was just an excuse to get away. He returned to the office where it was quiet and he could think. He sat down at his own desk and relaxed completely. His mind began churning over the developments so far established.

First of all, Rawlings had given his name as Mr. Q because he really expected to be accepted under that strange name. He did have a definite mission at the office. Certainly no man of Rawlings' caliber would ever think up anything as fantastic as using have recognized it. By not doing so, he proved he was either a liar or Rawlings had been duped.

Why? Peter wondered if Rawlings' work with portraits had anything to do with it. Conroy was interested in paintings, but only valuable masterpieces. Certainly Rawlings wouldn't have one of those. Not with his means. But Rawlings had evidently expected to get a lot of money. He'd run up bills, something quite unusual for a man of his frugal nature. Had he come to visit Conroy and collect? Conroy hadn't killed him. Of that much, Peter was positive. Conroy never had obtained the chance.

Then there was Parkes, the boarder who lived with Rawlings. It was odd that he'd been struck by a car and almost killed just at the time when Rawlings himself was being stalked by death. Was Parkes connected with these events somehow? He was inclined to take things that didn't belong to him. Joyce had frankly accused him of being a thief.

PETER found himself staring at the bench on which Rawlings had died. The murderer must have merely opened the door, slipped in quietly and struck before Rawlings even knew of his presence. That meant someone who was familiar with the office and who could move fast. Who knew exactly where Rawlings would be seated?

Jerry Hale, the ex-secretary? He had quit his job abruptly. Why? Or if the guilty man was not Hale, then there was Mitchell Conroy, the adopted son, who impressed Peter as being a type who would cheat at cards, lie if necessary or squirm out of any trouble. Perhaps Rawlings had, in some way, been deceived by Mitchell who was afraid of the results when his adopted father learned the truth.

As Peter sat there and pondered, he gradually became aware of an odd glitter from the floor near the bench. The glitter resembled the flash of a diamond and he jumped up. But it wasn't a diamond. It was just a bit of slightly curved glass reflecting the light in such a manner to create an illusion of the warmth and sparkle of a gem. Peter picked up the sliver of glass between his fingers and studied it.

After a moment or two, he emitted a startled whistle and reached for the telephone. He called up Joyce and asked her one question.

"I noticed your uncle's spectacle case on the lab bench," he said. "It was brand new. Had he purchased new glasses lately?"

"Why, yes," she replied. "He got them only yesterday. The others were broken somehow. My uncle was short-sighted. He could hardly see his hands without them."

"Thanks, Joyce," Peter said. "I'm beginning to get ideas. Nothing definite as yet, but at least it's something to go on. I'll call you later."

Peter went out, flagged a taxicab and went to Police Headquarters where he had a talk with the detective-lieutenant.

Peter learned that Conroy had at last succeeded in getting a message through to his attorneys and that a flock of them had already gotten busy putting through the various writs and papers necessary to release Conroy from jail. It is probable that the police would never have succeeded in incarcerating Conroy in the first place, with all his wealth and power, if the move hadn't been made on the spur of the moment. The detective-lieutenant already was regretting his impulsiveness. The heat was going on and the detective-lieutenant was looking glum.

The wealthy art collector apparently was glad to see Peter. He appeared to have forgotten his quarrel with Peter or that he had fired him. Now all of his wrath was directed toward the police.

"Ignorant fools!" he bellowed. "I told them I didn't know Q but they refused to believe me. Now they'll be sorry. Somebody on the police force is going to lose his job." He glared at Peter. "Where have you been? What have you been doing?"

"Working for you," Peter said. "Taking care of the office."

"Good." Conroy's frown disappeared. "Now I want to get out of here."

"You can go, sir, whenever you wish. You're free. The police told me so. But first I want you to answer a couple of questions. Do you trust your ex-secretary? Do you think your son, Mitchell, may know something about the murder?"

"That's insolence," Conroy roared. Nevertheless he answered the questions. "Hale worked for me over two years. I never discovered anything detrimental about his work. As for my son, he was adopted by my wife. She took him into the family just before she died. It was her idea. I didn't have anything to do with it. He was an infant and I hoped he would become a solid person, able to help me and even carry on my work after I was gone. He isn't that type. He gambles and cheats and lies. I can't break him of it. He's lazy and utterly without ambition. Also he's made a pal of Jerry Hale since he stopped working for me and I don't approve of it."

"But you keep him well supplied with money, don't you?" Peter persisted.

"That's his main trouble. Too much money. I've been far too indulgent, I guess. But if you think Mitchell had anything to do with the murder, you're crazy."

"Maybe," Peter answered. "Now one more thing. You collect paintings. Have you acquired any rare old oil paintings recently?"

Conroy seemed startled by the question.

"No. I do own some excellent canvasses. I bought the last one about a year ago."

That jolted Peter. It wasn't the answer he had expected. His theory for solving the murder was in danger of collapsing. Yet he was sure that he hadn't made a mistake. He asked to see the paintings and Conroy readily agreed to show them to him.

Peter let out a shout which summoned the keeper of Conroy's cell. When the man arrived, he was informed that the wealthy art collector was anxious to be released. The police were more than anxious to get rid of Conroy, now, and the formalities were concluded in record time.

A little while later Peter and the art collector emerged from the dingy stone building into the street. They stood on the curb, flagged a taxicab and set off for Conroy's home to inspect the art collection.

Peter Lang's pulses were beating fast with excitement. He knew it was up to him to solve the murder of Joyce Taylor's uncle, not only in behalf of Conroy and the police, but especially for the sake of Joyce Taylor. He could not afford to fail.

CHAPTER IV

Killer's Return

NO ONE was at home when Conroy and Peter Lang arrived at Conroy's home. The art collector lead the way upstairs and unlocked a door. He turned on the lights and Peter found himself in a magnificent art gallery. On the walls there were scores of paintings, evidently very valuable. Peter didn't know how much they were worth, of course. He just had to take Conroy's word for it.

Peter lifted each canvas from the wall and studied their backs in turn. Finally he uttered an exclamation of disappointment.

"I've been wrong," he confessed. "I had a theory, but it doesn't work out. Frankly, Mr. Conroy, I was convinced I'd find a painting with a small bit of canvas removed and then put back again. You see, Mr. Q was interested in duplicating the oil colors many of the old masters used in creating some of their finest works of art. I figured somebody had used his discovery to defraud you. But it doesn't work out."

Conroy sat down heavily. "Is this what you've been leading up to? It's nonsense!"

"Now, wait," Peter pleaded. "This much I'm sure of. Mr. Q visited your office some days before he was murdered there. You insist you didn't know him, that he came to see you without your knowledge or consent. Q was short-sighted and he'd broken his eye glasses. He could hardly see a thing without them. If I knew the answer to that, I believe the whole mystery would be cleared up."

"I haven't the vaguest idea what you're talking about," Conroy bellowed. "You're stupid."

Peter got up and walked over to the rows of portraits.

"Tell me which one is your most recent purchase, Mr. Conroy."

Conroy pointed out one oil that seemed actually to possess life, so brilliant were its colors.

"I acquired that painting just about a year ago. Lucky find. That landscape was known to exist, but nobody knew where it was."

"And the picture you purchased just before that one?" Peter went on. "When did you get it? I mean, how much time elapsed between the purchases of the landscape and the painting before that?"

"Well, you don't find these things every day," Conroy said. "I hadn't bought one for more than three years."

"And the last one is genuine?" Peter asked.

"Of course it is," Conroy answered angrily. "It came from one of the most reliable dealers in town. Are you trying to tell me I've been defrauded?"

"You'd better get some experts in to give you their opinion," Peter advised him. "Right away, too. I think somebody had switched paintings on you." There was an odd noise and Peter swung around fast. In the glass covered portrait before him, he had seen a suspicious movement. The back of the room was dimly reflected in the glass and Peter saw the heavy drapes covering one window, yanked apart. Then he caught a glimpse of a gun barrel.

He lunged at Conroy, bowled him over and fell on top of him. The gun blazed, only once. The bullet ripped a hole in the expensive rug on the floor. It had missed the wealthy art collector by a wide margin. But if Conroy hadn't been pushed out of the way, he would most certainly have been killed.

Peter offered no explanations. He sprang up and dashed for the wall where he took shelter behind a big chair. No more shots came. He took a chance, raced toward the window, and yanked the drapes aside. The window was open. It overlooked the back of the house. Peter heard someone running. He clambered out of the window as fast as he could and gave chase.

A shadowy form was slipping toward the corner of the house. Peter's long legs picked up speed. He drew closer to the figure. It was too dark to identify the man, but not so dark that he couldn't see him stop, raise one arm and point a gun. Peter dived.

Before the gun could go off, his arms had encircled a pair of legs and he had pulled the fugitive to the ground. Peter pinned his opponent's gun hand to the ground and then bent over the man to take a good look.

It was Mitchell Conroy, the adopted son.

"Peter," Mitchell panted. "I thought you were the fellow who fired that shot. I was afraid you intended to kill me."

The elder Conroy came hurrying out of the back door. He carried a flashlight and its beam struck Mitchell's face. Mitchell's adopted father groaned, shut off the flash and slowly walked back to the door. He acted as if, for once in his life, he had been beaten.

"Your story's plenty weak," Peter said. "Are you telling me you weren't the one who just tried to kill Mr. Conroy?"

"Let me up," Mitchell begged. "I'm speaking the truth. I came home and put the car away. As I walked toward the house from the garage, I heard the shot. Then someone ran toward me and I heard something fall. It was this gun. I picked it up."

IT WAS ridiculous. Peter snickered. "When a judge hears that yarn, you'll get about twenty years. Walk ahead of me, Mitchell. We're going into the house. No tricks, or you might not like what happens."

Half an hour later, Mitchell was repeating his assertions of innocence. Jerry Hale had arrived and stood by, mutely. The elder Conroy just kept shaking his head as if he couldn't believe the explanation.

"The facts are simple," Peter said to the old man. "You've already admitted that your son, Mitchell, was the one who negotiated for the purchase of that particular portrait. It's my idea that he bought an imitation, a fake, at several thousand dollars less than the genuine painting would have cost, and pocketed the difference. You trusted him. The imitation was so good that you never suspected there had been a substitution."

"I don't believe it," Conroy said. But his voice was weak. He wasn't roaring now.

"I'd advise you to have an expert look at your art gallery. As for Mitchell, he's your son. It's up to you whether he'll be turned over to the cops. But they're investigating Q's death, and sooner or later Mitchell will have to answer a lot of questions."

"I'll think it over." Conroy rose to his feet. His face had grown old and lined. He didn't look at his adopted son. "Thank you, Lang. I'd appreciate your silence. I want the whole matter dropped, I think. I don't know what I'll do. I can't say."

Soon after this Peter left the house. Jerry Hale went with him. Without a word to each other, they walked down the deserted street. It was early morning now. Finally they came to the place where their routes separated. They paused on the corner.

Hale sighed. "I can't figure out why Mitchell tried to kill his father," he said.

"That's an easy one," Peter said. "In the first place, he knew the truth about that portrait would soon come out. Secondly, if his father died, Mitchell would inherit a vast fortune. Besides, the police would think old Conroy died as the result of some plot in which Mr. Q also had a part. Q failed so someone else did the job. I turn off here. Good night, Hale. I'll lay odds that the portrait Mitchell bought for his father is phony. Otherwise, Mr. Q couldn't have been involved in the plot and there would have been no reason for his murder."

Peter walked away and kept going for ten minutes. Then he stopped abruptly and looked around. When he was sure no one had followed him, he started to retrace his steps for Conroy's house, moving at a rapid pace. He approached it from the back and found the art gallery window still open. Climbing through, he chose a dark corner and sat down to wait.

Two hours passed before he heard the front door open softly. A man appeared. He was carrying a large rolled object. Approaching a painting, one of Conroy's most recent purchases, he went to work. Peter didn't move until the intruder stepped back to admire what he had done. His task had been performed in semi-darkness. Only a thin streak of light came from the doorway to the hall.

Peter stepped out of his corner.

"I thought you'd come back, Jerry Hale," he said slowly. "And don't reach for a gun if you have one. The pistol you used to shoot at Conroy is in my hand. The gun you threw at Mitchell because you knew he would be fool enough to pick it up."

Jerry Hale gave a cry of despair. Then he began to plead with Peter.

"Listen. Conroy has more money than he knows what to do with. He'll never miss what I got. He won't even know what happened, because I've changed things back."

"I know," Peter said. "The portrait in the frame is now genuine. Q accidentally discovered the fake. I imagine someone had painted over the masterpiece and Mr. Q picked it up for a song. But when he came to study it, he discovered the truth. He removed the outer layer of paint, saw what was beneath and likewise knew that Conroy was supposed to own the original. So he asked for an interview with Conroy and talked with you instead.

"You had him come to Conroy's office, after hours, and instructed him to use the name of Q. That was clever because if he showed up when you didn't happen to be present and Conroy was, Conroy would think Mr. Q was an idiot and send him away. You represented yourself as being Conroy. Mr. Q's sight was such that he couldn't see much anyway, except at very close range. You agreed to buy the portrait. Q thought he was in luck and made a lot of purchases on credit."

"Listen to me," Hale urged. "We can both profit out of this."

THE interruption irritated Peter. "Shut up!" he snapped. "Later Q came with the portrait. You contrived, somehow, to break his glasses. Then you paid him, either in counterfeit money or with dummy packages made up as money. Without his glasses Q wouldn't know the difference.

"You probably intended to replace the phony portrait with the original, but again cupidity got the best of you. If Q died, you'd be in the clear and have the original portrait to sell to someone who'd keep the transaction quiet. So you drove out to Q's laboratories in your car, and waited. A man came out, dressed in Q's rather familiar coat and hat. You ran him down, but it wasn't Q. It happened to be a boarder who often borrowed Q's clothing.

"Realizing your error, you knew Q would see Conroy as soon as he learned he'd been cheated. You hurried to the office, waited until Q arrived, then slipped in and killed him. Whatever fake money you used to pay him off, you managed to steal back. I noticed someone had broken into Q's lab."

Hale was backing away slowly. "You're a fool if you don't come in with me."

"Did you hear that, Mr. Conroy?" Peter

called out in a loud voice. "I heard you coming down the stairs a few moments ago."

"I heard it." Conroy barged into the room, seized Hale and shook him until his teeth chattered. The rolled up canvas fell to the floor. Peter didn't bother to pick it up. He went over to the frame in which Hale had inserted the original portrait. Turning it over, he saw one of the little triangles in the canvas, like those Q cut to get his samples of paint.

Outside in the hallway, Mitchell Conroy was yelling into the telephone for police. Peter walked over and stood beside his employer. They both looked down at the trembling crook and murderer seated before him.

"A man makes a lot of mistakes," Conroy said. "I made a bad one when I misjudged you. I'm sorry. I want you to become my secretary, this time without me calling you a lot of hard names."

"That's a bargain," Peter said. "I'll be glad to work for you, Mr. Conroy, because now you've learned you can make boners too. Your biggest one was falling for my line about Mitchell being the killer. I wanted Hale to bring back the original painting. I knew he would. Possession of it would have been too dangerous from then on. He thought the police would believe that Mitchell tried to kill you so he could inherit your money and you'd fall for it, too, and quash the whole thing. I was sure Mitchell was innocent the moment you told me you let him have all the spending money he wanted. Why should he try to defraud you when he could get all the extra funds he needed without running any risk? Hale put that grenade into Q's pocket to make him seem like a fanatic, murder-bent. Hale probably obtained the grenade to blow up Q's lab if he couldn't succeed in breaking in. The stuff he passed for money had to be destroyed."

There was a tramp of feet in the hall. It was the police. They had come to take Jerry Hale away.

PERFUME OF THE INVISIBLE LADY
(Concluded from page 63)

ble?" the lieutenant asked. "This was a foolproof setup, as I see it."

"It almost worked," Craig admitted. "But I was suspicious. I gave the fake Jean a medal which I won. I told her it was Shorty's and that she certainly knew all about it because I was there when Shorty wrote her the story of how he'd won it. She said she remembered the letter and I knew she was a phony because no such letter was ever written.

"Besides—and like a bonehead I couldn't remember it until a short time ago—Jean's right hand carried a scar. A souvenir of her childhood days when she and Shorty manufactured a box kite which was to fly like a glider. She went up in it—and came down. She was cut pretty badly and Shorty told me about that scar."

The lieutenant nodded.

"Well, I think those two mugs you sent in will talk when they see Dunlap behind bars," he said. "Undoubtedly, they helped him."

"They did," Craig agreed. "The fake doctor kept Jean thinking she was too ill to go out. When I arrived, Dunlap told her it was Shorty who had come, and that Shorty must not know she was blind. It was a perfect opportunity to build up further the idea that Shorty was alive. But Jean came to Shorty's room in the middle of the night and stroked my uniform, thinking it was her brother's. That gave the game away so far as I was concerned.

"And then there was Max, the gardener. He didn't know the setup, but figured something was wrong. Probably heard from Dunlap that I was a fake, trying to wheedle money out of Jean. So Max got it into his thick skull that I ought to be driven away. Max is all right."

The lieutenant gestured. Dunlap, still silent, was dragged out. The woman who had pretended to be Jean, accompanied him, but she wasn't silent.

Craig squared his shoulders and marched up the steps. He paused in front of Jean's room, and took a long breath.

Perhaps, he thought, proper medical care would cure the blindness. He fervently hoped so, but what he had to do right now was ten times more difficult than his original mission had been. Then he smiled slightly. The real Jean would be like Shorty. She'd be able to take it.

He opened the door and walked in.

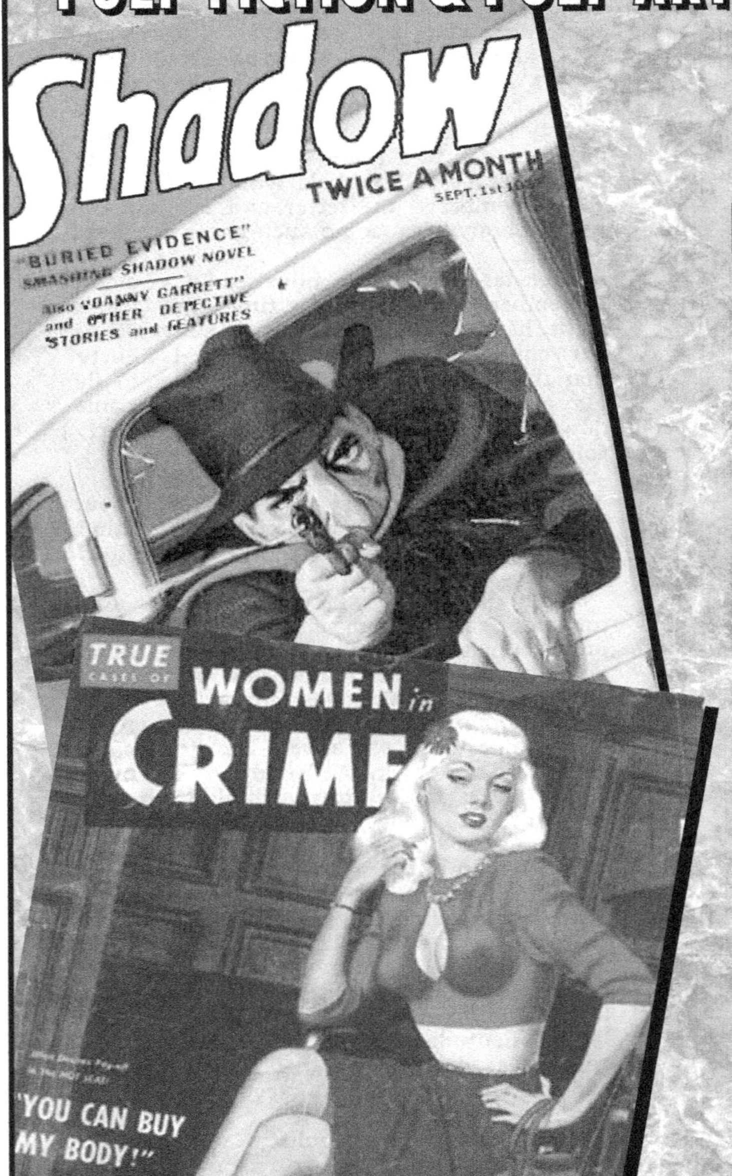

The Greatest Assortment of Vintage PULP FICTION & PULP ART on the East Coast

SATURDAY, November 1, 2008

RAMADA INN, BORDENTOWN, NJ

1083 ROUTE 206
NJ TURNPIKE Exit 7
10am-5pm
Admission: $6
($1 off with flyer)

Thousands of pulp magazines, vintage paperbacks and related movie-collectibles in the NY-Philly area

PULP™ ADVENTURECON #9

BOLD VENTURE PRODUCTIONS

For More Info: (609) 346-4184
www.boldventurepress.com • E-mail: boldventurepress@aol.com

The Black Bat had the knife in his hand when a flashlight was centered on him (Chapter VII)

MURDER ON THE LOOSE

By G. WAYMAN JONES

While the sinister plans for a monumental haul are being engineered by a vicious crew of jewel thieves, Tony Quinn flashes into rapid-fire action to check their evil crimes!

CHAPTER I

Under Cover

MRS. FRANKLIN P. ANKRUM wasn't fair, but she was fat, and considerably more than forty. She was also exasperated as she dropped the letter on the table.

"French" she exclaimed. "It's written in French and I can't read it. Just like Evelyn to do that. Whenever she writes something important—like an invitation to a party—she writes in French to show me she has traveled. Myra, if this keeps on, I shall be compelled to discharge you and hire a French maid instead."

Myra, blond, and trim in a maid's black uniform, held back the smile that quirked at the corners of her lips.

"If you don't mind, Madam," she said, instead of smiling, "perhaps I can read the letter."

"You?" Mrs. Ankrum exclaimed. "But you

AN EXCITING COMPLETE BLACK BAT NOVEL

aren't French. Well, read it. Yes, of course you may read it."

Myra read the note aloud with as much ease as if it had been written in English. It was an invitation to attend a bazaar which was to be held four days from then.

Mrs. Ankrum beamed. "Excellent, Myra! So in addition to your other accomplishments, you also can read French."

"I once worked for French people and they taught me, Madam," Myra murmured. "Perhaps you will wish to answer the letter in French. I could write it, so you would only have to copy it."

Mrs. Ankrum's eyes widened in pleasure. "Myra, that's an excellent suggestion! Tell her I will most certainly attend her bazaar."

Myra took a long, quiet breath. "And will you wear the Red Emblem, Madam?"

Mrs. Ankrum faced her neat little maid.

"Why do you ask?" she demanded abruptly. "The Red Emblem is one of the largest rubies in the world. It's worth a king's ransom—if there are any kings left. A congressman's ransom, at any rate. I never wear it except to the most important affairs. I certainly shall not be wearing it to any bazaar. What is your interest in this jewel, Myra?"

"Please, Madam," the maid said sincerely, "it is only that I hope some day to see it. I love beautiful things too. You do not suspect I might wish to steal it?"

Mrs. Ankrum shook her head. "I suspect everyone of wanting to steal it—there have been so many robberies lately. But you, Myra? Of course not. I'm sure you are too loyal to me. Anyhow maids are difficult to get and you're a most unusual one. I'm so well satisfied with you that I think I shall raise your wages."

MYRA was a most unusual maid. In the first place, her real name was not Myra, but Carol Baldwin. She was a college graduate and she worked in the organization of a mysterious figure known as the Black Bat. It was at his suggestion that she had obtained this job. Mrs. Ankrum was not the only person aware of the many thefts which had been occurring of late.

As Myra, the domestic, Carol Baldwin used little make-up and was quiet, and efficient. She was so prim and self-effacing that full attention would have had to be drawn to her for it to be realized that she was a girl who could create gasps in a blackout. Who could make movie test men blink in admiration, and who was not as fragile as she seemed.

Promptly at six-thirty, her day's work was done. She left the Ankrum apartment in this huge New York structure, took the servant's elevator to the ground floor and exited to a side street. Turning left, she walked rapidly to an avenue where there was a bus stop. By hurrying a trifle she might have made the bus now pulling up, but she didn't hurry. Neither did a hulking man who ambled casually over to the bus stop and leaned against a light pole.

He was an amazing person, built like a General Sherman tank, and his head seemed to be jammed down against his shoulders without the usual support of a neck. His arms were long and his hands resembled miniature footballs when the fingers were curled. Hands that could smash through a door or break a man's neck with one wrench.

Carol purchased a newspaper at a nearby stand, took up a position at the curb and opened the paper. She started talking in a low voice. The big man nonchalantly chewed a match stick and seemed to be paying no attention at all, but he heard Carol saying:

"Mrs. Ankrum isn't wearing the Red Emblem this week. She is afraid because of the burglaries. I'll keep my eyes and ears open when I reach that new home of mine tonight, and try to phone at the usual time. Stick around. If things go wrong, you appear as my boy friend, name of Hank Leonard. And if you have to go as far as hugging me to make it look real, put the brakes on those muscles, Butch."

The big man's features never even twitched. He stared casually across the street and when the bus came, he got on it after Carol—but he got off again a few blocks further on. Carol rode for twenty minutes before she finally alighted at a rather desolate stop for this great city.

There were no skyscrapers here. Once the section had been occupied by wealthy families who had built great brick houses. Now they had long since moved away and the houses were conducted as boarding or rooming houses by landladies who insisted the rent be paid every week without fail.

The last house down the dead-end street was the largest of them all. It contained thirty rooms, and almost that many maids, chauffeurs and gardeners lived in it. Carol had a small but comfortable room on the top floor.

She ate her meals there too, and they were meals that some of the employers of these servants couldn't serve—or did not. The cost of living here included dinner whether it was eaten or not. It invariably was, to the chatter of some thirty feminine voices.

Carol greeted several girls she knew and stopped to talk with a too slender, too heavily made-up girl who had initiated Carol into this particular boarding house. Her name was Linda, and she worked in the same house in which Carol's employer had an apartment. Carol had a strong idea that more than sheer coincidence had been responsible for Linda's having brought her to this boarding house.

The landlady greeted Carol with a warm smile. That is, if two thin, uncompromising lips like Mrs. Carter's could be said to smile warmly.

Mrs. Carter was lean and tall. She affected out-dated dresses with high necks and long, sweeping skirts. Her scrawny hair was piled on top of her head so that sometimes she looked like an animated mop. Her eyes were

"T." At the head of the table sat the landlady, supervising everything.

On her left was the enormously fat, squat man known as Jacques. His exact status in this weird household was not exactly clear to Carol, but she had noticed that the landlady took orders from him on occasion. On Mrs. Carter's right was a vacant chair, sometimes occupied by a hatchet-faced young man who said he was the landlady's son. His name was Compton—his first name, that is. His last, of course, was Carter. He was absent about as often as he put in an appearance. Carol didn't like him, but concerning

THE BLACK BAT

sharp, cold, forbidding, and they did not smile when her lips did.

Carol went to her room and changed to another dress. She smoked a cigarette, then carefully examined her trunk and suitcase. Both were locked, but both had been unlocked during her absence. These people here that the Black Bat had his eye on were taking no chances, but Carol was not worried, because the Black Bat had warned her not to take along any clothing or accessories of the sort a servant would not be likely to own or use.

PROMPTLY at eight, she went down to dinner. There was a huge dining room, with a table that once had been used for banquets. It was in the shape of a large

Jacques she felt something more than dislike. The feeling she had for him was akin to fear.

He seemed to be all chins and cheeks. His eyes were covered by a pair of thick glasses so that they were constantly obscured, but Carol had an idea those eyes would be hard and uncompromising. She knew well enough that they missed little.

A buzz of conversation filled the room when Carol entered. Talking was highly encouraged and Carol thought she knew why. One of the girls, for instance, was now embarked upon a description of a diamond necklace the lady who employed her was going to wear to some smart affair tonight, and everyone was listening.

"Two insurance c o m p a n y detectives

brought it," the girl was prattling. "They'll come after it tomorrow, and while I couldn't see, I think they came in an armored car. You should see the necklace! It sparkles like a hundred little fires. Mrs. Collier will be a knockout tonight."

The chatter went on and on. Carol listened to all she could, but took little part in it herself.

After dinner, Carol sat on the porch for a short time, and after a while she was called inside. The fat man had sent for her. He told her that Mrs. Carter had obtained some newsreels from Europe and they would be shown on the movie-sound machine in just a few minutes.

"Most interesting films," he told Carol, speaking in his characteristic clipped tones. "We have also a cartoon or two and a fashion film. We try to interest you girls—make you feel at home."

"You do," Carol said enthusiastically. "I can't wait to see the films!"

She wondered if the fat man's eyes were narrowed in suspicion, or if they were wide in blissful innocence. She wished those glasses were not so thick.

He followed her when she went into the dining room where the films were to be shown. The big table had been dismantled and stowed along one wall. Chairs were lined up, and a movie screen and sound projector were in place. Mrs. Carter's hatchet-faced son had materialized from somewhere and was inserting the film into the machine. His grin in Carol's direction was distinctly wolfish.

The fat man stood at the door, as if engaged in counting the boarders as they entered. Every boarder was expected to be present when, once a week, there was always something like this. Entertainment which couldn't be passed up. Everyone did attend. And invariably after such entertainment, the newspapers the next morning would carry stories about a fresh robbery. Sometimes it concerned the families for whom the servants who lived in this boarding house worked; sometimes not. Carol wondered if there were any other places of this type in the city.

She selected a chair as close to the door as possible. When the lights went out, she was determined to take a chance and slip away. There was a phone call to be made. A decidedly important one, considering what that foolish maid had said about a diamond necklace.

Under cover of the sound effects of an anti-aircraft barrage of the film, Carol managed to reach the front door and leave the house. She was quite certain no one had seen her. There was a drug-store two blocks away and she hurried toward it. With luck she might put through her phone call and return without being missed.

She glanced inside the drug-store before entering. There were a number of people there, but none who seemed suspicious. Carol entered and walked straight to one of the phone booths, opened her purse, and extracted both a coin and a small mirror. She propped the mirror up so that while she faced the phone, she could also observe the store entrance.

In a moment, after she had dropped her coin in the box, she heard the familiar voice of Silk Kirby, the Black Bat's personal servant, on the wire. Carol talked fast.

"Tonight Mrs. Harmon Collier's maid told how Mrs. Collier is wearing her diamond necklace to some affair at the Plaza," she told Silk. "In the morning it goes back to the safe deposit vaults and . . . hold it, Silk!"

IN THE tiny mirror Carol saw the hulk of Jacques. He was at the candy counter buying chocolates, but he was observing her too. He had followed her here! They were suspicious of her then. Carol quickly dropped the mirror into her purse.

"The fat man trailed me," she said into the phone. "I'll tell him I called my boy friend. Send Butch to the boarding house at nine-thirty to make it good. Butch's name should be Hank Leonard. Wish me luck, Silk. I'll need it if they ever get wise to me."

She hung up, stepped from the phone booth and walked briskly toward the door. Then, as if seeing the fat man for the first time, she stopped short and looked surprised and embarrassed.

"I—had a call to make," she said slowly.

The fat man smiled at her, though the movement of his lips was more suggestive of a leer. She mentally swore at those thick glasses again. They seemed to hide the man's soul—if he had one.

"So I see." He smirked at her. "But there is a telephone in the house. We strive to keep our guests comfortable and provide all conveniences. Did you not like the movie show, perhaps?"

"I want to get back for the rest of it," Carol replied. "I just had to call my boy friend, and I didn't use the phone at the house because . . . Well, some of the girls listen when I talk to him. I like privacy."

"Ah—so." The fat man seemed to be jeering at her. "Of course. He is a nice young man, this friend of yours?"

Carol nodded eagerly. "He's a war plant worker. Big fellow. You'll be surprised when you see him. He's coming to see me at nine-thirty tonight. I hope it's all right?"

The fat man took her arm, just below the elbow. His strong grip surprised Carol. She could have sworn he was as flabby as a chunk of blubber.

"There is a front parlor in the boarding house," he told her. "It is no crime for a pretty girl to have a sweetheart. Invite him to dinner some night. I'm sure Mrs. Carter will be glad to have him."

Jacques started weaving as he approached the Black Bat again (Chapter IX)

Carol felt a little more certain of herself. Butch would show up to alibi the phone call. But it was lucky she had used the mirror, and had spotted the fat man in time to warn Silk. Somehow she had an uncomfortable idea that the fat fingers now holding her arm could also grip her throat and never let go until she stopped breathing—forever. If this man should get the slightest proof that she was a spy in their midst, he would take drastic action.

Suddenly Carol found herself deadly afraid of him. He seemed hardly human, and the way he appeared to know everything that went on was uncanny.

CHAPTER II

Lesson in Violence

JACQUES, the fat man, was appraising "Butch" O'Leary an hour later. Carol hadn't come down from her room yet. Butch sat uneasily on the edge of a chair that threatened to collapse from under him because of his weight. It gave off a constant series of g r o a n s and squeaks.

The fat man had his head cocked to one side.

"Big fellow," he said. "Too big to fight. To fight well, I mean."

A statement like that was tantamount to waving a red flag in front of Butch. He rose and looked down at the fat man who, beside him, was almost diminutive.

"What's the idea?" Butch demanded. "I can fight. Good, too."

The fat man smirked and backed away a little.

"You are too big for good fighting," he repeated. "Too tall and clumsy. Here now —suppose we have a little sport. All in good fun. I'll bet you a cigar you can't push me into that corner."

Butch's arms opened wide and he moved forward. Fast, for a man of his bulk. He started closing those arms to encircle the fat man and jar him back against the wall. But inexplicably the ceiling took the place of the floor. The four walls spun like a merry-go-round gone wild and then Butch crashed down on his face.

He looked up when his wits stopped churning and registered sheer amazement. Not a hair of the fat man's head had been moved. He just stood there, grinning.

"Judo," he said. "The bigger an enemy is, the better it works. But I took advantage of you. You ought to know Judo, so this time I will promise not to use it. Attack me again, my friend. This time I will show you how to disable a man efficiently."

Butch got to his feet. Much more interested than angry, he accepted the challenge. Another rush carried him close to the fat man, and then Butch was jarred clear to his insteps. The fat man had thrust out his right hand, palm upraised, and Butch had run full tilt into it. Butch sat down without regard for dignity.

The fat man stepped closer.

"You see," he calmly explained, "it is done only with the heel of the hand. But there is much preparation first. The heel must be developed until it is like steel. You start when very young, methodically striking the heel against the edge of a board until you can crack the board with one blow. The heel hardens to the consistency of steel. It has no give, and even a tightly compressed fist has give."

"Hank!" cried a girl's horrified voice.

Butch grinned up at Carol who had stepped into the room.

"It's okay, Myra." Butch used her assumed name, just as she had used the one she had given him. "My pal here has been showing me a few tricks. Believe me, he knows 'em."

"Let me help you up."

The fat man extended his hand and jerked Butch to his feet. All two hundred and fifty-five pounds of him. Then the fat man faced Carol, smiled, and bowed slightly.

"Your friend is a good fighter," he said, "but he lacks a few tricks. Do you mind if I intrude and tell him some things about defending himself? I'm sure you will also be interested."

The fat man stayed there talking until almost midnight, until Butch finally arose and yawned. Jacques had given Carol and Butch not the slightest opportunity to talk privately. Not one sign had passed between them, for they were aware how closely those glass-veiled eyes were watching them. He even followed them to the porch, but turned his back discreetly for just a moment, to give them a chance to say good-by.

Butch enveloped Carol in a clumsy hug. She had time to whisper to him two significant words—"Warn Tony!" Then the fat man was beside them again.

She was certain, though, that he hadn't overheard her.

Carol went to her room shortly after Butch departed. Jacques stood at the foot of the stairs as she ascended. Carol hummed gaily, but she was not feeling gay. When she closed and locked the door of her room, she sat down near the window and began to worry.

If the Black Bat tried to forestall the inevitable attempt to steal Mrs. Collier's diamond necklace, Jacques would immediately suspect that she had telephoned the tip-off. By morning the fat man would know whether the robbery attempt had been successful or not, and if it failed, she would have little chance of escaping his wrath and that of his friends.

FROM the window she saw Jacques walking briskly across the back yard. He was heading for the next house, some two hundred yards to the rear. He lived there alone, so far as Carol had been able to determine. Her suspicions about that house listed it as headquarters for the slickest gang of jewel thieves on record. Jacques might be the head of them. He was ruthless and clever enough. Whether or not her suspicions about him were correct was among the things Carol hoped to discover here.

She didn't go to sleep. There were too many things on her mind. Earlier in the evening she had seen a panel truck drive out of Jacques' garage, and she knew by now that every time there was to be a robbery, that the same panel body truck went out. Somehow it was connected with the series of mysterious thefts which had the police and the insurance companies on edge.

The boarding house had long ago quieted down. Everyone was asleep, or supposed to be. Carol was certain that she alone suspected this super boarding house of concealing the criminal gang members she was certain it did. That was why the landlady could manage to provide really excellent quarters and meals of such high type and stay above water financially.

The place was merely subsidized by someone who profited from it as a cover.

At two in the morning, when all lights were out, Carol opened her door and crept down the hallway to the staircase. She was in time to hear the front door cautiously opened with a key. Then footsteps tiptoed across the floor and Carol heard Mrs. Carter's voice, and her startled gasp before a door closed on whatever followed that cry of surprise or horror—or both.

Carol had to take a chance. She went downstairs, her padded slippers making no noise whatsoever. When she reached the dining room, she saw light beneath and to the hinged side of the butler's pantry door. Edging up to the fairly wide crack where the door was hinged, she applied an eye to the crack and could look into the kitchen.

Mrs. Carter's son who had the impossible name of Compton, was there and clearly excited. Mrs. Carter was there also, but seemed far more worried than excited.

"We'd better get Jacques over here right away," she said. "He told me to call him if everything wasn't exactly right. You're sure the man was dead?"

"I stuck a knife into his chest right up to the hilt!" young Compton Carter said, with a curious mixture of pride and terror. "He let out a grunt or something, then started to fall down. I grabbed him so he wouldn't make any noise."

Mrs. Carter walked quickly to the rear door and snapped on a switch. Carol knew it controlled a light above the back porch, one that was never used. Now she knew

why. It was a signal to attract the attention of Jacques in his own house which was within easy sight of the back porch.

Carol shivered. Murder had been done! Clearly it wasn't the Black Bat who had fallen victim, for the killer would have boasted about that, since members of the underworld had long vied with one another for such a privilege. But murder—killing anybody—showed just how far these jewel thieves would go. More, one killing would inevitably lead to others. The Black Bat's hunch was turning out right, as his hunches, backed by logic and deduction, usually did.

Jacques arrived promptly, puffing a bit, which indicated that he had been running. Compton quickly told him what had happened.

"I got in, just like the map showed," the young man said. "It was easy. I waited until all the lights went out, then I gave them time to go to sleep. But something happened so the man didn't sleep. Anyway, not so soundly. I got the necklace—"

"Show it to me," Jacques ordered. "At once."

Compton reached into a pocket and extracted a shimmering strand of gems. Jacques held them at eye level, slowly rotated the necklace, then nodded heavily.

"Good! This is what you went after. Now! Did you kill the man or only wound him?"

"But I didn't tell you I—I used my knife. How did you know I did?"

"Idiot!" Jacques said smoothly. "There is blood on your shirt. Go ahead—talk."

COMPTON CARTER obeyed, speaking hurriedly.

"Well, the safe was easy and I was just hauling the necklace out when this man tiptoed into the room and jumped me. My knife was stuck in my belt. I just yanked it out and jabbed the fella with it. He's dead all right."

"And then you ran?" Jacques asked quickly.

"I went out the door, just as the plans called for. Nobody saw me enter or leave. It's in the bag, Jacques. Not a thing to worry about."

"Perhaps." Jacques frowned. "So far, I approve of what happened. Until now you have been a novice, but now your hands are bloodied. You will be a better man for that. What I wish to know is this. Did the appearance of that man of the house come so that you might assume he was ready and waiting for you? In short, was it a trap?"

"No," Compton Carter derided. "That bozo was half asleep and blinking like an owl. That's why it was so easy to stick him. Wasn't anyone else around and I bet his wife doesn't even know yet he's dead."

Mrs. Carter faced Jacques. "Why did you ask if it could have been a trap?"

Jacques was studying the necklace again.

"Well, I have been suspicious. That blond —the new one on the third floor—she seems just a bit too intelligent for her job. I'm probably wrong though. She slipped out tonight when the movies were on, and I followed her. She telephoned. Her boy friend came later, but if Compton had been trapped tonight, I would have known that she was a spy."

"You sent my son, when you thought it might be a trap?" Mrs. Carter said in a low, rasping voice.

JACQUES tucked the diamond necklace into his side pocket.

"Why not?" he demanded. "He wanted to join us. If he had been caught, they'd have found no police record. He'd have got off lightly, while any of the other men we use— well, they'd have been given the limit. If your son had been caught, we would have had him defended and paid him well."

"Sure you would!" Compton sided with Jacques. "Say—how about my cut, anyhow?"

"In due time." Jacques patted his pocket and smiled. "You know the routine. First, the necklace will be turned over to a certain party who will have it examined. If it is genuine, the gewgaw will be sold. You will receive the usual percentage paid to a tyro. Now remove your shirt. Quickly! I must get back."

"My shirt?" young Carter asked dully.

"It is bloody—as I told you. If I leave it here, your mother will burn it, perhaps, but that would do you little good. The police are plenty active in this business, and now that there has been a murder, they'll start hunting us harder than ever. The only way to destroy evidence of this kind is to apply acid to it. Turn it into a liquid and flush it away. Take off the shirt."

Carol quickly backed away from the door and made her way upstairs again, considerably shaken. But at least she knew several things that until now had been a complete mystery. Interesting items for the Black Bat. She also realized that the Black Bat had not acted on the information she had provided because he had sensed it might reflect on her.

This neglect had caused a murder, but that was something neither she nor the Black Bat could have predicted. If the life of Compton's victim had been spared by setting a trap, Carol's life might have paid the piper. She hadn't the slightest doubt but that Jacques had killed before and would do it again without the least hesitation.

Carol's next move was obvious. She had to see the Black Bat, but it would have to wait until morning. She went to bed, but sleep was a long time in coming. This was a house of murder and crime—not exactly a place conducive to restful slumber.

CHAPTER III

Lair of the Black Bat

IN THE morning Carol left the house with several other girls and took a bus to the apartment house where she was employed. She didn't enter though. Instead, she telephoned up to Mrs. Ankrum, asked for three hours off, and got the permission easily. The scarcity of servants would have made Mrs. Ankrum accede to almost any reasonable request.

Carol hailed a taxi and was driven to one of the best parts of the city. She paid off the driver four blocks from her destination and walked the rest of the way. When she reached one large house, with well-land-scaped grounds and shrubbery surrounded by a neat fence, she didn't even glance at it. But she knew well the plaque that was on the gate, inscribed with the owner's name— Tony Quinn.

Carol turned the corner at the end of the street before the impressive place, and headed down another street—a blind street. She gave one quick look over her shoulder, made certain she was not under observation and ducked through a garden gate she reached. She began running toward a small garden house, entered it, and stopped a moment to regain her breath.

Then she opened a skillfully hidden trap-door, dropped down into a tunnel and closed the door on top of her. In a few seconds she was ascending a ladder which led into a large, white-tiled laboratory. Someone moved rapidly toward the exit into the laboratory to help her. A firm hand gripped hers and she was hoisted up.

The man who greeted her could not have been called handsome. Not by a long degree. His features were too rugged for that, and around the eyes were deep scars. But he had a warm smile and friendly eyes.

This was Tony Quinn, lawyer, once district attorney, now appointed as a special district attorney, and—the Black Bat, a mystery man who took the law into his own hands and was well-known to police and crooks alike.

He led Carol over to a large leather divan and sat down beside her. Butch O'Leary, the big fellow who had pretended to be her boy friend at the boarding house, was smothering a straight-backed chair and smiling in welcome.

A third man stood near a small door that led into the house proper. He was the "Silk" Kirby to whom Carol had telephoned, a middle-aged man, almost bald, and of medium stature. Once Silk Kirby had tantalized police all over the nation as one of the best confidence men who had ever mulcted a ripe sucker.

That was before he had fallen from grace in his "profession" enough to come to rob Tony Quinn, during a lean period. But after a long talk with his intended victim, he had remained to work for Quinn as his personal servant. Now he was the Black Bat's loyal friend and confidante, a vast aid to him in his endeavors, because Silk Kirby was still as smooth as his nickname.

"Things happened last night," Tony Quinn said. "Unfortunate things, but when Silk told me that fat man had followed you to the drug-store, Carol, I was afraid to interfere. Now those crooks have added murder to their list."

"Compton Carter killed that man!" Carol said eagerly. "I overheard him bragging about it to his mother and Jacques. And, Tony, our fat man isn't the boss of this outfit. He took the necklace Compton stole and said it would have to be turned over to a certain party for appraisal before Compton could get his cut."

"I thought there would be some one higher-up than your friend Jacques behind all this," Quinn said. "The gang is too well-set, and works with too much cooperation not to have a clever leader. Any idea who it might be?"

"Not an iota. I doubt if anyone else at the boarding house knows, besides Jacques—and of course I couldn't read his mind."

"Equally of course," said Quinn, "we can't come out into the open, seize him and work him over. Wouldn't do much good anyway, from what Butch has told me of the man."

Butch leaned forward, his huge hands clasped tightly.

"That boy," he said "is dangerous. Me—I don't scare easy, but the fat man has got something. He set me back on my ear plenty fast. He's nobody I'd want to meet on a dark night."

"His kind become fragile once they are hurt," Silk spoke up.

BUTCH looked at Silk.

"Yeah," he agreed. "Only the idea is to hurt 'em before you get knocked for a loop yourself."

Quinn chuckled. "We'll take good care of Jacques in due time. Right now I have a few things to report. Nothing definite. As you know, this matter came before me in my capacity as special D.A. In the last thirty days there have been eleven hold-ups, as well as robberies in houses and other thefts where very valuable gems have been stolen. The police have made little headway, but thanks to the help of the three of you, we're beginning to get a start. Now that Carol has brought proof of a highly competent

Mason started when he saw the black automatic pointed at him (Chapter VI)

leader's existence, we have progressed even further."

"I'm glad I could help," Carol said. "But I don't see how that is so important, Tony."

"But it is. We have learned that all the families who have been robbed employed servants. Almost invariably those servants live in boarding houses much like the one where you are staying, Carol. Places that give too much for too little. They are run with one purpose in mind—to have a place where willing ears can listen to the gossip of these servants. News about parties at which valuables will be worn. Talk about the location of the safe in the house, or other spots used to secrete gems. Information about habits of the families, about doors and exits. Little by little the servants reveal—quite unknowingly—just what these crooks want to find out."

"It has certainly paid off," Silk opined.

Quinn nodded. "Indeed it has, but I'm still a bit suspicious. This mob of crooks must have a terrific overhead. The profits have been good, but not quite good enough to cover all their outlay and still pay them for their trouble. I believe the entire thing has been leading up to some big and decidedly important job. So far, not a glimpse of the thieves has been caught by their victims. They go about their work in an extremely businesslike fashion, which makes it all the more difficult to run them down. No trace of their loot has appeared on any market, either, which shows how cautious they are."

"If we could only find the man who runs the outfit!" Carol said, musingly.

"We're making a little headway," Quinn told her. "Butch and Silk have worked hard. I've taken advantage of my office to investigate certain factors. We have three fair suspects for the position of leader. The boarding houses, for instance—we know of three of them, so far—are all owned by one man who is the lessor. He is a real estate operator named Thomas Shirley, a cagey individual whose chief distinction is his love of money. Then there is an employment agency run by a William Jenks. From this agency many of the servants were supplied to those families which have been robbed. Jenks has no record, he has been in business for a long time, but has suffered badly of late because of the shortage of servants. He might have seen a way to recoup his fortune.

"Next, we have Sam Mason. Sam is a private detective who specializes in tracking down stolen jewels. His work is mainly done for insurance companies. They ask him no questions and he volunteers no information as to how he gets back the stolen stuff, but he does it, and capably too. One of these three men could conceivably be the leader of this gang of jewel thieves."

"My money is on Sam Mason, that private detective," Silk said. "In the old days I knew men like him and I know how they work. They're in on the job before it actually happens. The crook just turns the loot over to them, and after the insurance company has paid the claim, they move in to restore the property and get a fancy reward. The private detective calls it a fee. He splits with the crook, so of course he's as much of a thief as the actual one."

"True," Quinn admitted. "But Sam Mason's reputation is good. Of course it would be if he is as clever as the leader of this pack of wolves has shown himself to be. Carol do you think it's safe where you are? Murder has been done, and more will be done to conceal the first one if it becomes necessary."

Carol smiled. "I think I'm safe so far."

"Good. Now for some plans. We've got to make these crooks operate our way. Next time, I hope, you won't be suspected, Carol. Then I can move in as the Black Bat. Any of the other girls been doing any more talking?"

"Ann has," Carol said. "She works for the Paul Hampton's and she's been building up the rings Mrs. Hampton owns. They must be something from the way Ann talks. Mrs. Hampton wore them to the opera last week, but nothing happened. Maybe next time it will be different."

"Keep your ears open," Quinn advised. "The moment Ann says anything about when and where Mrs. Hampton's rings will be worn again, let me know. That's all for now. I think you'd best get back on the job."

"Tony," Carol said with a light frown, "there's one more thing. Perhaps it means nothing. But every time there is a burglary, Jacques goes out earlier in the evening and he always drives a station wagon. Maybe he makes contact with the leader and they discuss plans. But why use a car as conspicuous as a station wagon? He has a dark sedan in the same garage."

QUINN looked over at Kirby.

"Your job, Silk. Next time Carol warns us, you trail Jacques. He may even lead you straight to the man we want, although I doubt it. At any rate you may be able to determine the method of contact. They wouldn't use the telephone or a messenger."

Carol left immediately and soon after Butch departed. Tony Quinn picked up a cane. He walked toward the secret door which led into the library of his home. As he neared it, an amazing change came over him. His warm, friendly eyes suddenly became stony and fixed. The eyes of a totally blind man.

Indeed, everyone except Quinn's own little group believed him to be hopelessly blind. At one time he had been too, as the result of something that had happened when he had been an up and coming young D.A. pursuing crooks into their various holes and rapidly cleaning up this great city.

He'd been trying the case of an important criminal, basing his evidence on certain documents. In the middle of the trial, members of this crook's gang had tried to destroy the evidence by hurling a powerful acid upon it. Quinn had interfered and the acid had struck him in the face. He had been blinded almost instantly, and those deep scars around his eyes still remained as a silent witness of the tragedy.

He gave up his position as D.A., traveled all over Europe before the war, and to all clinics in this country. He was independently wealthy, willing to spend every cent he owned in order to see again, but money could not cure his blindness. At last, believing that he would never see again, Quinn settled down to the life of a blind man, living more or less a hermit's existence in his own home, with the reformed Silk Kirby as almost his only contact with the outside world.

It was at a time when things were at their lowest ebb for Tony Quinn that Carol Baldwin appeared. She came with a strange offer. Her father, a police officer in a small mid-Western town, was dying, the victim of gangster bullets.

He had followed the career of District Attorney Quinn and, knowing he had no chance to live, he wanted to give his eyes to Quinn. There was a little-known surgeon in Carol's home town, she said, who believed he could successfully perform the operation of replacing Quinn's dead corneas with Sergeant Baldwin's healthy ones.

Quinn went West and submitted to the operation and, soon after, Carol's father died. Quinn's sight returned, but he kept that a secret, because a new plan to fight crime and criminals had come to him. He knew the red tape that handicapped a public official in fighting crooks, and believed a free and independent investigator could make more headway. And that was when the Black Bat had come into being.

Attired in a close-fitting hood, made necessary because of the scars around his eyes which might easily identify him, somber clothing and crepe-soled shoes, the Black

Bat made his entrance as a crime investigator. His previous experience was a great asset, and his was augmented by certain physical traits he had acquired as a blind man.

His sense of touch had become highly acute, and his hearing was exceptionally good—Nature's compensation for his blinded eyes. When his sight returned, he did not lose the extra-sensorial aids he had developed.

Also, the operation produced some rather astounding and unlooked-for results. Tony Quinn could see in jet blackness as easily as he could in broad daylight. His uncanny eyes, penetrating darkness, could distinguish even pastel shades. Such a phenomenon was decidedly useful to him as a crime fighter.

Carol Baldwin had come East with Quinn and Silk Kirby, to join the Black Bat's organization. She had devoted her life to fighting criminals like those who had been responsible for her father's death.

Now no one except Carol, Silk, and Butch knew that Tony Quinn could see, or that he led a double life as a blind man and as the determined fighter known as the Black Bat.

Carol had proved to be a capable ally, and she and Tony Quinn had fallen in love. But neither of them ever mentioned that, knowing they could never marry while there was so much work for the Black Bat to do, and that always all their lives were in peril.

Butch O'Leary was a splendid ally, also. Tony Quinn had once befriended Butch who thereafter had devoted himself to his benefactor so loyally that he had been allowed to become a member of the little band. Butch while not the brightest of individuals, was faithful, and his enormous strength often became a valuable asset.

Only one outsider suspected that Quinn was the Black Bat—a detective captain named McGrath—and he seemed to spend all the time he could spare in an effort to prove it. With stubborn determination he clung to his opinion that the Black Bat was a crook himself, one who deserved nothing short of a prison cell, and he had vowed to accomplish that himself.

In plain terms he had announced that some day he would arrest the Black Bat, whom he was sure would turn out to be Tony Quinn. Even repeated examinations by the most noted experts who invariably declared Quinn hopelessly blind, had no effect on Captain McGrath.

In the case of another police official—Commissioner Warner, popular head of the force—it was different. Warner may at times have suspected Quinn of being the Black Bat, but he made no attempt to prove his suspicions true. He realized that the Black Bat was a most valuable ally of the police, and Commissioner Warner was not a man to examine such a gift too closely.

CHAPTER IV

Mysterious Journey

SILK drove Tony Quinn's car up to the entrance of the building where Quinn maintained an office in his capacity as Special District Attorney. Silk got out and helped the apparently blind Quinn alight. He held Quinn's arm and led him up the stairs while Q u i n n ' s c a n e tapped ahead of him, feeling out the way.

There was a visitor in the outer office. Captain McGrath, chunky, plainly dressed and a man of quiet efficiency, arose abruptly, walked directly in front of Quinn and extended his hand. It was just one of his ineffectual tricks to try and make Quinn reveal that he was not blind.

Silk had no time to steer Quinn out of the way and the blind man walked straight into McGrath, who backed up.

"Sorry," McGrath apologized. "I always keep forgetting you can't see. Or maybe I think you can. Right now I'm not worrying about that. Got a few minutes, Quinn? I want to talk to you about those jewel thieves."

Quinn invited him into the private office. McGrath sat down, crossed his legs and popped a cigar into his mouth.

"Strikes me a bit funny that the Black Bat hasn't come into this mess," he said. "You think it's because maybe he doesn't believe these thefts are important enough?"

Quinn smiled. His eyes, looking well to McGrath's left, were dead, staring orbs.

"I don't know, Captain. I don't happen to be a confidante of the Black Bat. Now, what did you want to see me about? Has anything new turned up?"

"No—and we've got to make something happen. There was a murder last night we're sure was committed by the same gang. So far we haven't the slightest trace of any of them. Sam Mason, the insurance detective, suggests we set a trap."

Quinn made a steeple of his hands. "It's dangerous, Captain. Last night these crooks showed their willingness to murder. They'll do it again. What is Mason's plan?"

"There's a family named Hampton. Paul Hampton's a wealthy engineer. His wife is attending some affair tonight, wearing seventy thousand dollars worth of rings. Enough to attract the gang. Now Mason suggests we have the newspapers print a story about those rings and make a casual mention about Mrs. Hampton wearing them tonight. If the crooks strike, we'll be plenty ready."

Quinn shook his head slowly. "It won't work," he said positively. "Such open advertising will scare the crooks off. Besides, you need the cooperation of Mr. and Mrs. Hampton and they aren't apt to risk their necks."

"Mason has already talked to them and they're glad to help," McGrath said. "We'll cover them from the moment they get the jewelry until it's back in the safe deposit vaults. The insurance company told Mason Mrs. Hampton intends to wear the jewelry tonight, and asked him to be on guard."

"It's your problem," Quinn shrugged. "Quite probably nothing will happen anyway. Is Mason intending to be with you?"

"Well—no. He did plan to, but says he's got something else to handle tonight. If I didn't know Mason well, I'd think he was deliberately trying to avoid being on the scene. But I'm going through with it. If we can land one of those crooks we'll make him talk."

"Good hunting, Captain," Quinn offered. "I still think it won't work."

The moment the door closed on McGrath, Silk placed an envelope on Quinn's desk.

"This is funny," he said. "I was opening the morning's mail and found this. It's addressed in a woman's hand, but inside the envelope there was only this blank piece of paper."

Quinn's eyes became alive again. He studied the blank paper, then the envelope.

"Odd!" he murmured. "Protect this paper, and envelope, Silk, until we can check for possible fingerprints."

Quinn put the envelope on the desk and lightly passed his fingertips across the sealed flap, still in place because Silk had used a letter opener. Sensitivity of touch told Quinn that the flap had been tampered with.

"It's been steamed open, then resealed," he said. "Application of additional glue has made the flap bulge slightly in spots. It was no error that we got blank paper instead of a letter. Someone wanted to tell us something and was circumvented. Well, eventually we'll probably find out what it's all about."

"What do you think of McGrath's scheme, sir?" Silk asked, as he put the envelope and paper away.

"I don't like it, Silk. Besides, McGrath is trying to kill a couple of birds with one trap. He took me into his confidence in hope the Black Bat would be on hand. He may be, at that, but well in the distance. Incidentally, the maid who works for the Paul Hamptons is the one who has been talking about Mrs. Hampton's rings. Remember Carol mentioning their names—and the maid, Ann?"

"Yes, sir. Maybe those crooks won't need newspaper publicity to make 'em act."

"Your job is to watch the house where that fat man lives," Quinn said, "and if he drives the station wagon out, trail him, see if he meets anyone. The station wagon must have some connection with the thefts—and last night's murder—because it is driven out every time a job is pulled. I want to know why."

A RUSH of normal business started then and Quinn went to work. At six o'clock Silk drove him home. Quinn made certain that the house was not under observation, then went straight to his hidden laboratory. There he studied the mysterious envelope and its blank enclosure. He proved now that the envelope had been opened. There were no prints on the paper though, except Silk's. The handwriting on the envelope was neat, slanted considerably, and obviously that of a woman.

He put it aside and pondered McGrath's trap for tonight. The Hamptons' maid would talk more at dinner. Jacques would hear her and set the wheels in motion for another robbery or holdup—unless the crooks read the item McGrath and Private Detective Sam Mason were having printed. Then they might smell a rat.

It seemed to Quinn that Mason was a trifle too eager. And he had taken pains to inform McGrath he wouldn't be on deck if anything happened. It sounded as if he meant to try to establish a fool-proof alibi.

Carol managed to phone after dinner and told Silk, in a few words, that the Hamptons' maid had talked about the rings. Silk relayed this information to Quinn who was seated in a well-worn leather chair before the fireplace in the library.

"Things stand just as they were," Quinn said. "Try to trail Jacques. Butch, as Carol's boy friend, is going to call on her and keep tabs there. I'll be going out—as the Black Bat, Silk. McGrath or not, I can't let those crooks get away with anything else. Not without a fight."

"Good," Silk approved. "Incidentally, sir, you haven't seen the evening papers. That is, I haven't read them to you as I always do. There is a most interesting little story."

"About the Hamptons and the diamond rings?"

"That's there too, but there is another. Some visiting royalty here now from one of the liberated countries, is going to throw a big party for a lot of important people two nights from now. The paper gives a partial list of those expected to attend and it sounds like the Social Register."

"And Tiffany's, no doubt," Quinn frowned. "Those crooks don't need talkative maids to get information. Every woman who attends that affair is bound to wear her best jewelry. It should make a haul large enough to tempt any band of crooks. I'm afraid it's what this particular gang has been waiting for. We'll have to make some countering plans, Silk. Find out all you can about it."

"Yes, sir. I think I'd better be on my way now."

"Darken the whole house before you leave," Quinn instructed. "Then if McGrath takes a notion to pop over, he'll think we're out. I don't need the lights anyway. And, Silk—phone me here as soon as possible, whether you find out anything or not."

Silk went to his room where he proceeded to don a disguise. Silk was no expert at this, but when he had been a confidence man, he had mastered two disguises. Both were simple, but effective. Selecting one of them now, he donned a gray wig, and added false eyebrows to make his own shaggier. A bit of cream rubbed into the face gave him a ruddy complexion. That was all, but combined with clothing typical of a movie mogul, or other financier, it made Silk another person.

After darkenning the house, in obedience to Quinn's instructions, he slipped out to the garage, changed license plates on one of the cars and drove away. When he reached the vicinity of the boarding house where Carol was staying and near which Jacques lived, he pulled up in an advantageous spot and doused the car lights.

More than an hour went by. He saw Carol returning to the boarding house with two other girls. Then the station wagon slid out of the driveway and Silk trailed it. He stayed far back, because Jacques would be naturally suspicious, but Silk was a past master at this

[Turn page]

business. He was certain Jacques had no idea he was being followed.

The fat man kept up a good pace until he reached a more populous portion of the city where he headed toward an exclusive residential section. Finally he pulled up in front of one of the few remaining private dwellings in this downtown area. Silk took careful note of the place, memorizing its illuminated number on the porch.

Jacques then whirled away to cross town. This time he came to a stop in front of a big apartment building where he stayed for about fifteen minutes. His third stop was before the sumptuous entrance of a large residential hotel.

SILK noted each stop, but was distinctly puzzled. Jacques never got out of the station wagon, didn't sound his horn—just sat behind the wheel and smoked cigarettes, the butts of which he snapped high into the air.

He drove through the city's largest park, but didn't stop. Far across town he did—in the middle of a dark, quiet block. Several other cars were parked on either side of the street, but they seemed to be unoccupied.

As the fat man drove away and headed for home, Silk had an idea that he had been neatly taken on a wild goose chase. Certainly Jacques hadn't delivered any message, nor had he come into even the slightest contact with anyone. And he drove straight home as if in a hurry to get there.

Silk watched him drive into the garage, and a few minutes later lights in his house were turned on. Silk sighed and gave up. As he drove away he was hoping he would be in time to tell the Black Bat of Jacques' strange actions. But the Black Bat had already departed on whatever mysterious errand demanded his attention.

CHAPTER V

Vanished Girl

CAROL, meanwhile, bided her time until after Jacques returned. At dinner, the maid employed by the Hamptons' had spoken her piece about the valuable rings. Jacques had gone home early. Mrs. Carter seemed unusually curt with her boarders, and her thin-faced son was nowhere about.

Carol watched Jacques drive off. She wanted to get into his house and examine it, and some time she hoped to get a chance to examine the station wagon he drove on these trips. But it was still early and Mrs. Carter bustled about, making rather frequent trips through the house as if to keep all her boarders under observation.

Carol did openly leave the house, walk to the drug-store and make a phone call to Tony Quinn. He agreed that an examination of Jacques' premises might prove interesting, but he warned her to be careful. Carol had made sure she hadn't been followed, but Mrs. Carter was standing in the doorway when she returned.

"My boy friend has been transferred to another shift," Carol said brightly. "I hope you don't mind if he calls on me about eleven o'clock. I'll send him home early."

"If you don't disturb the other girls, I have no objections," Mrs. Carter said over her shoulder, as she walked toward the kitchen.

Carol returned to her room. She saw Jacques come back, waited twenty minutes, then she slipped downstairs.

Mrs. Carter seemed to have gone out. Carol knew exactly what she had to do. She turned on the rear porch light—the one used to signal Jacques. Then she hurried through the back door, ran lightly in the direction of the fat man's house and concealed herself behind a tree.

Soon Jacques emerged, walking fast. He passed within a dozen yards of where Carol was hidden. She waited until he entered the boarding house, then she hurried toward his garage. It was locked, but the doors were equipped with ordinary tumbler locks. Carol opened her purse and took out several keys which Tony Quinn had manufactured in his laboratory. There were few locks they couldn't open and the one to Jacques' garage was not among these few.

Carol stepped in, closed the door behind her and went to the station wagon. She discovered that the windows were covered by curtains hanging inside the vehicle, but the front door was easily opened. Yet even from this point she couldn't see in back. A solid metal wall had been built there, cutting off the back of the wagon from the driver's seat.

She couldn't afford to spend much more time in the garage, for there might be more interesting things in the house. But Carol did notice one significant thing. There were two horn buttons on the wheel. One was coated with bright chrome and the other had been painted a dull brown.

This was interesting because of its uniqueness. She rapidly drew a good sketch of the interior of the place in her small notebook, ripped off the page and added a couple of notes. She inserted the paper in an envelope, addressed it to Tony Quinn, then slipped out of the garage, taking pains to lock up after her.

She glanced toward Mrs. Carter's boarding house, but the ungainly bulk of the fat man was nowhere in sight. Greatly relieved, she moved toward the back of his house, but decided against trying to effect an entrance there. If he returned, he would be sure to notice anything wrong, for he always came in the back way.

Carol hurried around to the front of the house which had been built close to the deserted street. She saw a mail-box a few steps from the house. Carol hesitated. She knew she was going to plunge into considerable danger, and already she possessed some meager information about the station wagon which might benefit the Black Bat. Was it worth while taking the chance of waiting to see whether she could get more information before mailing her notes?

Gripping the envelope addressed to Quinn, she hurried to the mail-box, affixed a stamp on the letter and posted it. She felt better after that was done. If she found anything else in Jacques' house, she could write another note or relay the information to Butch when he came to see "Myra."

Carol ran up on the front porch of Jacques' house. Again those keys which Tony Quinn had furnished served their purpose. She had the front door open in less than three minutes. There was a weak hall light illuminating the entrance. She closed the door quietly and stood there, listening, centering her attention upon the slightest squeak or pad of feet. She heard none and ventured further into the place.

IT WAS dark deeper along the hallway and she used a tiny flashlight which threw a yellow, weak ray. Aided by this, she began to examine each room. They were just ordinary rooms, expensively furnished, tidy and neat. There was not time to rummage in desks or bureau drawers.

She proceeded to the second floor, made her way to the extreme rear and looked over at Mrs. Carter's house. The porch light had gone out, but if Jacques had been moving back, she would surely have seen him.

There was one closed door upstairs. Carol turned the knob firmly, threw the door wide and stepped aside in the event of some attack from within. Nothing happened. She stepped into the room, turned her flashlight on—and gasped.

She saw a work-bench equipped with jeweler's tools. There was a small blast furnace for reducing metals, probably gold. Any large, modern jewel manufacturing plant might have been envious of such a place.

Carol moved closer to the work-bench. If she could find some of the gems recently stolen, she would have evidence enough on Jacques to warrant his arrest—unless the Black Bat wanted to handle the fat man in his own way.

She had picked up a red-plush case when the room started to swirl crazily. She grasped at the edge of the bench for support. Her flashlight hit the floor and darkness filled the room. But that darkness was sunlight compared to the gloom which enveloped Carol. She had hardly felt the blow on the head. It had been struck with scientific precision.

Promptly at eleven o'clock Butch O'Leary climbed the stairs of Carol's boarding house and rang the bell. He waited a few minutes when there was no answer. Then he rang it again. This time he drew results. Mrs. Carter, swathed in a voluminous bathrobe, opened the door.

"I guess my girl got sick of waiting," Butch said, and smiled at the landlady amiably. "I told her, though, I couldn't make it until eleven o'clock."

"If you are referring to Myra," Mrs. Carter said frigidly, "she moved out early this evening. She didn't say where she was going—didn't even give me any reason for leaving, but she's gone. Irresponsible—that's what she was, and you're well rid of her if you never see her again."

The door was slammed in Butch's face. For an instant he was tempted to tear it down and conduct a search of the place, but he realized that would do no good. Anyway, it was possible that Carol had seen trouble materializing and had made tracks for safety.

Butch turned slowly away, walked down the steps and onto the street. He headed back toward the bus stop. But he was wary. The Black Bat had taught him many tricks. He sauntered along the silent street like a puzzled, woebegone man, but his slow place was intentional. If anyone followed him, his shadow would be compelled to move just as slowly, and that meant ducking for cover, allowing Butch to extend his distance, then taking up the chase again.

There was someone behind him. Butch heard nothing, but he did spot a flitting shadow just beyond one of the street lights. Butch had purposely turned around at this point because he knew that anyone passing close to that light would leave a shadow.

Butch didn't even consider capturing the man after him. Not now, because all this meant that Carol had been taken prisoner. The Black Bat must be warned. Such pleasures as wringing a crook's neck would have to wait.

Butch reached the busstop, lit a cigarette and waited. The bus came along five minutes later. By that time four other people were waiting, but Butch was fairly sure none of these was the man who had followed him. When the bus pulled up, Butch was the first aboard. He dropped his coin in the fare slot and moved briskly toward the center of the bus.

There was a middle door exit, operated when a passenger stepped on a treadle. Butch saw a man dart from the shadows and hurry toward the bus. He got aboard last and as he fumbled for his fare, Butch stepped on the treadle, opened the exit door by this means, and the door closed automatically behind him.

As it did the bus lurched off. The shadow was still aboard, and that bus wouldn't stop again for half a dozen blocks.

Butch cut through a yard, heading for another street where there was more life. He spotted a taxi and hailed it. Inside it, he relaxed. He had thrown that trailer off. He was positive of it, but that did not alleviate the ache in his heart.

CAROL was on a spot and Butch felt like a deserter, running away like this. Yet orders were orders and he had been explicitly warned to do just this in case something happened.

It took a full hour for Butch to reach Tony Quinn's neighborhood. After leaving the taxi and seeing it drive off he took particular pains to be sure he was not observed. Then he went through the garden gate and in a few moments he was in the lab, frantically pushing a button which would warn Silk or Quinn that he had bad news for them.

Silk answered the summons and one look at Butch creased Silk's features into lines of worry.

"Carol?" he asked.

Butch nodded. "I don't know what happened, but that hatchet-faced landlady told me Carol had checked out. I was followed from the house, but I gave whoever it was the slip. What do you think we ought to do?"

"I know what I'd like to do," Silk said softly. "Go back and tear the joint down. But we can't—not until the Black Bat gets back. Somehow they must have got wise to her. All we can hope is that they haven't killed her. If she is being held for whatever information they think she has, Carol will be all right for a short time. She knows how to stall. Did you see that fat man, Butch?"

"Jacques? No! Look, Silk, take a tip from me. Jacques is fat and he looks like a bundle of suet, but don't get him wrong. He's plain poison. He knows more dirty tricks than a Jap and he's plenty smart. You know I don't scare easy, but I'm telling you I'd give Jacques a wide berth."

Silk whistled in amazement. "That's the first time I ever heard you admit being afraid of anything, Butch. Jacques must really be something."

"I met him," Butch explained seriously. "I know what I'm talking about. Jacques is a lug who'd rather kill than eat. . . . When will the Black Bat get back? He's got to know about this."

Silk looked at his watch. "It's after midnight. The party Mrs. Hampton attended was slated to break about half an hour ago.

If nothing happened the Black Bat should be here within a few minutes, but we can't depend upon it. Remember he's working alone. McGrath is on the job, too, and he'll have half an eye out for the Hamptons and an eye and a half out for the Black Bat. We've got to be patient, Butch. I'll bring in a pot of coffee."

CHAPTER VI

Phantom Killer

THE Black Bat minus his customary tight-fitting hood, sat behind the wheel of a cheap, dilapidated-looking coupé. It was parked close to the house where Mr. and Mrs. Paul Hampton were attending a party. Instead of the hood, the Black Bat wore a wide-brimmed hat, well turned down to hide the tell-tale scars around his eyes. The Black Bat disliked exposing himself this way, but circumstances demanded it.

A couple of times he noticed Captain McGrath emerge from the house. The police officer had men strategically planted around the section, although the Black Bat was half inclined to believe the crooks would make no attempt to get Mrs. Hampton's diamond rings. McGrath had advertised the party and the rings almost too well. Yet those rings represented an irresistible temptation to clever thieves. The stones were so large they could be cut and still be sizeable.

Finally the party broke up. The Black Bat knew the Hamptons' car and when it rolled off, closely followed by Captain McGrath and several detectives in another sedan, the Black Bat trailed along.

Naturally, he could not actually follow the Hamptons. McGrath's presence made that impossible, so the Black Bat contented himself with driving along an avenue paralleling the one on which the Hamptons drove. At each corner he slowed considerably until he saw Hamptons' car slide by the same cross street. Then the Black Bat speeded up, reached the next corner and repeated the process. The traffic lights on both avenues were coordinated and he had no trouble.

They were well uptown and not more than a dozen blocks from the Hampton home when their car failed to appear at the next intersection. The Black Bat turned up that side street, stepped on it and reached the corner, to park as close as he dared to the avenue. He got out, blended well with the shadows, and took a quick look around the corner.

The Hampton car was nosed in to the curb. Behind it was McGrath's police car with all doors wide open. Four men were fanning out as if in pursuit of someone, and lying in the road beside the Hampton car was a woman. The Black Bat could see the knife sticking out of her back. It was directly above the heart and there could be little question but that she was dead.

The Black Bat had a good look at Paul Hampton as the man talked to Captain McGrath. Hampton was about forty-five, tall, and athletically built. His hair was turning gray. At the moment he was overcome by grief. His shoulders drooped and his arms hung listlessly.

There was no time to study the scene further, for McGrath's men were approaching the spot from which the Black Bat watched.

and got it open without difficulty.

The Hampton apartment was nicely furnished. Not too expensively, but with excellent taste. He prowled through it, found Mrs. Hampton's bedroom and was somewhat surprised when he saw it was provided with three locks. One was a regulation door lock and the other two were heavy bolts. Besides these, there was also a stout burglar chain.

He came upon a diary which apparently the woman now dead had kept. It was just an ordinary diary and the latest entry consisted of a few words about the party she was to attend. There was premonition in the words she had written wondering if it was foolish for her to wear those gems after all the bur-

CAROL

He sprinted to his car, backed up as fast as possible and quickly headed into an alley. Not a moment too soon, for almost at once a detective hurried past. Radio cars also were converging on the scene.

The Black Bat had to take a chance. He pulled out of the alley, drove to the corner and turned into the avenue. No one attempted to stop him and he was soon safely away. Apparently the police were not searching for anyone in a car. The murderer, or murderers, must have made an escape on foot.

The Black Bat parked close by the service entrance to the apartment house where Paul Hampton lived. He entered the building, donned the black hood, and took the self-service elevator to Hampton's floor. In a moment he was working on the door lock

glaries and hold-ups which had taken place.

Hampton returned about an hour later and as he reached for the light switch, the Black Bat spoke from the darkness.

"Please don't turn on the lights, Mr. Hampton. And don't be afraid. This is the Black Bat."

Hampton's hand dropped from the light switch. He peered through the semi-gloom before kicking the door shut. Enough light filtered into the room so that he had a fair view of the eerie figure in black seated in one of the comfortable chairs in the living room.

"The Black Bat!" Hampton said hoarsely. "What do you want with me?"

"Information," the Black Bat answered. "Mr. Hampton, I want to help you find the men who murdered your wife."

"How did you know that?" Hampton

asked. "It happened only a little while ago."

"Sit down," the Black Bat said gently. "I was there, Mr. Hampton. Oh, not just when it happened, but only minutes afterward. I'd like the whole story—from your lips. Naturally, I can't go to the police, so I thought I'd come here."

Hampton sat down. "I hope you can help me," he said forlornly. "If anyone can, you're the man. McGrath says it was that band of jewel thieves and I agree with him. My wife and I worked with Captain McGrath to set a little trap. She was willing, and while I worried about it, I was talked into it. The fact that my wife would wear her rings was publicized. We were extremely well guarded at the party. On the way home I thought the thing had fizzled out, unless the crooks made an attempt to get the diamonds after we returned home. But McGrath was going to provide guards for the apartment too."

"Tell me just what happened," the Black Bat urged. "Did you see the man who knifed your wife?"

"No! No, I did not. He must have been in the back of the car although McGrath's men examined it before we drove off. Anyway, I was driving along when something hit me on the back of the neck. It was a terrific blow, delivered by a man of abnormal strength. I passed out, I guess, but as I did I somehow managed to turn the car into the curb, and I did hear my wife start to scream. It must have been cut off when the killer drove a knife into her back.

"Somehow I got the car door open and fell out. My wife didn't die instantly. It was one of those rare cases where a person lives a few seconds after the heart is pierced. She got out too, before she collapsed. It was horrible. The police car was fairly close behind us although it had stopped for a red light. Captain McGrath told me he didn't dare go through it in case the crooks were watching and would guess it was a police car. McGrath and his men did the best they could. But the killer, whoever he was, got away clean. I never saw him."

"Did McGrath or any of his men?"

"He said not. They were almost a block behind us when it happened. There were several places where the killer could have gone. At any rate he disappeared. The diamonds, of course, had been wrenched from my wife's fingers . . . Black Bat, I'm not going to stop until I see the murderer of my wife behind bars! I'm going to do all in my power to circumvent any further attacks of this kind by those crooks. I'm an engineer by profession. I know how to plan, and I won't rest until that gang has been broken to bits! I know your reputation and I appreciate your offers to help. I'll do anything you suggest."

"Later," the Black Bat said slowly. "I haven't any real clues yet. These men are clever, you see. Incidentally, I looked over your apartment. Not from curiosity, but to make certain I was alone. I noticed your wife had a dread of crooks. Her bedroom door was secured like a bank vault."

Hampton put a hand to his forehead and slowly massaged it as he spoke.

"She did that recently, after this crime wave started. Betty was deathly afraid of burglars. She must have had some sort of feeling about what was to happen. And I laughed at her! I was the big know-it-all. I—"

Hampton looked up. The chair which the Black Bat had occupied was empty. He turned on lights. The Black Bat had quietly slipped away.

Meanwhile, he had reached his car. He had one more stop to make. It was some distance away and in another apartment house much like that in which Paul Hampton lived.

When the Black Bat arrived there, the corridors were deserted and silent. He stopped in front of a door on which was a brass plate bearing the name of Sam Mason—private detective who seemed to have too much luck in recovering stolen gems which had been insured.

THE Black Bat rang the bell. Mason came to the door and gave a startled exclamation, partly because of the weird figure he faced and partly because of the black automatic pointed at his chest. Mason was short, lithe, and had bright bluish-green eyes. He was fully dressed, even wearing a hat. He backed up a few steps and raised his hands.

"Sorry about the gun," the Black Bat apologized, "but I am a man who is wanted by the police and you're a detective."

Mason managed a weak grin. "I promise not to try and take you, Black Bat. As if I could! You're here about the murder of Mrs. Paul Hampton, aren't you? I heard about it over the radio just a minute or so ago. I also know what you want with me. Somehow you have learned that I helped engineer the trap Captain McGrath wanted to spring. I swear I had no idea it would backfire this way!"

"And why didn't you accompany the party?" The Black Bat closed the door behind him, but his gun remained steady. "As a detective working for insurance companies, you should have tried to help spring your own trap."

Mason looked worried. "I don't expect you or anyone else to believe this, Black Bat. I'm almost inclined to think I was framed. I meant, all along, to help protect the Hamptons. But I received a letter asking me to be at the corner of Woodruff Avenue and State Street at precisely eleven-thirty. There were two one-hundred-dollar bills enclosed and a promise of more if I would take the case that would be offered me. The letter also stated that if no one showed up, I was to be there again tomorrow night. I thought McGrath could handle things, and a two-hundred-dollar fee isn't to be sneered at. You don't believe me, do you?"

"Let me see that letter," the Black Bat ordered, and when Mason reached for his pocket, the Black Bat's gun rested lightly against the middle button of his vest.

Mason handed over the letter. The Black Bat glanced at the handwriting on the envelope and almost whistled in surprise. It matched the oddly slanted writing on the strange envelope he had received. The one which enclosed nothing but a blank sheet of paper.

The letter itself was just as Mason had described it and was, of course, unsigned. The Black Bat tucked it into his pocket.

"Frankly, Mr. Mason," he said, "I do believe you, but I'll keep the letter. If you get into trouble and need it I shall know about it and see that the letter is returned to you. There is nothing else? No clues, however meager, as to the identity of the gang?"

"If I had some clues, don't you think I'd tell you?" Mason exclaimed. "What profit would there be for me to cover up for a killer?"

Mason's eyes glowed with a desperate light. His thin body twisted with agitation as if it were made of bone and nerves and nothing else.

"You haven't always been exactly friendly with the law," the Black Bat observed. "The police in the past have known you to keep a buttoned lip when you could have talked. I ask you again. Do you have any clues?"

"Not one." Mason shrugged. "Look, I know crooks. It's my living to know them and do business with them. Certainly I circumvent the law sometimes and the cops don't like me especially, but I have to produce stolen gems. If I don't, I have no job. Sure, I know who committed a number of robberies, but I consider my dealings with crooks highly confidential. If I betrayed one of them, I'd never make another contact."

"I understand," the Black Bat said. "Have you ever been contacted about any of the jewels stolen lately—presumably by this gang?"

"No, and somebody in this gang has killed two people so far. He, or others, will kill more. If they contact me, I'll turn them in. The consequences won't matter because I believe this gang to be the most dangerous I've ever known about. Murder breeds more murder and if I associate with them, sooner or later I'll be on the receiving end."

"A wise deduction," the Black Bat said. "Turn around now. Keep your hands up."

When Mason obeyed, the Black Bat made his exit. He was soon driving the coupé back to Tony Quinn's house—and the agony of discovering that Carol was in danger.

CHAPTER VII

Murder Over His Shoulder

BEFORE the Black Bat could remove his outfit, Silk was telling him about Carol. The Bat said nothing for a few moments, but betrayed his nervousness by pacing up and down the lab. Then he yanked off the hood.

"Carol's danger is extremely grave!" he said then. "That jewel thief gang again exhibited their ruthlessness tonight by killing Mrs. Paul Hampton. Yet we must reason things out and have faith. Butch, you and I are going to the Carter boarding house. Silk, you stay here in case Carol finds an opportunity to get in touch with us. And, Silk, did you trail that station wagon?"

Silk took a notebook from his pocket and related the odd route taken by Jacques. The Black Bat noted down the addresses and seemed puzzled.

"Jacques made the rounds of the homes of every man we suspect," he said. "Tom Shirley, the real estate dealer, lives in the private dwelling where Jacques made his first stop. William Jenks, who runs the employment agency, lives at that hotel, and Sam Mason resides in the apartment house where Jacques also stopped. The side street on which he made his last stop doesn't seem to fit in with anyone so far involved. Didn't he get out of the station wagon, blow the horn, blink the lights, Silk? Give some sort of a signal?"

"No, sir—he did nothing but park. I don't understand it, sir."

"Neither do I," the Black Bat said musingly. "Jacques had a purpose, of course. He knew that Mrs. Hampton would wear her diamonds and he was tipping off someone —perhaps the head of the gang, who could then issue orders for the robbery. Jacques and this leader know that Shirley, Jenks and Mason are under suspicion. Jacques drove to each address so they'd share that suspicion."

"Then one of them must be the big shot," Butch broke in. "The other visits were made just to cover up the real one."

"Unless all three visits were blind ones and Jacques somehow transacted his business on that dark side street," the Black Bat said. "We really haven't progressed far enough to be sure of anything. I'd like a look at that station wagon. Maybe I'll get the chance. Ready, Butch?"

Butch drove the coupé to the neighborhood of Mrs. Carter's boarding house. It was totally dark. When Butch parked at a safe distance from the place, the Black Bat gave him his orders.

"Bang on the door. Ring the bell—make a lot of noise. When Mrs. Carter answers, insist on seeing Carol. Create all the disturbance you can without getting loud enough to bring the police. That will keep her and anyone else who may be on guard so busy I'll be able to effect an entrance through the rear. Make it last about five minutes, then stalk off. Watch out for a tail. Now get started."

The Black Bat in his somber clothing seemed to vanish in the darkness when he was a dozen yards from the car. His eyes penetrated the gloom easily and obstructions which would have tripped a man with normal sight were visible to him, so he could avoid them.

As he reached the back of the house he heard Butch demanding to see Carol, pretending to believe she wouldn't see him because of a spat they'd had. Mrs. Carter's voice was low and venomous as she tried to shoo Butch away.

The cellar door offered excellent possibilities for the Black Bat, since it was equipped with a cheap lock. Hurriedly he opened the lock, stepped into a musty cellar and looked around with his uncanny eyes that swept away the blackness. The cellar was littered with old furniture, empty barrels and packing cases. He had started across the floor when he came to an abrupt stop, hearing a metallic squeak from the opposite side of the cellar.

Gun ready, the Black Bat moved forward silently. This might be the headquarters of the gang—some hidden room off the cellar. But his hopes of finding Carol there were quickly blasted. The noise came from an old bed against the further wall. On it lay a man securely trussed up and gagged. From descriptions furnished by Carol, the Black Bat knew the man was Compton Carter, the landlady's son.

IF THAT gag hadn't been in place, Carter would have screamed in terror, for it shone starkly clear in his eyes. This was a stroke of good luck for the Black Bat. Compton Carter had been made a prisoner for some reason and he would be sure to talk. He was an active member of the gang—a killer, in fact. Weak too, judging by the cut of his chin and the fear in his eyes. Faced with the prospects of the electric chair he probably would talk.

The Black Bat changed his mind about searching the house now. Chances of Carol being there were slim anyway, for there were too many boarders in the place. Compton offered the best possibilities. The Black Bat bent over the man.

"They're going to kill you," he said softly. "You know too much. Your life isn't worth a dime, but I'll help you. I'm going to take

you out of here. I don't trust you enough to remove the gag or the ropes now. I will later. Don't try to struggle."

The Black Bat hoisted young Carter and draped him over one shoulder. Then he quietly made his way back to the cellar entrance. Above, he heard the front door slam and Mrs. Carter's footsteps clicked across the floor. Butch must have departed.

The Black Bat opened the cellar door and peered out into the darkness. He saw or heard nothing. Silently he climbed the steps to the back yard and started running lightly toward the small garage. His burden gave a convulsive series of kicks.

"Cut it out," the Black Bat warned, "or I'll tap you on the chin."

The movement stopped. The Black Bat cut through two yards and saw the coupé in the distance. He also saw a uniformed patrolman ambling slowly along. The Black Bat crouched quickly, hoping the darkness was intense enough to shield him. He slipped his prisoner off his shoulder and laid him on the ground.

Then the Black Bat gasped. His prisoner was dead! There was a large haft of a knife protruding from his back. Those convulsive struggles had been caused when the knife had been driven home.

The Black Bat stood up and peered toward the Carter House. Someone had been hiding behind the back porch or around the corner of the house, where he could see what was going on and still not be seen even by a man with the Black Bat's strange vision.

Of course the knife had been thrown—and by an expert. If anyone had tried to slip up close enough to deliver this fatal thrust, the Black Bat would have heard him.

The Black Bat studied the handle of the knife. There might be fingerprints. With gloved hands he worked the blade out of the wound.

He had forgotten the patrolman until suddenly a flashlight cut the darkness and centered on him, half-crouched, with the knife in his hand. Turning swiftly, the Black Bat raced away. A gun cracked twice, but he evaded the ray of the flash and darkness protected him.

The cop was running in his direction. The Black Bat dropped flat in a little gulley. He could see the patrolman who was not using his flash now, probably afraid it would only make a target of himself. He passed close by where the Black Bat was hiding. As soon as the officer was some distance from the gulley, the Black Bat arose and sprinted for the coupé.

Butch had the motor turning over and as the Black Bat climbed aboard, the car started moving. The Black Bat quickly exhanged his hood for the large black hat.

"Step on it, Butch," he said. "I found young Carter in the cellar, alive, but tied up and a prisoner. I carried him out, but on

SILK

the way to the coupé someone threw a knife. Young Carter is dead, but what's worse, that cop saw me as I extracted the knife from Carter's body. He must have believed I'd just killed him. He recognized me, without doubt. McGrath will go into a frenzy now. He'll probably get to the house as fast as he can, to speed things up."

When they reached Tony Quinn's home, Butch did not head down the street in front of it. He took the street behind the house. The Black Bat got out, climbed a wall, and ran for the garden house. He was stripping off his regalia as he raced along the tunnel.

The lab was empty. He quickly donned the familiar trousers and gray tweed coat of blind Tony Quinn. Seizing his cane, he approached the secret door, his eyes dead and staring. He opened the door a crack and heard voices at the front door. Silk and Captain McGrath! The detective had lost no time after the patrolman had phoned in the news of Carter's death.

QUINN hastily seated himself in his accustomed chair in front of the fireplace.

"Silk!" he called. "I'm not asleep. I came downstairs half an hour ago."

Silk made a move to usher McGrath into the room, but the detective barged past him.

"Sorry, sir," Silk murmured to Quinn. "Captain McGrath seems to be exceptionally excited tonight. I thought you had retired and I refused to awaken you."

"It's all right, Silk. Now, Captain—what are you excited about?"

McGrath eyed Quinn closely, then shrugged disgustedly. Quinn certainly looked like a placid blind man.

"You know I think you're the Black Bat and that you can see," McGrath said. "I've always thought so and no number of eye doctors can convince me otherwise. Perhaps I'm a fool. I think not. The Black Bat, Quinn, has helped the police many times. Unquestionably, we should be grateful to him. Some are, but in my opinion, the Black Bat is just as much of a law-breaker as any of the criminals he tracks down."

"Which you have remarked time and again," Quinn said wearily. "I'm tired, Captain. Come to the point and stop making ridiculous accusations."

"They may not be so ridiculous. As I was saying, the Black Bat has killed men, but it was always in self-defense. So much I concede, but tonight you—that is, the Black Bat —was seen stabbing a man to death! A cold-blooded, deliberate murder. Why he did it, I don't know, but an honest patrolman saw the crime committed."

"The Black Bat has never killed indiscriminately," Quinn said slowly. "However, what he does is no concern of mine. Shall I repeat that I am not—"

"No! I've heard it too often." McGrath's voice had an edge in it. "I've always said I'd bring the Black Bat in some day. I will! But now that I know he's a murderer I'll shoot to kill when I see him. I shall issue instructions to every police officer to shoot on sight. When I take the hood off the Black Bat, he will be dead. I just wanted to warn you."

"Why me?" Quinn retorted irritably. "Look here, Captain, you may hunt down the Black Bat all you wish, but there happens to be something else which requires detective work too. The murdering gang of jewel thieves. Tomorrow I want you to come to my office and bring Tom Shirley, William Jenks and Sam Mason with you, Nine-thirty. Is that understood?"

McGrath relaxed somewhat. "Yes. But that warning still goes. I think—"

"Good night, Captain," Quinn said flatly.

McGrath glared, then stalked out. After he had driven away, Silk returned to Quinn and found him worried.

"Up to now," Quinn said, "McGrath has been an interesting nuisance. But he's turned dangerous—with reason too. And Carol is still missing. We're progressing backward, Silk."

CHAPTER VIII

Contact Man

QUINN was up early the next morning, at work in the lab. He compared the handwriting on the envelope which had contained a blank sheet of paper with the writing on the letter which Sam Mason had received. They were identical, as he had known they would be.

His e n v e l o p e could m e a n s e v e r a l things. Someone had written something of importance and the letter had been replaced with the blank sheet of paper. Or the letter had contained valuables, extracted by a crook. Or it might be the work of a crank. District Attorneys sometimes received such things.

Now, however, the letter was tied up with Mason's and both somehow were mysteriously connected with the jewel thieves.

Silk entered the lab, much excited. He extended a letter to Quinn.

"It just came in the first mail, sir. That's Carol's writing! Maybe it's a tip where she is."

Quinn hastily slit the seal and extracted the note and sketch. He studied both before looking up at Silk.

"Carol wrote this before she was taken prisoner," he said then. "She had an idea something might happen to her. Carol saw Jacques' station wagon. It's a peculiar vehicle. You can't see into the back of it and there are two horn buttons. This doesn't help us find Carol, but through her work, we may have a clue. How about the morning papers? If she is being held for the ransom of my exit from the case there might be an ad. Certainly they couldn't communicate

with the Black Bat in any other way."

Silk hurried to get the papers. Two of them did carry personals which read:

B. B. Contact Mason at once. Patient growing weaker. Don't fail.

Quinn frowned. "So Sam Mason is in on it. We're going to the office now. Mason will be there with Captain McGrath and those other two men at nine. Wait for about an hour after he leaves, then phone him. Say you are the Black Bat and get the facts. Frankly, Silk, I'm more worried than I've been in years. That ad may even be the work of Captain McGrath. In his present state of mind, he's capable of it and we can't afford to take any chances. We've got to remember that Carol's predicament is serious. Silk, if they've killed her, so help me, Captain McGrath is going to find out that the Black Bat is a killer! Now get the car out."

Captain McGrath and the men involved in the case were waiting when Quinn arrived at his office. Paul Hampton also was there, and after Quinn had been told who he was, Hampton explained why he had come.

"I'm working with Sam Mason," he told Quinn. "It was my wife who was murdered last night. I want to help find the men who killed her. Naturally, I can't join the police, but I can work with a private detective—and I'm working on a scheme to outwit those crooks. You'll know all about it when I have it detailed."

"Very good," Quinn said. "However, if you do wish to inform me of such a scheme, please arrange to do it privately. You see, Mr. Hampton, I have half an idea that the man who directed the murder of your wife is here now."

There were gasps of astonishment and Tom Shirley, the real estate man, grew ruddier than normal. He had a shock of hair that stood up straight, like the quills of a bristling porcupine. At the moment he was decidedly the porcupine type.

Sam Mason's expression didn't change at all. William Jenks, the employment agency man, laughed a trifle too loudly.

Quinn's apparently blind eyes sized up these men closely.

"Yes, gentlemen," he went on. "I make no personal accusation, mind you. Yet Mason, for instance, is in a position to run a gang of jewel thieves and be smart about it, with his vast experience. Mr. Shirley, you own several places which are operated as rooming houses. Actually they are run for one reason. The boarders are servants of people owning precious gems—wealthy people. The servants know when the gems will be worn, where they are hidden, and when they arrive and leave the house. You own these places —all of them that we have so far discovered."

"But I own fifty places that are leased as boarding houses," Shirley protested. "This is preposterous!"

"No, it isn't," Quinn told him quickly. "Coincidence cannot be so strong as to make you the sole owner of the three or four places of which we know. I will concede this, though—those places may have been leased from you and run by the crooks to throw suspicion upon you and confuse the issue."

"Where do I come in?" William Jenks was still chuckling. "Wait—I can guess. The servants who talk too much all come from my agency."

"Quite right," Quinn nodded. "Servants employed by nine victims of this gang came from your agency. Now here again, a deliberate attempt to throw suspicion on you may have been made. Incidentally, how is your business doing right now?"

JENKS lost his grin, and scowled instead. "None of your business, Mr. Quinn. You sound as if I were on trial. I refuse to be intimidated."

"It's nothing like that," Quinn said. "But you are suspected. Tell me—just why do you keep running your employment agency when help is so hard to get? You pay big rent for your offices, too big for the fees you take in. Is it a charity organization?"

"Well, I—" Jenks lost his bluster. "Oh, what's the use trying to kid a man like you? You have the whole Police Department to run down things like this. Banks will open their books to you. All right—I do lose money. I haven't made a dime since the war began. But before that, I had worked up an excellent business and I want to hold it intact. I've been putting plenty of money into it. I'll put more."

"That's all I wanted to know," Quinn said. "And I believe you, Mr. Jenks . . . Mr. Shirley, you are not like Jenks. You are making so much money some people think of you as a profiteer. What about that?"

Shirley glowered and spoke angrily. "I work for what I get. I'm not a thief. I saw a shortage of real estate coming so I invested heavily. It's paying dividends, but that doesn't make me out a jewel thief or a killer."

"It certainly does not," Quinn agreed. "However, gentlemen, you now realize why all of you have had a certain measure of suspicion directed your way. I've had you investigated. I even know what you were doing last night when Mrs. Hampton was murdered. Jenks, you and Shirley have airtight alibis for that time."

The two men glanced at one another and seemed greatly relieved until Quinn spoke again.

"Which doesn't mean much. The man who heads this gang of thieves and killers would be certain to have an air-tight alibi. He doesn't perform the robberies himself. He merely directs some capable crooks and takes most of the profits. Now consider Sam Mason. He has no alibi at all. Captain McGrath told me what happened to you last night, Mason. Interesting."

Mason shrugged. "It fixes me all right, but you need more evidence than that, Quinn. I'm warning you—I know my rights and I've got backing. The insurance companies believe in me and they'll battle for me. I rate aces with them. Mr. Hampton can tell you that. Why, I've already taken him to several companies, told the officials I thought his plan to catch the crooks was good, and they accepted my word for it."

"What plan?" Quinn asked.

Mason grinned. "We're not talking yet, eh, Hampton? The fewer people who know about it, the better. But I'm saying this much—those crooks won't lay their hands on the cheapest bauble that will be flashing around the party for the Duchess—"

"Shut up, Mason!" Hampton broke in. "We agreed secrecy was our best bet. Don't ruin everything."

"I'm sorry," Mason said. "I was a little het up, I guess. Quinn had me rattled—making me out the leader of those rotten jewel thieves and killers."

"That's all, gentlemen," Quinn said. "I want you to know where you stand. And let me repeat, the real crook may be throwing suspicion on you because he knows you are open to it, and that the more people who are suspected, the more confusing the issue becomes. Silk, please show these gentlemen out. And thanks to all of you for coming to see me."

Captain McGrath didn't go with them Instead, he hunched his chair closer to Quinn's desk.

"What was the idea of that?" he demanded. "If one of them is the man we're after, he'll be doubly careful now."

"I agree, Captain. He'll be so careful he may give himself away. Because, you see, this business has been petty so far—"

"Petty?" McGrath roared. "Listen! Those rings stolen from Mrs. Hampton last night were worth seventy thousand dollars. Do you call that petty?"

"Peanuts," Quinn declared placidly, "compared to what those crooks are really after. Captain, you don't look far enough into the future. Tomorrow night there is to be a grand party in honor of two foreign dignitaries. Everyone who can wangle an invitation will be there, all dressed up in their finery. That includes gems—real ones, not the paste imitations they wear to theaters and the opera most of the time. There should be a million dollars worth of gems at the affair. Tantalizing for a crook like the man who is now operating."

McGRATH blinked. "Good night! I never thought of that. That's what Mason had started to tell us about when Hampton interrupted him. Well, I'll arrange a guard that will stay close enough to the party to tell us how many times each diamond shimmers. And to do that I'd better be on my way right now."

"And will you forget about the Black Bat until this is over with, Captain," Quinn said. "Trying to handle two things at once makes a man serve each poorly."

"Yeah," McGrath's cold cigar bobbed up and down, his eyebrows arched, and his eyes grew dark. "Yeah—I'll handle only one thing. But if it comes to a choice, I'll take the Black Bat. The murderer who wears a black hood and pretends he's such a little helper to the Police Department. By the way, are you planning to attend that party?"

"I will probably be there," Quinn said. "I have an invitation."

"Then I'll be there too, and my invitation was extended to me a long time ago—on a badge."

McGrath slammed the door after him.

"He may be a difficult problem," Silk said, and sighed deeply.

"He already is," Quinn groaned. "I used to like having him prowl around. It lent spice to our little game, but now he's gunning for us, Silk. I'll have to think of something. You phone Mason shortly in answer to the ads."

Silk went out. He returned about an hour later, showing none of the excitement he felt. He waited patiently until Quinn had disposed of routine matters, then closed and locked the door of the private office.

"Mason received a letter and some money this morning," he said. "The money was a retainer. The letter informed him that he was the go-between with you and Carol on the ends. Those killers know Carol works for the Black Bat. Or strongly suspects it. Mason was sent a sealed enveope to deliver to the Black Bat. He suggested a certain spot in Central Park, but I overruled him. I told him to get into his car at eight tonight and start driving at random. That the Black Bat would stop him somewhere. That's the safest way."

"And the best." Quinn leaned back in his chair and cocked both feet on the edge of the desk. "Butch will have to do it, in the Black Bat's hood. Mason may have told McGrath about this and if so, Mac will be right on our necks. Find Butch and give him his instructions."

"Yes, sir."

Silk arose and headed for the door. Quinn stopped him with a word.

"Silk, another thing. I want you to practise imitating my voice. Get the inflections and the tone. Try it out on Butch. Perhaps this is all nonsense, but if I do need my voice in a place where I can't be, then you'll become most useful."

"Yes, sir," Silk answered vaguely. "I'll do my best, sir."

His tones bore a fair resemblance to Quinn's.

CHAPTER IX

Crimson Magic

SOON after dark that night the forces of the Black Bat were at work. Butch had gone off to meet Sam Mason—but only after Tony Quinn had made certain that neither Mason nor McGrath were setting a trap.

Silk and the Black Bat were on their way to Mrs. Carter's boarding house. As usual, the Black Bat wore his wide-brimmed hat, and he had taken great pains to make sure before they left that McGrath had not been hanging around the house.

"We're going to give our killer some rope," the Black Bat explained. "Enough to hang him if he accepts it. Tonight, Silk, you and I are planning a crime. I found out today, that certain social affairs will be attended by certain women who will wear jewels. If our plans work one of those women will be held up or her home robbed."

"I don't get it," Silk admitted. "But suppose you do set this trap, and the woman who is to be robbed is killed?"

"She won't be. First of all, I shall try to make certain it won't be a stick-up, but rather a breaking and entering job while the woman and her family are asleep. No burglar is going to go out of his way to commit murder. It's safe enough . . . You'd better bounce across the sidewalk half-way down the next block and drive the car into that empty lot. Behind the tree, where it won't be seen."

Silk obeyed, and in a moment the car was well concealed from the street. The Black Bat got out.

"Come along, Silk. You and I are going to tackle the fat man. Jacques!"

"Jacques?" Silk gulped. "He's dangerous. Even Butch is afraid of him."

"But we're not. I want to test a couple of things and he is necessary to my plans. In fact, Silk, I intend to hand Mr. Jacques a knife and encourage him to kill me."

"You—what?" Silk gasped.

"You'll see. But from under cover, Silk. He must not lay eyes on you. Take along that coil of wire, the gag and the blindfold. We're going to need them—I hope."

The Black Bat and Silk made their way to Jacques' residence near Mrs. Carter's house. Silk hid behind the garage while the Black Bat glided to the back door, invisible in the gloom. He gained admission to the house without much trouble and after passing through the kitchen, he stopped in the middle of the dining room to listen.

He had a faint hope that Carol might be here, and if so he could do two things at once. But no sound reached him to bolster such hopes.

He examined the first floor and found nothing, then crept up the staircase as noiselessly as a ghost. He saw the same closed door which Carol had spotted and approached it warily.

Now his sensitive ears picked up a faint hissing, like that made by a Bunsen burner in his laboratory. He rested a black gloved hand on the doorknob, drew a gun, and began slowly to twist the knob.

its holster. Jacques lowered his half-raised hands and his pudgy form seemed to stiffen. The Black Bat sat down and crossed his legs like a man wholly at ease because his enemy looked too flabby to be dangerous.

"You are going to take me to where that young lady is being held," the Black Bat said. "Oddly enough, she doesn't work for me, but you'll hardly believe that."

Jacques curled his flat lips. "Then why are you so interested in her?"

"Because she probably knows something that would interest me. Like the identity of the man you work for. Anyway you probably intend to kill her and I can't permit that."

BUTCH

There was no sound at all as he swung the door open. Jacques was bent over his work-bench, intent upon his task. The hissing came from a small blast furnace which was in operation.

"Would those be Mrs. Hampton's diamonds?" the Black Bat asked casually.

Jacques didn't whirl around to face this unexpected danger. He laid down a pair of forceps, removed a jeweler's loupe from his right eye and replaced his glasses before he arose. Then he turned slowly. Fat jowls were placid, eyes were obscured behind the thick glasses.

"Ah—so," he said smugly. "The Black Bat! You have received a certain message already, but you refuse to abide by our conditions. It will not be healthy for the young lady."

The Black Bat stuffed his gun back into

JACQUES shrugged and nonchallantly picked up a small bar of metal. He seemed to be examining it minutely, and spoke without looking up.

"Black Bat," he said slowly, "you are outside the law. I have never believed that you don't profit from your work. You could profit tremendously if you worked with me. Take this little bar. It is pure gold and yet it represents a small fraction of the profits. There are diamonds and rubies, sapphires and pearls. I am a jewel expert. I know how to alter the appearance of stones so they can be resold without much depreciation of value. Together we might—"

Suddenly he flung the small, heavy bar of metal. And if his intended victim hadn't been sure he was about to become a target, the gold bar could have injured him seriously. As it was, the bar whizzed harmlessly through the air because the Black Bat had flung himself sideways out of the chair to the floor.

With a bellow of rage, Jacques charged. The Black Bat's legs came up. As Jacques bent to seize the intruder's throat, the Black Bat kicked him neatly under the chin. Jacques went reeling back, squealing with pain. But he came on again—in a wild charge. Jacques knew how to fight, and he possesed tremendous energy. He lacked only one thing—restraint. He forgot to keep a cool head, and the Black Bat didn't.

Jacques ducked under the Black Bat's swing and seized a wrist with both hands. He arched himself to throw the Black Bat against the wall with a judo twist. Instead, the side of the Black Bat's hand came down against Jacques' neck—a crippling blow against nerve centers that sent Jacques to his knees.

The Black Bat stepped back and waited. He wanted Jacques to absorb more punishment than this. The fat man shook his head, growled in rage, and started weaving as he approached the Black Bat again. He was like an animal coming in for the final attempt to disable his foe. If he failed, everything would be ended, so Jacques was cautious. His fat jowls were quivering and his mighty shoulders were tensed.

Then the Black Bat confused Jacques by doing the unexpected. He started a charge, so swiftly that Jacques had no opportunity to straighten up for defense. All he could do was try and wrap massive arms around this black-clad fighter. But it was too late for that. The Black Bat's fists lashed out, battering Jacques' face and head until he staggered backward. Another well-aimed punch, and he sat down hard.

The Black Bat bent over him, and in his gloved hand was a heavy, long-bladed knife.

"All right, Jacques," he said sternly, "talk! Where is that girl? Talk—or this knife will make you."

Jacques massaged his jaw before he answered defiantly.

"You wouldn't use a knife. Not the Black Bat! I know you are too civilized to resort to torture. I am not afraid of you!"

The Black Bat straightened up and carelessly placed the knife on Jacques' workbench. He picked up his chair and sat down again. Jacques arose warily, as if expecting the Black Bat to charge him again. When he didn't Jacques quietly placed himself between the Black Bat and the knife, so tantalizingly near on the workbench.

"All right," the Black Bat said. "I can made you talk. I am not a torturer—but I can have you thrown into a cell on charges of being an accessory to murder. I know you are the right-hand man of someone who directs these crimes. You establish places where servants of wealthy people congregate and talk. You listen and determine certain facts. These you transmit to the head of the outfit and he passes on the news to professional thieves. The loot is turned over to you and altered into salable products in this room. Are you satisfied now that I could have you jailed?"

"First," Jacques said, "you have to close the cell door on me. Words do not place a man in prison. The fact is, you will never talk about this!"

Covertly—Jacques thought—his right hand slipped around and seized the knife. Holding it high, he charged at the Black Bat. But the Black Bat was prepared. Leaping to his feet he raised the chair and parried the knife thrust with it. All in one smooth motion. Before Jacques could get the knife into position for another thrust, the Black Bat dropped the chair, closed in and delivered two hard blows to the chin. Jacques didn't sit down this time. He fell down and lay quiet.

THE Black Bat went to the window, raised it, and whistled softly. Silk came out of the shadows and in a few minutes he was busy tying and gagging Jacques. He removed the knife from the fat man's limp hand.

"It must have been rather dangerous for you, sir." He looked up at the Black Bat.

"No. I wanted to see whether or not Jacques would throw the knife. He did not, which is proof he doesn't know how. It eliminates him as the murderer of Compton Carter, something I had to find out. Compton was probably killed by Jacques' superior. Tie him firmly and make sure he can't work the gag loose. Then stow him in that supply closet and leave him there. He's going to be stiff by tomorrow night, but the wages of crime do not include comfort."

The Black Bat and Silk made their way to the garage, after Jacques had been disposed of. The Black Bat got into the station wagon.

"I thought this is what we'd find," he said, as he finished his swift examination of it. "Jacques couldn't openly approach the leader of the gang. Therefore he had to get word to him about prospective jobs through this means. Crimson magic! In the back of the truck is equipment generating infra-red light. There is a steady beam which can be interrupted by pressing this second horn button. To send signals, the beam is broken in that manner. The beam is invisible except to a photo-electric cell through a lens fitted with the proper filter.

"Somewhere along the route over which you followed Jacques, this other receiver was ready to take the signal. We're going over that route tonight. When we reach the first stop, you are to do exactly as Jacques did. I'll be crouched down out of sight, but I'll send the signals. This means is so unique that they'll hardly have a code established. Just good old Morse."

For the next hour and a half Silk drove to the various spots, stopped, and the Black Bat compressed the second horn button to interrupt the beam of invisible light and send a message. They operated in front of the residence of Tom Shirley, William Jenks, Sam Mason, and finally on that quiet side street where there were always several cars parked.

This completed, Silk drove the station wagon back to Jacques' garage. While Silk entered the house to check on Jacques, the Black Bat slipped over to Mrs. Carter's house.

The angular woman was hustling about the lighted kitchen. The back door was not locked so the Black Bat stepped into the kitchen. Mrs. Carter whirled to face him. She shrank back, then spoke in a low, venomous tone.

"The Black Bat. You murdered my son! Killed him without giving him a chance! I hope you die the same way!"

"I did not kill your son," the Black Bat interrupted. "I found him in the cellar here, tied up and gagged. I carried him out. Outside someone threw a knife. Perhaps at me, perhaps with the idea of killing him. He died —rather justly because your son killed a man with a knife too. I want to know why he was a prisoner in his mother's house."

"I didn't know he was there," she said slowly. "And you're lying. You did kill him! Why should any of the others? He was helping them."

"Perhaps, Mrs. Carter. However, your son was not a man of strong character. A murderer never is. He might have worried about his crime, seen the face of his victim too much. Perhaps he weakened, and they thought he might talk. That's why he was made a prisoner. I'm sure of only one thing —that I did not kill him. He was murdered by someone else. Not by Jacques, because that fat man isn't a knife thrower. Perhaps it was the man who controls Jacques. You know him, of course."

"I know nothing," she answered tartly. "I only run a respectable boarding house."

The Black Bat nodded. "When I finally prove who killed your son you will talk, because you loved him no matter what he turned out to be. I wanted to tell you this— to let you think it over. I don't believe you know the identity of the man who operates this criminal organization. He is much too careful to permit that."

The Black Bat was backing toward the door when his eye fell upon an open cook book. Some notes were written on the margin of the exposed pages and the handwriting was identical with that on the mysterious envelope he had received, and the same hand had written the anonymous note to Sam Mason. The Black Bat tore out one page of the cook book.

"A tempting dish," he said. "I'll take this along. Are those your notes, Mrs. Carter?"

"Of course they are. I hope you poison yourself on that recipe! I hope—"

But she was talking to herself. The Black Bat had stepped through the door and disappeared.

CHAPTER X

Clues in Color

AT THE laboratory, the Black Bat and Silk found Butch waiting restlessly.

"I trailed Mason to a quiet spot, then I put on one of your hoods," he told the Black Bat. "I stopped him and he gave me this envelope. There's something heavy in it."

The Black Bat opened the envelope, removed a letter and a metal vanity case.

"Carol's," he said. "Included as proof they have her a prisoner. The letter instructs me to drop out of this case and stay out. It says that the first time I show up, Carol will die. The letter was written by Carol, but it contains no hints as to where she is being held. The crooks would see to that. She adds that it is at her own suggestion that the vanity case is included and that on the surface of the cake of powder she was impressed the print of her thumb, as definite proof."

The Black Bat opened the vanity case. If he had any hopes that it might contain a clue, they quickly faded. There was nothing in the case but the solid cake of powder.

"Odd," he said slowly. "Carol would have sent us a message if she possibly could and she is ingenious about things like this. Yet there seems to be nothing. Certainly her thumbprint can't tell us where she is, though she did rather emphasize it. We'll have a look."

The Black Bat carefully dusted the top of the powder cake with a chemical which would bring out any prints. None appeared. He rubbed his chin and frowned. Carol's message meant something. She wanted him to look for that print, yet there was none.

"Perhaps it's on the back of the cake," he muttered.

With a pair of forceps, he carefully lifted the cake from the vanity case. The back of the cake was smeared with a substance that looked much like bloody soot.

"Now what does she mean by this?" he demanded.

"Looks to me like the whole business was dropped on a dirty floor," Silk offered hopefully.

"No," the Black Bat said. "This stuff was

deliberately smeared onto the cake. Boys, I'm going to be busy for a time. Silk, you'd better go into the house and stand guard. Butch, catch a few winks if you like. I may be two or three hours at this job."

Then the Black Bat went to work. In this lab he had everything needed for the most careful analysis. He scraped the dark sooty substance from the back of the cake and dissolved some of it in a solution. He proceeded then to put it through a qualitative analysis.

Much sooner than he had expected, the Black Bat was finished. He called Silk and Butch to the laboratory.

"Carol did smear that soot on the under side of the powder cake," he explained. "We would never have looked for it, had she not made certain we would by telling us of a non-existent thumb-print. She realized that I'd be puzzled and put the black substance through an analysis. Well, I did. The soot is from some chimney, I believe. It contains more strange elements than I've encountered for a long time. There is strontium in it and copper and iron. Cobalt and chromium and several other metals.

"At first, I couldn't make much sense out of it, then I recalled that each one of these metals is used to create a different color in rockets and other fireworks. So where many of them are found in one sample of residue that indicates some kind of a plant where either fireworks or signaling munitions are made.

"Silk, start calling up manufacturers of fireworks. See if anyone connected with that business knows of an abandoned fireworks plant either in town or not far away."

"Can't I do anything?" Butch asked.

"Take a couple of submachine-guns out of the arsenal, check them and bring extra ammunition," the Black Bat told him. "If we do find an abandoned fireworks factory, Carol will be there. I think she somehow contrived to gather a sample of soot from a testing chimney, where fireworks are shot off experimentally."

"Oh, boy!" Butch rubbed his hands. "You and Silk take the tommies. Let me whack the lugs who are holding her with my bare hands. I promise my mitts will do as much damage as the bullets."

Silk came back from the telephone.

"There is such a factory," he said. "Just one. The firm had to expand when they went out of the fireworks business and into munitions. They couldn't enlarge their quarters so they moved the whole thing. The three-story building they abandoned is on the outskirts of town. Near the river. I've got the address."

"Get out one of the big cars," the Black Bat ordered. "Switch marker plates. We're going after Carol now!"

It was more than an hour later when three men cautiously approached the old fireworks factory. There were no buildings close to it. Safety regulations provided for that. It gave every indication of being deserted. Windows and doors were boarded up and it looked like some vast tomb.

ALONE, the Black Bat went forward through the night and examined the building. He found a small door which was not sealed, but he was afraid to try and gain entrance by it. Even a skeleton key or the tools he carried with which to open locks made some slight noise, and if Carol was in here her guards might hear it. This was a ticklish business, because those guards would have orders to dispose of Carol the instant anything happened.

The Black Bat found a hatch leading into a storage cellar, beside the rear loading platform. He tackled the padlock, and in a few moments had it open. He had his gun in his hand as he slipped through. Butch and Silk, armed with tommy-guns would come quickly if he signaled, but at the moment stealth was the important thing.

The cellar led under the building and to an elevator shaft. Down this shaft came voices. Those of at least three men—and Carol's. The Black Bat's heart pounded like a hammer. She was alive! And unhurt, judging by the conversation.

But to rescue her would be difficult. The elevator ropes could be climbed noiselessly and easily. An attack could be made upon her guards, but there were problems. The conversation above indicated them definitely.

Carol was talking.

"But even if you three men don't kill me— if this boss of yours does—you'll still be accessories and get the chair. All for nothing too. I'm a plain housemaid. I don't know a thing about the Black Bat except that I wish he was right here now."

"Wouldn't do you any good," one of the men said. "And how many times do we have to explain? We been tellin' you for the last four hours that if the Black Bat puts his oar in, the boss is comin' here to send a bullet through your head. We told you how he telephones every thirty minutes. If we don't answer, he'll know somethin' is wrong and make his getaway."

"Let him," Carol said. "When he phones again, don't answer. He'll run for it. You can let me go and I'll never say a word."

"Look," the same man sighed patiently. "The boss has his hands on all the stuff we've been swipin' for him. We haven't got our cut yet and we don't work for the love of it. We want what's comin' to us. Now shut up, will you? Or talk about something else."

Quietly the Black Bat withdrew and returned to Silk and Butch. He talked to them in whispers.

"Carol is in there and safe—so far. She's

guarded by three men who won't kill her. They are part of this gang of professional thieves and burglars, but they are not murderers. What makes things bad is that the leader telephones every thirty minutes. If there is no answer, he'll run for it. Or else come here to murder Carol. We could trap him, possibly, but the evidence against him wouldn't be strong. We couldn't testify against him and I've got to prove that he, and not I, stabbed Compton Carter."

"So what do we do?" Butch asked.

"It's your party, Butch. I'll help you slip into the place and show you where Carol is being held. Hide in the building. If things go wrong, free her. If things remain serene, just don't do anything until midnight tomorrow."

Butch blinked. "I'm going to be awful hungry by that time, but okay. I'll take the tommy-gun in case things get too hot. At midnight I grab the bozos."

Shortly afterwards the Black Bat emerged from the building alone and relocked the hatch.

Then he joined Silk.

They made one stop at an outlying drugstore where Silk telephoned Captain McGrath, told him he was the Black Bat and ordered him to arrest Mrs. Carter and hold her. He hung up before McGrath could deliver a blistering condemnation of the man whom he believed to be a cold-blooded, sinister killer.

CHAPTER XI

Set-up for Crime

NEXT day was a busy one. Silk Kirby made a swift visit to Jacques' house and determined the prisoner was safe, with gag and blindfold intact. He checked on the fireworks factory by driving near it. All seemed serene, and it would not have been if Butch had been spotted or gone into action. There would have been visible scars about.

McGrath came to Quinn's office with the news that he had arrested Mrs. Carter at the behest of the Black Bat, but that she claimed it was all a mistake and she knew nothing.

"Hold her," Quinn ordered. "We know those boarding houses are part and parcel of this scheme. Perhaps the Black Bat will get in touch with you and tell you how to make Mrs. Carter talk. We can hold her for twenty-four hours . . . What about those suspects?"

"All under observation," McGrath answered. "Personally, I think you're wrong, but I do admit there is enough evidence

[Turn page]

to make them suspicious. Also, I might add the Black Bat hasn't been so active since I warned you I'd shoot him on sight."

"Perhaps he heard you." Quinn grinned. "The man seems to be everywhere, according to your version of his activities . . . Now about the party tonight. You have taken steps to see that it is well protected?"

"Like Fort Knox. Mason called this morning and insisted that the scheme he's worked out with the insurance companies is a honey, but he wouldn't tell me what it is. Says I'll find out tonight."

"Let's make certain Mason's scheme isn't too deep, Captain—so good that it works in reverse," Quinn said. "A haul at that party would net more than a million dollars in gems. Those crooks will take any risks for a chance at loot like that. I'll see you there— early—so you can look around and tell me what you see."

As McGrath departed to make all arrangements, Quinn was satisfied that things were working out smoothly. The leader of the crooks would not try to contact Jacques. He always left the contacting up to the fat man and, so far as the leader knew, Jacques was on the job and had furnished him with a profitable tip last night.

Quinn studied the newspaper accounts of the latest robbery. A Mrs. Warlock's home had been skillfully entered and a string of valuable pearls stolen. It was obviously the work of the same gang which worked with such smooth efficiency.

Quinn had expected that holdup. He was gratified about it.

"Because," as he told Silk, "I now know who is behind this. Without realizing it, the leader gave himself away last night. Now let's go home and get dressed. I look forward to an exciting evening. . . ."

The affair in honor of the foreign dignitaries was lavish. Given in the home and on the grounds of a large estate, more than two hundred guests, among them the wealthiest and most important people in the country could be easily accommodated.

Silk drove up in Tony Quinn's big car, parked, and got out. He opened the door and helped blind Tony Quinn, in evening dress, to alight,

Quinn was warmly greeted on all sides as he entered on Silk's arm. Captain McGrath was there. He took Quinn aside.

"Something happened all right, sir," he said. "I prophesy that we'll have no trouble at this shindig because the ringleader of those crooks is locked up. What do you think of that?"

Quinn looked amazed. "If that's true, Captain, you deserve a promotion and a medal. Tell me about it."

"Well, ever since you listed Mason, Shirley and Jenks as suspects, I've had them watched. Early this evening, Shirley barged out of his place with two bags and made a bee-line for the airport. My boys picked him up. He told me his sister was dying in Seattle, and that he had to reach her quickly. He showed me a telegram containing the news. I called the telegraph office and they had no record of such a wire. Then I phoned his sister and she told me she had sent no wire and that she was feeling fine. Shirley insisted a man in a messenger's uniform delivered the wire, but my boys didn't see him go in or out. Shirley was trying a getaway and lied when I nabbed him."

"Good work," Quinn said. "Still, if he hasn't confessed, we can't be absolutely certain. Anyway, even if he is the man we're after, he would have had time to make arrangements with his gang. They may tackle the job without him. They may not even know he's been arrested."

"I thought of that," McGrath grumbled. "But they won't get away with a thing. Sam Mason is here, of course. Paul Hampton is with him and Hampton has a private detective's badge. They told me about their scheme."

"Ah yes, the foolproof method of protecting the jewelry. What is it, Captain?"

McGRATH'S frown showed that he was uneasy.

"Well," he said, "Hampton and Mason figure this way. All the jobs have been pulled after a party. Therefore Mason is having an armored truck come here for the jewelry and has arranged with the women to turn their stuff over to him and some insurance company detectives before they leave. A bank is going to allow the armored truck to transfer the stuff to their vaults."

"Did you double-check everything?" Quinn asked. "Remember, Mason is on our list of suspects too."

"I called every insurance company involved and they backed him up. I phoned the armored truck company and they told me everything was okay. Maybe I won't land those crooks tonight, but they won't get any loot. All the jewelry owners agreed to the scheme because they've been scared stiff with so many robberies and stickups going on."

"I shall breathe much easier then." Quinn smiled. "By the way were those three suspected men all accounted for last night?"

"They were. They are so scared of being implicated they didn't budge out of their homes. Incidentally, I went to the funeral of Mrs. Hampton this afternoon. Just on the chance the killer might show up. But Hampton identified everyone present. Anything else for now, Quinn?"

"No. You have things in hand. I can enjoy the party now. If nothing happens, then I think you will be able to feel certain that Shirley was behind it and the thing fizzled with his arrest."

Before McGrath left, Silk appeared with an elderly man in tow. A man who, like Quinn, carried a cane and had the staring eyes of a blind man.

"It's Mr. Claremont," Silk said to Quinn. "He wanted to talk with you."

"Mark!" Quinn said happily.

He clasped hands with the blind man, their arms guided by Silk. McGrath walked off.

"We'll probably be in the way here, Mark," Quinn said. "Suppose we retire to some comfortable nook and have a long chat. Frankly I came here only because I heard you'd be present."

"Nice of you to say that," Mark Claremont beamed. "Silk will find a quiet place for us."

Silk did. An upstairs room. Silk had a servant bring drinks and informed the man that he, Silk, would be in attendance on the two blind men from then on.

Quinn and Claremont talked of law cases— Claremont was also an attorney. They talked politics and the war. Downstairs, the entertainment was in full swing, spilling out into the large gardens. Neither paid much attention to it. They talked on and on, until at last the end of the evening's festivities downstairs was in sight.

Suddenly Quinn, while still talking, arose quietly. Claremont was answering Quinn's rather involved question as Quinn donned black clothing and the hood of the Black Bat. Just as quietly, Silk slipped into the chair which Quinn had occupied. Silk carried on the conversation in an excellent imitation of Quinn's voice.

The Black Bat slipped out of the room, made his way to the rear of the house and reached the garden by descending a trellis.

By moving to the outskirts of the grounds, he avoided being seen. As he approached the front of the house he saw a heavily armored truck swing around. Four men got out. Two held submachine-guns and took up positions. Two more were inside the truck. The first pair stopped at Captain McGrath's order and produced papers that seemed to satisfy the police official. Then they entered the house.

When shortly they emerged, they were carrying large boxes which were carefully passed to the men inside the truck. The Black Bat looked for McGrath, but he had disappeared.

It was going to be difficult, for McGrath's men would have orders to open fire on the Black Bat at sight. McGrath himself might forget about a possible robbery and concentrate on capturing the Black Bat.

THE Black Bat reached for his gun—and froze. A flashlight beam centered squarely on him. "Don't make a move!" McGrath's chilly voice whispered. "I figured you'd show up, so I've been prowling around watching for you all night. Slow now—reach."

"McGrath, you're an idiot!" the Black Bat whispered back. "Those men with the armored car are crooks. They're getting every last bracelet and ring. The stuff is being handed to them! If you let them get away, you'll be broken to a patrolman."

McGrath laughed shortly. "You'll have to think of something better than that. I checked on that armored car and those men. Everything is in order. Are you getting your hands up or do I put a slug through you?"

The Black Bat slowly raised his arms. McGrath moved forward in the most triumphant moment of his life. The steel door of the armored car slammed shut and the Black Bat groaned. Tires grated, and the truck started moving off.

"All right," the Black Bat said, "you've got me, McGrath, but a million dollars in jewelry you are supposed to protect is on its way in the hands of crooks! Go ahead, take off my hood. See who is beneath it and arrest me for murder. But you won't convict me! It will be the last arrest you ever make!"

CHAPTER XII

Flaming Cocktails

McGRATH'S gun slanted downward a trifle. He was not as sure of himself as he had been a moment before. But he was just as determined to yank off the Black Bat's hood.

He reached for it. A gloved hand shot out and closed around his wrist. The gun didn't go off. It simply dropped into the grass. McGrath was swung around like a top. When things stopped whirling for him, he looked down the muzzle of his own weapon.

"I've never lied to you," the Black Bat said softly. "I've never doublecrossed you. I didn't kill young Carter. I know who did. McGrath, I'm giving you back your gun, butt first. Is that evidence enough that I need your help? The armored car is almost out of the driveway now. We haven't a moment to loose. If I'm wrong, you have me at the mercy of your gun. But for heaven's sake, man, act!"

"All right," McGrath said. "I'll take a chance. I've got a fast car. We can overtake the truck easy."

"Drive the car around to the garages in back," Quinn said. "We'll need more than guns to stop that traveling tank. Pick me up there—and you might send word to your men that I'm not to be molested. Step on it, Mac! If we slip, we're both done."

"You are, anyhow," McGrath growled, but he hurried away.

The Black Bat hastened to the garage. He came out of it clutching four quart bottles and a gallon can. He hopped into the car beside McGrath.

"Step on it!" he ordered. "I'll fix these cocktails for the men in the truck. This is going to be dangerous, Mac. They'll shoot the moment they know we're after them."

McGrath was racing the car down the driveway. He turned into the street after the armored car and sent the gas pedal to the floorboard. He jerked his head toward two machine-guns in back of the car.

"What good are machine-guns?" Quinn asked. "That truck is armor-plated. The guns will come in handy, though, when the crooks spill out. And they will, unless they get in a lucky shot somehow."

McGrath drove faster than he had ever driven before. They topped a hill and, half-way down it, the headlights of a car heading in their direction swept across the armored truck which was rolling at a good clip.

Quinn was pouring gasoline from the gallon can he had taken from the garage into the four bottles. Without a word he reached over, raised McGrath's coat and yanked out his shirt-tail. He ripped several strips from it, drowning McGrath's objections with harsh urging for him to make better time. He shoved strips of cloth into each bottle and loosely fitted a cork into the neck of each.

They were getting closer to the armored car now.

"Pass them!" the Black Bat ordered. "Don't try to cut in front. Just keep going."

McGrath nodded and swung the wheel a trifle. At that moment, guns began to flame. The windshield cracked in a dozen places. Slugs whined alongside the police car, smashed into the hood and into the highway near the the tires. McGrath kept going, though he knew that at this speed one bullet could send them on a journey to oblivion.

Heedless of the whipping bullet, the Black Bat calmly lit a match and touched it to the wick of the first bottle. He leaned out of the car and hurled the bottle. It hit the road just ahead of the truck. Two more bottles splattered the truck and the fourth covered it with flame that seemed to extend little crimson fingers down the sides and creep into the firing slits.

The shooting stopped—so did the truck. It veered off the road, nearly turned over, and crashed against a tree. The rear door opened and men popped out. The Black Bat held one of the submachine-guns in his arms now and he pulled the trigger.

It was over in a few moments. He lined up the crooks and placed them under McGrath's gun. Then he climbed into the police car and told McGrath he would send detectives.

They arrived in short order, took over and McGrath drove back to the estate, in time to witness the end of the affair. Detectives indicated one of the large rooms and when McGrath burst in, Mason and Paul Hampton were facing the Black Bat, across a large desk. On that desk lay a large knife.

"Mason," the Black Bat said, "you've been an unknowing stooge. Hampton used you as he used everyone else. He thought up this slick scheme and had you propose it to the insurance company. But Hampton owned that armored truck. The other hold-ups were performed more for effect than profit, all leading up to this big event. Certainly the men on the truck had their papers in order. They'd built things up to this."

HAMPTON said nothing, but he was pale and once he looked down at the desk.

"But—but Hampton's own wife was killed by those crooks!" Mason protested. "It doesn't seem possible that—"

"It is. He wanted his wife to die. He murdered her. There were no crooks that night—besides Hampton. He's handy with a knife. Mrs. Hampton wasn't in on this business. But she was getting wise and Hampton had to kill her. She even wrote Tony Quinn a letter explaining about her husband, but Hampton found it where she had hidden it until she could get a chance to mail it.

"Naturally he couldn't simply destroy it, but he did have another woman—Mrs. Carter—address a fresh envelope in which he placed a blank sheet of paper. Mrs. Hampton probably didn't look at the handwriting when she took her letter from its hiding place to post it. The anonymous letter you got, Mason, fixing things so you had no alibi, was also written by Mrs. Carter."

Hampton clenched his fists in rage. "You're absurd!" he thundered. "I loved my wife."

"You did, when she had a lot of money—before you went through it. Then you bought her those diamonds—with money you got from the gems you'd already stolen. Those rings would be a motive for an attack upon her."

"Prove it!" Hampton raged.

"Of course," the Black Bat agreed. "Last night the home of a Mrs. Warlock was robbed. You ordered your professional thieves to do the job after you got what you thought was a message from Jacques. But I sent it. I was in that station wagon, for it might interest you to know that Jacques and Mrs. Carter are prisoners. I visited the neighborhood of each suspect, and signaled with infra-red who was to be robbed. A different person for each suspect.

"Those I named for Mason, Shirley, and Jenks were unmolested. The one I flashed on that quiet street where you were hidden concerned Mrs. Warlock. When she was robbed I knew you were responsible, for it had to be someone in that group of suspects which included you—though you did not know it.

"You tried to confuse things by making suspects of the other men you drew into your scheme, even compelling Shirley to make an attempt to take a sudden trip when you had one of your men deliver a forged telegram to him. You played safe by making use of professional crooks who, if arrested, could take it without talking. Young Carter was different, so—"

Hampton suddenly scooped up the knife, seizing it by the point of the blade. His arm went back in a flash, before McGrath could raise his gun. The knife flew from Hampton's fingers—and landed squarely in the middle of the desk. McGrath's gun exploded and Hampton screamed wildly as he headed for a window. He stopped short, and gently slid to the floor.

He tried to get up. He was like a punch-drunk fighter who refuses to give in to unconsciousness.

Finally, he gave up the struggle and went limp where he lay.

"Thanks, Mac," the Black Bat said. "That squares everything. I knew Hampton killed Carter by throwing a knife into his back. I knew he would look for a chance to pick up this knife I purposely left on the desk. I wanted him to show that he was a knife thrower—but he didn't know that particular knife was weighted so that nobody could throw it.

"You'll find that Hampton's wife was so afraid of him that she had several locks put on her bedroom door. She lived in constant terror, but didn't dare come to the police . . . Mason, give McGrath a hand with Hampton. Hurry—if you want him for the chair. And Mac, if you tell Mrs. Carter that it was Hampton who killed her son, and not the Black Bat, she'll talk her head off."

McGrath and Mason were so busy with Hampton that they did not notice it when the Black Bat faded out of the scene. . . .

WHEN an ambulance arrived, there was a look of satisfaction on Captain McGrath's face as he watched Hampton being packed into it. It had been a good night. Then he thought of the Black Bat and Tony Quinn. A servant told him that Quinn, Silk and Mark Claremont were in one of the upstairs rooms.

McGrath went there, smiling at the thought that Quinn would not be there. Or even if he was, Claremont would admit Quinn had been gone for a while. McGrath felt that he would have a right to gloat.

He opened the door. Quinn looked up blankly. Claremont stopped talking. McGrath asked questions, and Claremont laughed.

"Why, of course Tony has been here all the time. Every moment. Why?"

"Yes," Quinn said, "why? Isn't everything all right downstairs? I stopped worrying when I knew you had things under control."

"Everything is fine," McGrath growled. "Except me. I think I'm going slightly batty."

He exited in a hurry. The other two men, guided by Silk, went downstairs and heard the story. Then Silk and Quinn drove home. Carol was there, with Butch.

"It was a cinch." Butch grinned. "I took those three bozos easy. They didn't even want to fight. The cops got 'em by now."

Quinn took Carol's hands in his own. "I hated to leave you with them, Carol, but there was nothing else to do. Hampton would have suspected if we had freed you." Quinn looked over at Butch. "Nice work. As a reward you may go to Jacques' house and prepare him for the police. Silk will show you where he is."

"Boy!" Butch rubbed his hands. "Boy, have I been looking forward to this!"

HIGH ADVENTURE
KI-GOR, THE JUNGLE LORD
DOUBLE FEATURE
ZOMBA HAS A THOUSAND SPEARS
HIGH ADVENTURE
BLOATED DEATH
by
JOHN GRANGE
A New Book-Length
HIGH ADVENTURE
CAPTAIN DANGER
A Complete Novel of Rip-Roaring Air War
Action Featuring the Whirlwind Ace of Aces
By LIEUT. SCOTT MORGAN

Made in the USA
Monee, IL
07 July 2026